A HARVEST OF AMISH BLESSINGS

MINDY STEELE   RACHEL J. GOOD
JENNIFER BECKSTRAND   TRACY FREDRYCHOWSKI

Cover design by Tracy Lynn Virtual, LLC

ISBN: 979–8-9919988–6-4 (paperback),

979–8-9919988–5-7 (ebook)

CONTENTS

THANKSGIVING ON HUCKLEBERRY
HILL
Jennifer Beckstrand

Chapter 1	3
Chapter 2	17
Chapter 3	26
Chapter 4	37
Chapter 5	47
Chapter 6	64
Mom's Apple Pie	71
About the Author	73

HELPING HANDS
Mindy Steele

Acknowledgments	77
Chapter 1	79
Chapter 2	89
Chapter 3	97
Chapter 4	103
Chapter 5	111
Chapter 6	121
Chapter 7	130
Chapter 8	139
Chapter 9	148
Chapter 10	154
Amish Madhouse Cookies	157
About the Author	159

SEASONS OF THE HEART
Tracy Fredrychowski

Chapter 1	163
Chapter 2	176
Chapter 3	184
Chapter 4	196
Chapter 5	206
Chapter 6	215
Chapter 7	227
Epilogue	236
Paper Bag Apple Pie	239
About the Author	241

LETTERS OF GRATITUDE
Rachel J. Good

Chapter 1	245
Chapter 2	251
Chapter 3	260
Chapter 4	266
Chapter 5	273
Chapter 6	283
Chapter 7	291
Chapter 8	298
Chapter 9	305
Chapter 10	313
Chapter 11	320
Mammi's Pumpkin Pie	327
About the Author	331

THANKSGIVING ON HUCKLEBERRY HILL

JENNIFER BECKSTRAND

CHAPTER 1

$\mathcal{A}$nna Helmuth woke up with an unwelcome and unfamiliar feeling at the base of her throat. She rolled onto her back and opened her eyes. She couldn't see the ceiling —the early Wisconsin morning was as black as pitch—but she knew what was looming over her head. There was a little glop of plaster just above Felty's pillow shaped like a lumpy mushroom and another glop to the left that looked like an ice cream sundae. A smear of plaster right above her head could have been a baseball, a Granny Smith apple, or a pizza, depending on how hungry Anna was on any particular day.

Anna reached out her hand to give Felty a pat, but all she felt were the smooth, cold sheets. *Ach*, he'd already gotten up to milk the cow.

Anna growled and sank back into her pillow. They really should get rid of that cow. She blew a puff of air from between her lips. Not get rid of it. She couldn't hurt Daisy's feelings like that. But they definitely needed to find their beloved cow a new home. A couple of grandsons came every day to help Felty milk the cow and feed the chickens, but today was Thanksgiving, and Felty had told the grandsons he would milk

Daisy himself. "You should be with your families on Thanksgiving Day."

As if Felty and Anna weren't family! As if the grandsons would rather be anywhere than with their delightful grandparents on Thanksgiving Day.

Anna cringed at the very idea that she was getting along in years. Felty thought he was old, but Anna refused to give in to that kind of negative thinking. She was only eighty-six and had at least fifteen productive years ahead of her.

Anna swallowed hard, remembering the unpleasant emotion sitting at the base of her throat threatening to choke her or at least send her into an uncontrollable coughing spell. The feeling wasn't hunger or thirst or weariness or even peevishness. She was profoundly melancholy, a word her grandson Jonah had taught her out of his thesaurus. To Anna, *melancholy* sounded like something she'd grow in her garden, a fruity gourd bred with a strange variety of broccoli. That was a much more cheerful definition than what melancholy actually meant: sad, miserable, downhearted. And discouraged.

Anna was melancholy from the top of her head to the tips of her toes, like an unwanted fruit that hadn't been picked for the Jell-O salad and on Thanksgiving Day, no less.

She got up, lit the lantern, and went into the bathroom to brush her teeth. Might as well have fresh breath while sitting around the house doing absolutely nothing to prepare for Thanksgiving Day. No pie making or turkey basting. No cheesy jalapeño banana bread. No oyster carrot salad. No family. No friends. No one for Thanksgiving but her, Felty, and Sparky the dog. Worse, Sparky didn't care what day it was as long as she got fed.

Anna heard Felty come in the front door and whistle all the way down the hall. "Life's Railway to Heaven," one of his favorites.

He came up behind Anna in the bathroom and wrapped

his arms around her waist. She spit out her toothpaste a little too forcefully. "Felty, how can you whistle at a time like this?"

Felty frowned. "At a time like what?"

Anna rinsed her mouth and patted her lips with a towel. "At a time when nobody loves us and everybody thinks we should be put out to pasture."

Felty fingered his beard, which was a handsome salt-and-pepper gray. "I'm pretty sure everyone still loves us."

Anna shook her head. "How could they, Felty? They won't even spend Thanksgiving Day with their poor, decrepit, boring parents."

"We're not boring."

She smacked her toothbrush on the counter. "Of course we're not boring. You have titanium knees and a fascinating tattoo. I have a melanoma on the bottom of my foot and three broken bones. *Ach, vell,* I *had* a melanoma on the bottom of my foot, but I do have a very interesting scar in its place."

"I nearly froze to death in Korea, and you knit potholders for the entire neighborhood. What's more exciting than that?"

Anna slumped her shoulders. "They don't love us anymore."

"Of course they love us." He gave her that grin that always made Anna's heart skitter over her ribs. "Who couldn't love you? You're the most lovable person in the world."

"*Ach,* Felty, you have to say that. You're stuck with me."

"For sure and certain, I'm glad of that."

"I sent out twenty-seven invitations to Thanksgiving dinner, and every last one of our children and grandchildren declined the invite. Even Vernon Schmucker said no."

Felty sprouted a slightly nauseated look on his face. "You invited Vernon Schmucker?"

Felty didn't like Vernon Schmucker. Anna didn't especially like Vernon either, but his *mater* had gone to Florida for Thanksgiving, and Anna had a heart for motherless children,

5

even though Vernon was in his forties and made a pest of himself at every opportunity.

She swatted away Felty's concern. "Don't worry. Vernon isn't coming. Neither is anyone else." She counted on her fingers. "Both Esther and Titus say they want to celebrate Thanksgiving with their own families this year, as if you and I aren't their family too. Abigail and Dan heard the weather was going to be bad, and paying a driver is expensive. Diana and Crist are spending the day with Wilma in Wautoma, the grandchildren are scattered to the wind, and everybody else is too far away." Anna's lower lip trembled. She felt more melancholy than ever. "We've been put out to pasture." Anna couldn't help the tears that trickled down her face.

Felty wrapped Anna in a bear hug. "Now, now, Annie, I can't see that we've been put out to pasture. We raised our children to be able to manage without us. They all have families of their own. In truth, we've been trying to get rid of them since the day they were born."

"*Ach*, Felty, what a thing to say! I never wanted to get rid of my children."

Felty chuckled. "I'll bet Vernon Schmucker's *mamm* would like to get rid of him."

Anna cuffed Felty on the shoulder. "Don't tease me, Felty Helmuth. Vernon is a special case."

Felty thumbed his suspenders. "I'm looking forward to our own private Thanksgiving Day. It will be very relaxing. You don't have to brine a turkey, and I don't have to carve it."

Anna slumped her shoulders. It would be a lot less work, but she was still melancholy about it. "Thanksgiving dinner will be two peanut butter sandwiches and a jar of pickles."

"What about potato chips?"

Anna sighed. "I suppose I could open a bag of potato chips."

Felty burst into a smile. "I love potato chips."

They made the bed together, just like they had for over sixty years, Anna feeling glum about her life and wishing her children cared about old people as much as they cared about themselves. After breakfast, they did the dishes and watched at the window as the sky turned from gray to midnight blue to black, then gave way to a smattering of snow. It snowed lightly at first, then harder and harder until the flakes were so thick, Anna could barely make out the outline of the barn not a hundred yards from the house.

Felty motioned toward the big picture window in their kitchen. "It's probably just as well the family isn't coming today. We wouldn't want them out in this storm."

"It's just as well I didn't bother to get a turkey," Anna said. A trifling winter storm like this wouldn't have deterred a truly faithful child or grandchild. What was a little snow to those who truly loved their grandparents?

Felty was undaunted, which was slightly irritating. Anna wanted to wallow, and she didn't want to be reminded that she was putting a damper on Felty's happy Thanksgiving Day. "What if we did something special today, just the two of us?"

Anna took a deep breath. Her extended family had abandoned her, but she still had a *wunderbarr* husband who never complained about her cooking and wouldn't harm a fly —literally. Any spiders, insects, or creepy crawlies that made their way into the house were scooped up in a Mason jar and released into the wild. Felty had a heart for animals and other helpless things.

"I'm sorry. Felty. I know self-pity is a waste of time, but I just can't seem to pull myself out of feeling melancholy."

Felty leaned forward as if he hadn't heard her. "Feeling what?"

"Today would be a *gute* day to clean out the hall closet. It's a big chore, and I'm already in a bad mood. Or maybe we should purge the fruit cellar. We have canned apricots down there that are older than most of our grandchildren. The Health Department would probably arrest us if they knew." Anna perked up at the thought of getting arrested on Thanksgiving Day. Surely the officers down at the station would share their turkey and cranberry sauce with a forlorn and lonely *mammi*.

Felty grimaced. "That's not really what I was thinking of."

Anna didn't want to ask, because she wasn't in the mood for anything cheerful, but she did anyway. "What did you have in mind?"

"We could take a walk in the snow."

She glanced out the window. "We'd die out there, Felty."

His lips twitched upward. "How about a game of Life on the Farm?"

"I'm sorry, Felty, but Life on the Farm is boring. I live life on the farm every day. I don't need to play it."

"We could do some chair yoga."

Anna cracked a reluctant smile. "Now you're just being ridiculous."

Felty's eyes lit up as a new idea came to him. He opened the junk drawer and pulled out a pencil and notepad. "Okay, Annie, since you're being so contrary, how about this? Let's write a list of all our grandchildren who still need spouses and make a plan to get at least one of them married this year."

Her heart leapt in her chest. Felty usually tried to talk her out of her matchmaking schemes. He must really be desperate to cheer her up. "*Ach!* Just the thing." She grabbed the pencil and notepad from Felty and planted herself in the kitchen chair opposite the window so she could watch the snow come down while she made her list. It was a beautiful snowstorm, much nicer to look at from inside her warm kitchen. Her sour mood shifted slightly as she watched the snow descend from the sky like feathers from a giant's pillow fight. She tapped the pencil to her lips, then wrote, "Unmarried Grandchildren" at the top of the first page. "Should we make a list of all our unmarried grandchildren, or just the most likely candidates?"

"It seems to me that the most likely candidates need the least amount of help."

Anna's eyebrows traveled upward. Felty was always so smart. "*Gute* thinking, dear. But it's also true that our grandchildren are superior in every way to other people's grandchildren. So if we go by the standard of most and least likely candidates, none of our grandchildren would need help finding spouses."

Felty stroked his salt-and-pepper gray beard. "True, Annie. Maybe we should abandon our list and do some chair yoga."

Felty was obsessed with chair yoga. Anna had to put a stop to it. "What about Sarah Jane's boy LaWayne?"

"*Vell*, Annie, I think we should match grandchildren before we help our great-grandchildren."

"Hmm, I suppose that's true, but they'll all need matches eventually." She wrote LaWayne's name at the bottom of her paper, just in case they had to come back to him.

"What about one of the Annies?"

Felty had a heart for the "Annies" in the family because their naming had created a huge kerfuffle. Their daughter-in-law Frieda Jane still hadn't completely gotten over it. Frieda Jane had named her first daughter Annie, after her *grossmammi* Anna. Then six months later, Peter and Clara named their baby Annie for the same reason. Frieda was very irritated about it, but Clara insisted that it wasn't fair for Frieda Jane to get dibs on everybody's favorite *mammi*. A year later, David and Ruth also named their daughter Annie, and Frieda Jane had almost suffered a heart attack.

"There are a lot of Annies."

Felty pinned her with a smug smile. "I told you they still love you, even if they're not coming to dinner. You're so popular, three of our sons named *dochters* after you."

9

Anna waved her pencil in the air, swatting away Felty's attempt to make her feel better. "That was years ago. They've all changed their minds." Still, she wrote "Annie Helmuth" three times on her list.

Felty made a few suggestions, which Anna thought very admirable, especially since he would rather do chair yoga than play matchmaker. Anna wrote down Max Helmuth, Mathias Junior Nelson, Wilma Zimmerman, and Frannie Lapp. Anna had always thought that "Frannie" was a little too close to "Annie" for comfort, but Frieda Jane hadn't said a word about it.

Anna nearly jumped out of her skin when a pony cart and rider passed in front of the window. "Did you see that, Felty? Who in the world would be out on a day like this?"

"It was definitely better that everyone stayed home."

She was unconvinced and unmoved. "At least they should have all *wanted* to come."

Anna joined Felty at the window, and they watched as the rider guided the pony cart into the barn, emerged a few minutes later, and headed toward the house. She was bundled in a puffy black coat with a midnight blue scarf around her neck and face, a pair of black mittens on her hands, and a lavender beanie stretched over her black bonnet. The beanie and bonnet combination was a strange look but a *gute* way to keep her head warm. She wore a sturdy pair of boots and what looked like sweatpants under her dress. The beanie and coat were caked with snow. She'd been out in the storm for half an hour at least. Anna was sure it was someone she was related to, though she couldn't see her face. Who else but a very responsible grandchild would put the pony and cart in the barn so tidily like that?

Whoever she was, she seemed the sensible sort, having dressed appropriately for the weather. But she also seemed the *not* sensible sort, having gone out in this terrible storm in the first place.

She clomped up the porch steps in those sensible winter boots, and Felty opened the door before she had a chance to knock. She brushed the snow off her coat and beanie, stomped her feet on the rug, and came into the house. Felty shut the door behind her.

"Irene!" Anna exclaimed, clapping her hands, then immediately feeling guilty that she had completely left Irene off her matchmaking list.

Irene pulled the beanie and bonnet off her head and the scarf from her face, her cheeks bright red and her nose glowing like a red Christmas light. "*Hallo, Mammi.* I came to spend Thanksgiving with the only people in the whole world who love me."

Irene was a lovely girl, but she tended to be dramatic and impulsive. There were plenty of people who loved her, unlike Anna, whose children couldn't even be bothered to come for Thanksgiving.

Anna snatched her list from the table and stuffed it into her apron pocket. Irene never needed to know her *mammi* had neglected to put her on the list. "It's *wunderbarr* to see you, dear, but it's quite dangerous to come through such a terrible storm."

Irene pressed her lips together and ripped off her mittens. "*Mamm* kicked me out of the house."

Anna eyed Irene doubtfully. "In a snowstorm?" Irene's *mater*, Sallie Mae, wasn't one to lose her temper over much of anything.

Irene blew a puff of air from between her lips and rolled her eyes. "*Ach, Mammi,* she's being completely unreasonable." She pitched her voice a little higher. "I said, '*Mamm,* I'd rather go to the dentist than spend one more minute in this house,' and she said, 'Well, if you're going to be so snippy about it, why don't you go to *Mammi* and *Dawdi* Helmuth's house and see if they'll give you some sympathy.' Can you believe it? She said I'm snippy. I said, '*Mammi* and *Dawdi* love me. They don't think I'm snippy.'"

"Of course we don't," Anna replied, not sure she was following the conversation. "But then your *mamm* kicked you out?"

Irene lowered her eyes. "She didn't kick me out exactly, but I know when I'm not wanted. I bundled up, hitched Patty to the cart, and came here. I hope *Mamm* is worried sick about me. I hope her Thanksgiving is ruined. She can't treat her own daughter like that and not suffer the consequences."

Anna still wasn't following what all the fuss was about. "Treat her daughter like what, dear?"

Irene plopped into a kitchen chair and peeled off her boots. "She has no right to tell me what I can and cannot do. I'm in *rumschpringa*. I can do whatever I want."

"That's not completely true," Felty mumbled, but Anna could tell he didn't want to upset Irene, so he kept his voice low. He took Irene's coat, scarf, and hats and hung everything on the hooks by the front door.

Anna stretched her smile a little wider. "What is it you want to do during *rumschpringa*? Your *dawdi* has a tattoo, but I'd advise against it."

Felty nodded. "You'll regret it the rest of your life."

"And you'll get hepatitis." Anna pointed to the stove. "Would you like some hot cocoa to warm you up?"

Irene nodded.

Anna filled the teapot with water and set it on the stove. "Andy Miller took up smoking during *rumschpringa*, and now his teeth are yellow."

"Oh, *Mammi*," Irene said, smiling affectionately. "I'm not going to get a tattoo. Not yet."

"Not *yet*?"

"And I wouldn't smoke even if you paid me a million dollars. It gives you wrinkles, and I don't want to look old before my time."

"I don't want to look old before my time either," Anna said.

Irene stood, came around the counter, and put her arms around Anna. "You look beautiful, *Mammi*. Your skin practically glows. Any woman would kill to have your skin tone and your high cheekbones."

"She's still the prettiest girl in Wisconsin," Felty said.

Anna pressed her hand to her cheek. "I don't think my cheekbones are any taller than average."

Irene pulled the tin of hot cocoa from the cupboard. "Miriam Beechy is going to Milwaukee, and she wants me to come with her. We can get jobs at one of the breweries and split the rent for an apartment. Doesn't that sound like an exciting adventure?"

Felty peered at Irene over his glasses. "You want to work at a brewery?"

Irene nodded enthusiastically. "Miriam says they're always hiring because they have to make ten million barrels of beer a year."

Anna's eyes nearly popped out of her head. "That's a lot of beer."

"Doesn't that sound like the funnest job? I just need enough money for bus fare and a deposit on an apartment. And maybe food for a few weeks until I get a job. But *Mamm* won't give me any money, and *Dat* agrees with her. They say Milwaukee is too far away and too dangerous for an Amish girl. They say I can have a perfectly fine *rumschpringa* here in Bonduel, but how am I supposed to have an adventure in the middle of nowhere? There's nothing in Bonduel but cows and chickens and soybeans." She slumped her shoulders. "There certainly aren't any boys worth mentioning."

Anna's ears perked up. This was the perfect situation for a

matchmaker. "I could help you find a boyfriend. We just need to make a list."

The teapot whistled, and Irene slid it off the burner. She angrily spooned powder into three mugs, poured water, and stirred the cocoa in each mug as if she were beating eggs for a souffle. "I don't need a boyfriend, *Mammi*. Boys tell you they love you and promise to marry you, then they decide to go to Pennsylvania for a whole year, and they don't even bother to tell you. You have to hear it from their sister, and then your heart breaks and you decide you'd rather be in Milwaukee than anywhere near a stupid boy."

Hmmm. That was oddly specific.

Anna picked up her mug before Irene could break it with her vigorous stirring. "*Cum*, dear. Bring your mug to the table, and tell me and Felty all about it."

Irene handed Felty a mug, wrapped her hands around her own mug, and sat down. "*Ach, Mammi*. All I want to do is go to Milwaukee and have an adventure. Is that so unreasonable?"

Anna patted Irene's hand. "You skipped over the part where a boy broke your heart."

"I don't care about stupid boys," Irene said, looking anywhere but at Anna.

Anna glanced at Felty with an apology in her eyes. "Boys can be stupid, but it seems like you care very much."

Irene took a sip of cocoa and immediately spit it back into her mug. "Hot," she said. She blew into her mug and took another sip. "Truly, *Mammi*, I don't even care about him anymore." She drew in a shaky breath. "He's been coming around every week for more than a year, and three months ago he told me he loved me and wanted to marry me. I actually thought he was sincere. Then yesterday, his *schwester* announced he's leaving for Pennsylvania in January to do an apprenticeship. *For a whole year*. Doesn't sound like he's madly in love, does it?" She tossed her head back and laughed bitterly, like her heart was broken. "So now I truly don't care. I just want to go to Milwaukee and make beer and have an adventure. It will be really fun, and *Mamm* just doesn't understand."

"What's his name?"

Irene sat up straighter. "I'm done with him. His name will never cross my lips again."

Felty's eyes twinkled. "I like a girl who has the courage of her convictions."

Anna sat back in her chair and studied Irene's face. This was going to be a hard case, but Anna was up for the challenge. She'd been a matchmaker long enough to see that Irene's perfect match was What's-His-Name. She was obviously deeply in love with the boy, and he was deeply in love with her, but she had jumped to several conclusions and had obviously misunderstood What's-His-Name's intentions. Trying to make Irene see reason wasn't going to do any good. She'd have to use reverse physiology. Or reverse psychiatry. Or reverse psychology. She was never sure which was which. Anna forgot all about her uncaring family. Helping Irene see the error of her ways would be a wonderful-*gute* Thanksgiving activity. "I'm so glad you came to us for help, Irene. You must stay for Thanksgiving dinner. We're going to help you forget all about What's-His-Name and make a plan to get you to Milwaukee."

"We are?" Felty asked.

Anna nodded. "That beer isn't going to make itself."

Irene bloomed into a smile. "Oh, *denki, Mammi*. I knew you'd help. You're the only person who understands me."

Poor Irene had no idea how true that was.

Felty smiled. He understood too, but he wasn't one to call attention to himself or crave recognition. He quietly went about his business, not needing any credit or appreciation. That was why no one ever suspected him of being sneaky. He got away with a lot more that way.

Anna sighed. She really shouldn't have thrown such a tantrum about Thanksgiving. Irene was going to be very disappointed. "The only problem is that it's going to be a pitiful Thanksgiving dinner. You came all this way, and we have nothing to fix. I didn't even bother to buy a turkey."

Irene was suddenly wildly cheerful. There was nothing like a little bit of validation to make a person feel better about everything. She clapped her hands as if the thought of a turkey-less Thanksgiving was the most *wunderbarr* thing in the world. "We don't need a turkey to have a proper feast. Show me what food you've got, and I'll cook up the best Thanksgiving dinner you've ever eaten."

Anna wasn't going to argue, but it wouldn't be the best Thanksgiving dinner without turkey and cheesy jalapeno banana bread. There were no bananas and no jalapenos, and why had she been so stubborn about buying a turkey? She had let her temper get the better of her, and now Thanksgiving was ruined, and Irene would probably never marry What's-His-Name.

Irene rifled through the cupboards. "Noodles, corn, flour, pinto beans. I could make biscuits and a hearty soup." She opened the fridge. "Apples and eggs. Lots of vegetables. Three containers of sour cream."

Anna blushed. "I always forget I have it and buy more at the store. A well-stocked fridge can't be without sour cream."

Irene grinned. "I agree."

"The good stuff is down in the fruit cellar. I've got seven pints of my famous huckleberry raisin jelly and tons of spaghetti sauce."

"Let's go down and see," Irene said.

They all looked out the window when they heard a low, distant rumble. Something with a loud and obnoxious motor was coming up Huckleberry Hill.

CHAPTER 2

They gathered around the front window to watch as a massive motorcycle lumbered up the hill. Anna squinted. "It's a tricycle. A giant tricycle."

The fake motorcycle had three wheels, one in front and two behind. It was shiny black with red pinstriping, three substantial headlights, and a very comfortable-looking cushioned seat. Long white locks of hair stuck out from under the rider's black helmet, and he wore a black leather jacket with all sorts of patches on the sleeves. "Oh dear," Anna said. "He must be freezing."

The tricycle-motorcycle slipped and slid up the hill. The rider revved the engine, and the wheels spun furiously before they found traction on the road and catapulted the motorcycle forward to flat ground.

"Who is he?" Irene murmured.

Anna held her breath as the rider killed the engine, slipped off his trike, and stomped up the porch steps. She couldn't see his face because of the helmet, but he had broad shoulders and a frightening skull patch on the front of his leather jacket. Was he here to murder them? Steal their Thanksgiving dinner?

Give them a ticket for not having a turkey in the fridge? Surely a man who drove a trike couldn't be dangerous, could he?

Felty opened the door before the man knocked. He was much more trusting than Anna, although no one, not even a robber, should be out on a cold day like this.

"Hello," the man said, his voice deep and scratchy and oddly shaky, as if Felty made him nervous instead of the other way around. "I'm looking for Abraham Schwartz."

Felty motioned him inside. "Come in, come in, before you turn into a popsicle."

The man took off his helmet and brushed the snow from his jacket. Though he didn't have much hair on top, it was long and very pretty, flowing over his shoulders and down his back like a cascade of white ivy down a black leather wall. His equally white mustache drooped past his lips and met the goatee on his chin. He wore a fuzzy turtleneck sweater under his leather jacket that looked cozy, but not thick enough to keep him properly warm on a day like this. "Um, no thank you. I don't want to intrude. I stopped at the house down the hill, and they directed me up here."

"You stopped at the Tuttles?" Anna asked. The Tuttles were Anna and Felty's nearest neighbors, lovely Englischers who lived a half mile down the road. Anna sometimes used their phone for emergencies.

He nodded. "I'm just wondering if Abraham Schwartz lives here or if you know where I can find him."

Anna couldn't bear the thought of sending the robber out into the storm. "We don't know Abraham Schwartz, but please come in and get warm."

The man gazed longingly into the house before shaking his head and taking a step back. "I'm sorry to bother you."

Anna wasn't about to let him get away with that. She stepped onto the porch in her slippers and boldly hooked her elbow around his arm. When you were eighty-five years old, you could get away with a lot of bad behavior. "I won't be able to sleep tonight for thinking you're frozen to death on the side of the highway on your cute little trike."

He looked both surprised and deeply offended. "I don't want to be rude, but unless you want to see a grown man cry, don't ever tell a biker his ride is cute."

"No need to be so touchy. It's freezing out here." Anna yanked on his arm, and he relented and let her lead him into the house.

Without letting her eyes stray from his face, Irene took a few steps backward just as Felty took a step forward. "Can I take your coat?"

"If I could just warm up and get directions to the nearest gas station. I . . . I appreciate your hospitality." The biker shrugged off his jacket, which had a huge skeleton hand stitched on the back.

"Is that applique or embroidery?" Anna asked. "I know how to do both, but I've never tried to do it on leather."

Irene snapped out of whatever daze she was in. "Um, would you like some hot chocolate?"

The man pulled off his black leather gloves and flexed his fingers. "That's very kind, but have you got anything stronger?"

Irene wasn't qualified to make beer yet, if that was what he wanted.

"Coffee?" she said.

"That's better."

Anna pointed toward the comfy sofa where Sparky was lounging. "Come and sit down. Would you like a blanket?"

"No thank you, but I might take my boots off, if you don't mind. My feet went numb about thirty miles back."

"Of course," Anna said. "I'll fetch you a bowl of warm water to soak them in."

He got a funny look on his face. "Uh, I guess that would be

helpful." He sat on the sofa and unlaced his black, clunky boots. They must have been the biker fashion, because they seemed very impractical for normal footwear.

It was rude to stare, but the situation was so out of the ordinary, Anna couldn't help herself. Besides, Felty and Irene were staring. Anna was just following the crowd.

Felty sat next to him. "I'm Felty Helmuth. This is Anna, and this is our granddaughter Irene."

With some effort, the man pulled off his right boot. "I'm Abraham Schwartz."

Felty tilted his head to one side. "You're looking for yourself?"

Anna frowned. "Lloyd Packer's son went looking for himself, and Search and Rescue had to pull him off a cliff."

Abraham didn't look up as he worked on his other boot. "I'm Abraham Senior. The other Abraham is my son." His voice trailed off as if he were ashamed he had a son, but then Anna realized that he must have been ashamed he didn't even know where his son lived.

Anna was nosy, but she tried to respect people's privacy—unless they were related to her. But Abraham was sitting in her living room, and she would never learn his tragic story if she didn't ask. *Ach, vell,* she just assumed it was a tragic story, because what kind of father lost track of his own son? She wouldn't ask Abraham that question. It seemed harsh, and she could attract more flies with honey than vinegar. She filled her mopping bucket with warm water and set it on the floor next to Abraham. "Tell us about your son," she said, smiling sweetly, as if she didn't have a devious bone in her whole body.

Deep lines etched themselves into Abraham's face. "I'd rather not."

Well. Anna wasn't one to be put off so easily. "Is he tall?"

Abraham scrubbed his fingers through his beautiful white hair. "I'd better go. I've taken up enough of your time."

Anna drew her brows together. Surely Abraham hadn't found her question offensive, had he? She bit her tongue. What if Abraham Junior was unnaturally short or had lost his legs in a car accident? What had Anna been thinking, asking such an insensitive question?

Felty saved the day. He always did. "What would it hurt to wait out the storm? You won't get very far out there, and it seems you don't know where you're going."

Abraham glanced at Anna, probably wondering if she would ask any more prying questions. "But I've interrupted your Thanksgiving celebration. Thanksgiving is for family, not perfect strangers."

Well, in case he hadn't noticed, Anna was pretty thin on family today. She had almost forgotten how downhearted she was, but the sadness returned when she thought of her children sitting around a table, laughing and talking, glad she wasn't there. "Why don't you stay for dinner? It's too cold to go out, and nobody else is coming."

Abraham narrowed his eyes as if he didn't completely believe her. "That's . . . that's very kind of you."

"But I have to warn you, there is no turkey or cranberry sauce. We do have some huckleberry raisin jelly and five quarts of spaghetti sauce. Plus all the chow-chow you can eat."

A memory traveled across Abraham's face. "I haven't had chow-chow for thirty years." His expression immediately hardened to stone. "It's very Amish of you to invite me, but staying for Thanksgiving is really too much. I would never take advantage of your kindness that way. I can eat at the gas station."

Felty propped his elbows on his knees. "Don't forget to entertain strangers, because you might entertain an angel without knowing it." That was one of the reasons Anna adored Felty. He always had a scripture in his back pocket for emergencies.

Abraham seemed to wither like a flower in an early frost. "I'm no angel. I can guarantee that."

"You could be looking at it backwards," Anna said. "Let strangers feed you Thanksgiving dinner, because they might be angels in disguise."

Abraham cracked a smile. "I can't argue with that."

"Good." Anna decided not to tell him that he wouldn't be getting any cheesy jalapeno banana bread. The disappointment of no turkey was bad enough.

Irene brought him a steaming cup of *kaffee*. "Is black okay?"

Abraham's face relaxed into a comfortable smile as he put his nose to the rim of the cup and breathed in. "There is nothing I like better than a hot cup of coffee. Except maybe a gas station hot dog. Those things taste like cholesterol on a stick."

WHILE ABRAHAM WARMED HIS FEET, the four of them talked about what they could make for Thanksgiving dinner. Everything depended on what Anna had in her kitchen. Irene volunteered to make biscuits to go with the huckleberry raisin jelly, and Abraham wanted to make his famous five-alarm chili. Anna didn't even know what five-alarm chili was, but it sounded a little bit dangerous. They also agreed on chow-chow and buttered noodles because Abraham said he had a hankering for both.

Not bad for an impromptu Thanksgiving meal.

Irene gave Anna a hug. "*Mammi*, you have spent more than sixty years making Thanksgiving dinner for your family. Let me cook so you can relax."

Anna patted Irene on the cheek. "That is very kind of you, dear. It's tradition that I make the cheesy jalapeno banana bread, but since I don't have the ingredients, I'll let you cook. I can fold the napkins. Felty and I took an oregano class, and I can make them look like swans. Or roses. Or artichokes."

"Origami," Felty said.

Irene's smile stuttered briefly. "I'll sure miss your cheesy jalapeno banana bread."

Felty let Abraham wear a pair of his old slippers, and they all got to work. Anna sat at the table to fold napkins. There were only four of them, but it usually took her about fifteen minutes to fold a swan. She wanted to have plenty of time in case Abraham preferred an artichoke.

Abraham had no trouble lighting the LP gas stove, and he seemed very comfortable in her kitchen. Most Englishers stared and stuttered when they met Amish folks. Abraham was more familiar with the Amish than he was telling. Anna had to bite her tongue to avoid asking any questions that would drive him back into the storm. She studied him out of the corner of her eye, looking for any signs of Amishness in his demeanor, but the spider tattoo on the back of his neck and the snake up his arm made it hard to fathom how he could have been Amish.

She had to do more prying. But carefully so Abraham wouldn't suspect. "Abraham, I'm sorry I called your trike cute earlier. I didn't know that was an insult."

Abraham inspected the bottles on Anna's spice rack. "No worries. I'm just a little testy about my ride. I used to own a tricked-out Harley, but I got in an accident and wrecked my knee. The three wheels give me more stability, but they also get me teased a lot."

Anna pretended to concentrate intently on her paper swan. "Do you have someone to take care of you and your knee? Like a wife or a girlfriend?"

Abraham shuffled his feet. "I don't really have anyone." He turned, and Anna could tell he was pretending to concentrate intently on the spice rack. "I've made a lot of mistakes. Big ones. I want to make amends, but it wonders me if it would be better to just let it go and disappear."

It wonders me was most definitely an Amish phrase. Anna was more curious than ever and especially eager to help Abraham make amends for whatever it was he'd done. Anna was pretty sure the amends had something to do with his son and all those big mistakes Abraham said he had made.

"Never trouble trouble till trouble troubles you," Irene said. She was rolling out biscuit dough, but Anna could tell she was thinking very seriously about what Abraham had said. Did she regret making such a fuss about going to Milwaukee? Had she burned a bridge with What's-His-Name that she couldn't rebuild?

Abraham nodded. "Exactly. Maybe certain people would be better off without me in their lives. I'd only stir up trouble that's been underground for many years."

Felty set four plates on the table. "A boil will fester if it's not tended to."

"*Jah,*" Anna said, hoping to give Abraham a little encouragement. "Once Irene's *dat* got a sliver in his palm, and he was so stubborn, he refused to let me take it out. A pocket of pus formed around it, and . . ."

Irene whirled around. "*Mammi!* Maybe not before we eat."

Anna formed her lips into an "O." "I'll save that story for later. But in my experience, trouble only gets worse unless it's attended to. Like blisters or mold in the refrigerator."

With a concerned look on her face, Irene opened the fridge and stuck her head inside. After a few seconds, she drew back and closed the door. She wouldn't find any mold in that refrigerator. Anna would never stand for it.

Abraham tilted his head and glanced out the front window. The snow was still coming down like autumn leaves on a windy day. "Do you hear that?"

Anna caught her breath. The cheery sound of jingle bells wafted up the hill.

Irene's eyes widened then narrowed. She growled softly. "There's only one person I know who puts jingle bells on his horse before Christmastime. And I'm never speaking his name again as long as I live."

CHAPTER 3

$\mathcal{A}$nna abandoned her swan and went to the window. For sure and certain, she loved that big picture window. She always knew exciting things were coming before they came. "Is it What's-His-Name?" she said, trying to keep the delight out of her voice.

Irene folded her arms and stood at rigid attention. "If he thinks I'm going to forgive him just because he came all this way in a snowstorm, he has another thing coming."

If What's-His-Name had indeed come all this way to fix things with Irene, then he already had Anna's approval. He was obviously a smart young man. Intelligent young men made matchmaking so much easier. Too many boys were as thick as a slab of lard.

A one-horse open sleigh, just like in the song, glided up the hill as if it had just touched down on a runway. The handsome boy holding the reins wore a straw hat and a brilliant white smile. He lifted his gloved hand and waved at the house. Irene scoffed.

It was definitely What's-His-Name. Who else would make Irene so angry?

Ach, vell, her *mamm,* her *dat,* her *bruder* Titus, and Titus's herd of unruly goats. Irene got mad about a lot of things.

There were three other people in the sleigh with What's-His-Name. Three Englischers, by the looks of it. A woman wearing a thin coat sat next to What's-His-Name with her arms clenched tightly around two small children. The children were wrapped in what looked like a bright red scarf.

"That's the scarf I knitted him last year!" Irene said. Was she mad that What's-His-Name had shared his scarf or mad that he had the nerve to use it when he had so deeply offended her?

What's-His-Name guided the horse to behind Abraham's trike. He quickly jumped down, took the two children from the woman's arms, and hurried up the porch steps. Once again, Felty opened the door before the knock.

What's-His-Name didn't even wait to be invited in. "Their car slid off the road near the bottom of your hill, and now it won't start. I got them up here as fast as I could." With a quick glance at Irene, he handed one screaming child to Felty and one to Anna and dashed out of the house. He reached out his hand to the woman, who had managed to alight from the sleigh, but she waved him away. "I'll unhitch the horse," he called.

The woman blew into the house, and Felty shut the door behind her. She took the smaller child from Felty. His eyes were puffy, his nose ran like a faucet, and he clutched the red scarf in his little fists as if it were his only friend. Poor thing. He couldn't have been more than two. The woman shushed him and pressed her lips against his forehead. "It's okay, Jude." She looked around the room with her warm, sad brown eyes. "I'm so sorry to intrude like this."

She burst into tears, and Abraham was suddenly right next to her. He patted her awkwardly on the shoulder. "You're safe now. No need to cry about it." He obviously wasn't used to trying to make someone feel better, but Anna could tell his sincerity ran deep, even if he couldn't express it well.

The little girl in Anna's arms squirmed and reached for her mother, nearly piercing Anna's eardrum with her screams. But Anna had reared thirteen children. Nothing rattled her. "Her hands are like ice. Let's get them into a warm tub."

The woman squared her shoulders, wiped her face, and followed Anna down the hall to the bathroom. Anna drew a lukewarm bath as the woman stripped both her children and set them in the tub. The girl calmed down almost immediately as the water washed over her. The boy continued screaming for another five minutes, but the color returned to his cheeks, and he stopped shivering.

Sitting next to the tub, the woman unrolled some toilet paper and blew her nose. "Thanks for your help. I don't know what we would have done."

"What's your name?" Anna said.

"I'm Brandy. This is Jude and Hazel."

Anna tried to get Brandy to make eye contact. It didn't work. "Are you trying to get somewhere for Thanksgiving?"

Brandy's eyes filled with tears again. "Not anymore."

"What's-His-Name says your car died."

She swiped a tear from her cheek. "After it slid off the road. Four cars passed us, but nobody stopped to help, and I couldn't get cell service." She wrapped her arms around her legs and buried her face in her knees. "I don't know what I'm going to do. My cards are maxed out."

"I'm glad What's-His-Name came along when he did."

Brandy sniffed and lifted her head. "Do you not know John?"

"He looks familiar, but he's not in my district." John. That was a nice name. Jesus's favorite apostle was named John. Then again, the other John, Jesus's cousin, got his head chopped off. Anna drew her brows together. Was that important, or were there too many random and unnecessary facts floating around in her brain?

Why wasn't she acquainted with John? She frowned. She was failing in her responsibilities. As an expert matchmaker, she needed to know all the unmarried young people in all five districts in Bonduel. She should have knitted all of *die youngie* matchmaking potholders by now. Potholders were a time-tested way to get two people to fall in love with each other. "We should get you and these little ones into some dry clothes. I have a dress you can wear, but nothing for the children. We could wrap them in blankets and hang their clothes by the pellet stove to dry." She handed Brandy a fluffy white towel.

Brandy pulled Jude out of the tub and wrapped him in the towel. "I loaded our suitcases into John's sleigh before we abandoned our car."

Anna was already halfway down the hall. "I'll ask him to fetch them." Suitcases. Brandy wasn't local. Was she headed to family for Thanksgiving? Some people still wanted to spend the day with their grandparents, even if Anna's own family didn't.

John was just coming in the front door with a suitcase in each hand and a cellophane-wrapped basket tucked under his arm. His smile seemed to be a permanent fixture on his face, never wavering even when his gaze flicked to Irene, who stood at the stove with her back to everyone, apparently intent on ignoring him. He set the suitcases on the floor and the basket on the table, narrowly missing Anna's half-folded swan. He reached out his hand to Anna. "I'm John Bontrager. We haven't met, but I've seen you at the market, and Irene has told me all about you." Irene's name stuck in his throat for a fraction of a second. "My *dat* is Gary Bontrager. He fixes Englischers' motor homes."

"*Ach,* I know your *dat,*" Anna said. "Mostly by reputation. They say he can fix anything. But I don't have a motor home, so I haven't felt the need to introduce myself."

John pulled the hat from his head, sending a cascade of water droplets onto the floor. "I walked the motorcycle into the barn too. I hope that's okay."

Abraham looked up from his five-alarm chili bubbling on the stove. "I really appreciate it."

Anna wrapped her fingers around the long handle of the bigger suitcase. "I need to get these to Brandy."

"Let me." John grabbed the handles of both suitcases.

Anna motioned for him to follow her down the hall. "Thank *Derr Herr*, you saw Brandy was in trouble. Where were you headed on this snowy day? Most people are hunkered down with their families."

The wheels of both suitcases whirred down the hall. "I was coming here, of course. I'm madly in love with Irene, and she's very angry at me. I came to make things right."

"I had you pegged for a smart one the moment I saw you, John Bontrager."

"Not smart enough to keep her from getting mad at me in the first place."

"She wants to make beer in Milwaukee."

His grin drooped. "I know. She's really mad."

John set the suitcases outside the bathroom door and retreated down the hall. Anna knocked. "Brandy, here are your clothes. Let me know if you need any help."

She returned to the kitchen. John stood with his arms folded, leaning against the wall, staring at Irene, probably hoping to get a private moment to talk with her. It didn't look promising. Irene acted as if he wasn't in the room, and besides that, she was watching her biscuits in the oven, boiling noodles, and chopping apples all at the same time. She had always been a deft and efficient cook. Two pie shells sat next to her on the counter. When had she found time to make those? Anna was overjoyed. There would be pie for Thanksgiving!

She almost hated to ask, but the little ones would need something to eat, and Anna didn't think five-alarm chili would be safe. "Irene, do you think you could make some macaroni and cheese for the children? I have three boxes in the cupboard."

Irene turned, smiled at Anna, then glared at John. "Of course, *Mammi*. That won't take but a minute."

John glanced at Anna and scrunched his lips together. Coming here was a nice gesture, but actually getting Irene to forgive him was going to be much harder. What had Irene said? That John was going to Pennsylvania for a year and hadn't told her? Yep, John would have to do a lot of groveling before Irene would even agree to look at him.

Anna bustled to the end table in the great room and pulled out a fluorescent pink potholder from the drawer. Nothing but the most garish and exciting potholder would do. She handed it to John. "Give this to Irene. The way to every woman's heart is through a potholder."

John seemed confused and appreciative at the same time. He'd definitely be grateful later.

Brandy came into the great room carrying Jude and leading Hazel by the hand. The children both wore threadbare red pajamas and slippers. Their feet would be warm. Brandy was dressed in dark purple leggings and a large, gray sweatshirt that looked like it had swallowed her whole. Anna made a mental note. Brandy would need stockings, because the wood floors were icy cold.

Brandy sat down on the sofa, pulled her children tight, and seemed to shrink into a tight ball of fear and despair. Her face was streaked with tears. Anna couldn't blame her for indulging in a good cry. She was among strangers, away from home, and she didn't know that Anna was planning to invite her to stay for dinner. Of course, if she knew there was no turkey, she might not want to stay. "I sorry for barging in on your Thanksgiving."

She showed Anna her phone. "As soon as I can figure something out, I'll get out of your hair."

"I won't hear of it," Anna said. "You're eating Thanksgiving dinner with us. We can sort out the rest after that. But I must warn you, there's no turkey. It will be a very mediocre Thanksgiving."

From his place at the stove, Abraham studied Brandy with concern. "Do you like five-alarm chili? I could make it one-alarm chili if you've got a sensitive stomach."

Brandy dabbed her nose with a wad of toilet paper she had balled in her fist. "I have a turkey."

"You do?" Anna said. She tried not to let her happiness run away from her. It was too much to hope for.

Brandy hesitated and looked down at her hands. "We got a Thanksgiving care package from the church, and it has a turkey in it. It's already smoked and everything."

John pointed to the basket on the table. "Is this it?"

Anna got excited for about three seconds. Then she had to be realistic. "We can't eat your turkey. The church gave it to you."

"I want to share it. You saved me and my children from frostbite and who knows what else. I'm embarrassed at how stupid I was. My tires are bald, and my car is twenty years old. I didn't plan things out very well. I should have taken the bus."

"Who wants to be on a bus on Thanksgiving?" Abraham said. His voice was gruff, but the compassion in his sky-blue eyes was unmistakable. He went to the kitchen table and fingered the care basket tied up with a bright red ribbon. "What else you got in this care package?" He pumped his eyebrows up and down.

A giggle burst from Brandy's mouth. "Go ahead and open it."

The curiosity was too much for everyone, including the children. They all gathered around the table as Abraham ripped off the bow and tried to untie the ribbon around the cellophane with his thick fingers. Anna took pity on him and pulled a pair of scissors from the drawer. He cut the ribbon, and the cellophane fell open like a blooming flower. The biggest thing in the basket was the turkey. Abraham set it on the table. It wasn't huge, just a modest-sized turkey breast, but plenty for the eight of them, especially with the chili, noodles, mac and cheese, biscuits, chow-chow, and pie.

Ach, they'd be eating leftovers for days.

Abraham motioned to Brandy. "It's your basket. You should do it."

Brandy pulled out two cans of green beans, a can of cream of mushroom soup, a can of corn, and a small box of instant mashed potatoes.

"I love those," Anna said. "I use them to make potato chocolate cake."

The stuffing mix seemed to trip Brandy up. She went very still as she studied the directions on the back as if there were a secret message hidden in the recipe. Tears pooled in her eyes, and she blinked them back like her life depended on it. "Nobody should spend Thanksgiving alone. Not even people who deserve it."

Abraham pressed his lips together and shifted his feet. "For what I've done, I deserve to spend the rest of my days alone and lonely. Even on Thanksgiving."

"Nobody deserves to be alone," Felty said in that gentle, adamant way that always made Anna glad to be his *fraa*. "God loves us all and wants us to love each other, no matter how hard that is sometimes."

Brandy took a deep shuddering breath, but the tears had dried up. "I'm a horrible person."

"I'm way more horrible than you are," Abraham said.

"John is the most horrible person ever," Irene said, lifting

33

her chin and glaring at John still holding up the wall by the door.

Anna couldn't believe that John Bontrager was the most horrible person ever. Had Irene met Vernon Schmucker?

John raised his hand, one corner of his mouth curling upward. "I'm horrible because I made a decision without consulting the girl I love, and now she's mad at me."

Irene sniffed into the air. "I'm not mad. I've already moved on."

"I'm the most horrible," Anna blurted out. "I decided not to buy a turkey out of spite, and I've ruined Felty's Thanksgiving."

"You haven't ruined anything, Annie Banannie."

A low, rumbling laugh came from deep within Abraham's throat. "It's not a contest. We can all be equally as horrible."

Brandy cracked a smile. "I guess we can."

Felty stroked his beard. "We just need to remember that Jesus swallowed up all our horribleness and took it on Himself. It's the best reason to be thankful."

"Amen," Abraham said, his booming voice echoing through the entire house. He looked at Brandy. "What else is in that treasure chest?"

At the bottom of the basket was a can of pumpkin pie filling, but it wouldn't be much good without a pie crust and an oven. Abraham pulled out the last things in the basket: four caramel apple suckers. He slipped the wrappers off two of them and handed them to the children.

"You'll ruin their dinner," Brandy said, without an ounce of protest in her tone.

"We've already established that I'm a horrible person. I ruin children's dinners without remorse."

Even though the sucker was almost as big as Jude's head, he opened wide and popped it into his mouth. Hazel licked her daintily, as if she was afraid it would end up tasting terrible.

They decided to eat the turkey and leave the rest of the basket for Brandy to take home. Anna would have liked to have stuffing with her turkey, but she didn't dare suggest it seeing as how the mere sight of the box made Brandy so upset. Just to help her feel better, Anna went to her bedroom and got Brandy a thick pair of stockings to wear while Felty carved the turkey. Irene put the pies in the oven, and everyone sat down. There had been such a kerfuffle earlier that Anna had only had time to fold one swan. She gave it to John because he needed a little extra Thanksgiving cheer. Irene in turns ignored him or glared at him, and he looked a little dejected.

Anna had already made a plan for John and Irene. Everyone else at the table was in on the plan, even though not a word had been spoken about it. For sure and certain, they were all hoping that John and Irene would get back together. Anna watched as Abraham and Felty sat on either side of Brandy and her kids. Anna slipped into the chair next to Felty so Irene and John would be forced to sit together. "Felty, may we say a prayer out loud this time and hold hands as a sign of fellowship?"

"Of course."

Irene was just barely polite enough to take John's hand, though she wasn't happy about it. She wore her outrage like a badge.

"Before we start," Abraham said. "I have to warn you about the chili. Anna has an excellent spice rack. She's got five types of paprika and three varieties of hot chili flakes. I got a little carried away, and now it's more like six-alarm chili than five-alarm chili. I would advise anyone under the age of ten and over the age of thirty not to eat it."

"But Abraham, you're older than that."

He chuckled. "I'm used to a lot more spice than this. I can handle it."

Anna raised her eyebrows. "So only Irene, John, you, and Brandy are allowed to eat it?"

"That's correct."

"I can't eat anything spicy," Brandy said. "It gives me heartburn."

Irene nodded. "Me too."

Felty laughed. "It looks like the chili is all yours, John and Abraham."

"I'll do what I can," John said.

Just as they were about to bow their heads, they heard another low rumble coming up the hill. Anna glanced at Felty in confusion. Was it another trike? Whatever-it-was stopped before it came into view from the window. After a long minute, a plump, round figure came into sight and lumbered up the porch steps.

Anna's heart lurched. "But . . . he wasn't supposed to come."

Felty winced. "He must have heard about the turkey."

CHAPTER 4

*O*ernon Schmucker had come to dinner after all.

What a disappointment, and just when the day had started to look up! There were two apple pies in the oven, Brandy wasn't crying anymore, and a small but adequate smoked turkey sat in the middle of the table, sliced and ready to eat.

Anna bit down hard on her bottom lip. It was her own fault. At the height of her irritation with her family, she had invited Vernon to Thanksgiving dinner. But he'd turned her down and positively assured Anna he wasn't going to come. What had changed his mind?

This time, Felty wasn't eager to answer the door. Vernon knocked, and Felty took his time getting out of his chair. He didn't want Vernon here, but Anna also knew he didn't want to scrape a frozen Vernon off their porch come springtime. Felty opened the door and acted as hospitable as ever, even though Anna was sure he was clenching his teeth in annoyance. "Well, *hallo,* Vernon. I thought you weren't coming." *Hoped you weren't coming* was more like it.

Breathing heavily, Vernon waddled into the house, the

sweat trickling down his face. Vernon was in his early forties, unmarried, with a hearty appetite. Anna had made the mistake of encouraging Vernon to court more than one of her granddaughters, and Vernon sort of thought of himself as part of the family. He took off his hat. "My *mamm* is in Florida, and she made me a Thanksgiving dinner before she left, but I got hungry and finished it off last night. *Mamm* always makes sure I get three square meals a day. I knew she wouldn't want me to starve on Thanksgiving. I went next door to Sensenigs' house, but they couldn't squeeze me in at their table, so Ike Sensenig offered to bring me here on his four-wheeler."

Anna snorted, then clapped her hand over her mouth in dismay. It was rude to snort, even at Vernon Schmucker. For sure and certain, Ike Sensenig was as happy as a clam to pass Vernon off to Anna and Felty and make him their problem instead of his. Ike was irritatingly proud of his four-wheeler. He'd gotten permission from the bishop to buy it for his business, and it surely brought Ike great pleasure to dump Vernon at other people's houses on Thanksgiving Day.

"He dropped me at the crest of the hill, which I thought was very rude, but he said I could walk the rest of the way."

"Well, yes," Felty said. "It's only another hundred feet from there."

"Like I said, very rude." Vernon took off his hat. "Looks like I'm just in time. What's for dinner?"

Anna jumped to her feet and grabbed another place setting for Vernon. She would have liked to put him in the barn to eat, but that seemed a little drastic, even for someone who'd come uninvited. Anna frowned. Vernon *had* been invited, and she had been the one to invite him. There was no one to blame but herself. *Ach*, sometimes she wished she weren't quite so impetuous.

Irene scooted away from John to make room for Vernon to sit between them, but Anna wasn't having any of that. She'd worked very hard to get John and Irene together, and not even Vernon would tear them apart. "Here, Vernon," she said. "Sit between John and me." This would mean that she would have to hold Vernon's hand during the prayer, but she would sacrifice herself for John and Irene's sake. It was what any *gute* matchmaker would do. Anna had broken her arm, sliced a chunk out of her thumb, and knitted dozens of potholders all in the pursuit of finding suitable spouses for her grandchildren. She could certainly hold Vernon's hand for a prayer.

"Pass the biscuits," Vernon said.

"Vernon, we haven't prayed yet."

Vernon made a face. "What are we waiting for?"

Felty directed everyone to hold hands. Vernon's hand was clammy, despite his having just come in from the cold. Anna pressed her lips together and thought of Irene and John on their wedding day. The result was worth the sacrifice.

"Dear Heavenly Father," Felty began. "We are grateful to have friends here, new and old. We are grateful for this food, grateful for willing hands that prepared it, and grateful that John and Irene, Abraham and Brandy and her kids found their way to us today."

Had anyone else noticed that Felty hadn't mentioned Vernon?

After the prayer, Vernon asked for the biscuits, beans, turkey, and chow-chow, and Felty kindly reminded him to take one thing, then pass it to the right.

"Jam," Hazel said in delight, her earlier ordeal apparently forgotten with the prospect of huckleberry raisin jelly. Abraham spread some jelly on her biscuit, and she gobbled it up like a baby bird.

"These biscuits just melt in my mouth," John gushed. "Irene is the best cook in Bonduel."

Vernon's head snapped up, and he pinned his gaze on Irene. "You made the biscuits?"

Irene nodded, a look of alarm flashing in her eyes.

Vernon wiggled his eyebrows up and down, which he did often in the presence of single young women. He seemed to think it made him intriguing or attractive or some other such nonsense. "They're really good. Better than my *mamm*'s. Do you want to come to my house and fix dinner for me tomorrow night? My *mamm* will be gone for another three days, and it's been ages since I've had a good plate of biscuits and gravy. I can show you my fly-tying workshop. I tie my own flies and catch all kinds of fish. Do you know how to cook trout? I'm looking for a *fraa* who can fix trout correctly. Most girls cook it too long. You're awful skinny though. How can you be a good cook and be so skinny? I'm not going to rush into anything until I taste your trout."

Irene stiffened like an icicle in January. Vernon never made any bones about the fact he was looking for a *fraa*. He certainly wasn't shy about it. Overbearing was probably a better word. It was a dilemma every girl faced when confronted by Vernon. Amish girls were naturally polite and kind, and they didn't want to be rude, but agreeing to anything Vernon asked was out of the question.

To Anna's delight, John immediately jumped in to rescue Irene. "I'm afraid Irene can't fix you any meals or come to your house or make trout." He smiled as if he were talking about the weather. "You're more than twice her age, and she's not interested in being your *fraa*." He reached over, snatched Vernon's bowl, and ladled some chili into it. "Try some of Abraham's chili. He'll be offended if you don't."

Abraham eyed Vernon menacingly. Anna could tell it was all for show, but Vernon didn't know that. "Yes, I will."

Vernon licked his lips as his gaze pinged between Irene and Abraham. He dipped his spoon into the bowl and took a tiny bite. His eyes grew wide as his face turned bright red. He reached for his water glass and took several gulps.

Abraham narrowed his eyes. "Good?"

Vernon could only nod.

Anna could almost see the smoke coming from Vernon's ears. He took several more swigs of water before stuffing a whole biscuit into his mouth and falling silent. Anna smiled to herself. Lord willing, chili would keep Vernon quiet for at least twenty minutes.

Irene looked, really looked, at John for the first time today and smiled at him, though her manner was guarded. One nice thing about Vernon was that he made every other boy in the room seem attractive by comparison. Maybe Anna didn't mind him so much.

John took a healthy bite of Abraham's chili and sighed in satisfaction. "That is wonderful-*gute* chili. The best I've ever tasted."

Abraham looked surprised. "You like it?"

John grinned and took another bite. "I like spicy foods. It clears out my sinuses. Vernon, if you want to avoid a cold, you should eat two or three bowls full."

Vernon looked as if he'd just stepped off the boat after a long and bumpy trip.

John set down his spoon. "I want to clear the air, and since Irene doesn't want to take a walk and talk in private..."

"It's thirty degrees out there!"

John chuckled. "Since Irene refuses to be alone with me, I am going to bare my soul to the entire group." He didn't seem to feel bad about baring his soul to everyone. Anna was liking him more and more. She hated to be left out of other people's private business.

Irene's blush traveled all the way to her scalp. "I'm not interested, John." But she was lying. She looked extremely interested, and her fingers had turned white curled around her glass.

John pretended he hadn't heard her. "I have loved Irene since eighth grade."

"Oh, that's sweet," Abraham said.

Anna smiled. The five-alarm chili cook obviously had a soft spot.

"Three weeks ago, my cousin wrote and asked me to come to Pennsylvania for a year to work with him in his woodshop making tables and chairs. I want a good job to support Irene and my children, and if I learn the business, I can come back here and start my own. Carpentry is what I've wanted to do for many years."

"That's true," Irene mumbled.

He looked at Irene and talked to her as if she were the only person in the room. "I should have consulted you, but I thought you would say yes without reservation. You're only eighteen, and I think it's wise to wait until we're both a little older."

"I'm old enough" was Irene's reply.

John nodded. "I should have asked you."

Irene folded her arms. "You should have."

"I got married when I was nineteen," Abraham said. "I was plenty old."

Irene looked archly at John. "See?"

Brandy tilted her head to one side. "Does your wife like that you ride a motorcycle?"

Abraham grimaced. "She's . . . uh . . . we're not together anymore."

Brandy slumped in her chair. "I'm sorry. I just wondered if disagreements like that can be worked out, or if there's hope for any of us. Sounds like there's no hope."

Anna reached over Felty and patted Brandy on the arm. "Of course there's hope, dear. One time I got so mad at Felty, I made him sleep in the barn. Another time, I threw his boots out of the house and into a mud puddle."

Felty wrapped his fingers around Anna's hand. "I deserved it. I'd tramped dirt all over your clean kitchen floor."

John focused solely on Irene. "I wrote to my cousin and accepted his offer, and I was going to come to your house that very evening to tell you. Then my horse threw a shoe, and *Dat* needed help with a refrigeration system on one of his motor homes. Before I could get to your house, you saw my *schwester* at the market, and she let it slip that I was leaving. I don't blame you for being mad, but I really was going to tell you. I'm sorry you heard it from Lilith instead of me." John looked at Irene with so much love that Anna's heart melted.

Irene didn't look as if *she* would melt anytime soon, but her mouth was a little softer around the edges. She ripped her biscuit apart and buttered it with zealous fervor. "But if you love me that much, how can you stand to be away from me for a whole year?"

"She's got a point," Felty said. "I can't stand to be away from Annie Banannie for more than a few minutes."

Anna reached out and patted Felty on the cheek. "*Ach,* you've always been so romantic, but we do both have to go to the bathroom occasionally."

John dared to reach out and brush an errant strand of hair from Irene's cheek. Irene flinched but didn't slap his hand away like Anna half expected her to. "Irene, I want to marry you so bad my bones ache, but ultimately, this apprenticeship will allow us to marry sooner. A year is a long time, but I'll write you every week, and you'll be in my thoughts every second. I'll come home for a visit at Christmastime."

Irene lifted her chin. "And my birthday."

John's lips twitched upward. "And your birthday. And if you want to go to Milwaukee to make beer, I'll support it, but don't do it because you're mad at me. I couldn't bear it."

Irene huffed out a breath. "I can see the wisdom of your decision, John."

He burst into a smile and curled his fingers around her wrist, which was resting on the table. "I'm so glad."

But Irene didn't act as if it had been settled. She pulled away from John's touch. "But it's plain my feelings don't matter to you. You're only thinking of yourself."

"That's not true."

Abraham cocked an eyebrow. "That's exactly what you're doing."

Irene gave Abraham a self-satisfied smile. "Thank you." She turned to John. "You made your decision without caring how I would feel."

"I care how you feel."

"Not enough to ask me first. I'm sure I would have come around to your way of thinking, but it stings that you didn't need or want or seek my opinion. You didn't care about my feelings enough to ask the question."

Anna was once again thoroughly ashamed of herself. All this time, she had assumed Irene was overreacting, but John had behaved quite selfishly, whether he realized it or not. Maybe John wasn't as good a match as Anna had thought. She shouldn't have been so quick to give him that potholder.

John's mouth fell open. "That's not what I . . ."

Irene picked up a buttered noodle from her plate and waved it at John as if she wanted to slap him across the face with it. "I won't marry someone who doesn't care about my feelings."

John's cheerful confidence disintegrated before Anna's eyes. "I care, Irene. You have to believe I care."

"Do you?" She motioned to everyone around the table. "Because you didn't even ask if I wanted to have this conversation. You just plunged ahead because it was what you wanted. You've ruined Thanksgiving."

But there was turkey and pie. In Anna's mind, it was a

highly successful dinner, even though Vernon Schmucker was there.

Abraham cut a piece of turkey into bite-size pieces for Hazel and glanced at John. "If you don't care to hear your wife's opinions, then she's just a housekeeper and a roommate."

Everyone's head snapped toward the window as they heard another thunderously loud vehicle coming up the hill. Now it was getting absurd. Anna had wanted a crowd for Thanksgiving, but Huckleberry Hill was starting to feel like a bus terminal.

Felty glanced at her doubtfully. "Who else did you invite?"

"Nobody." Anna took a deep breath. "We can't cram another person at this table unless we put in another leaf."

A platinum blue behemoth of a truck pulled in front of the house. Brandy gasped and jumped to her feet so fast, her chair clattered to the floor behind her. Abraham stood too, righted the chair, and put his arm around Brandy in a very fatherly gesture. Abraham had a rough exterior, but Anna had learned long ago never to judge a book by its cover.

"Somebody you know?" Abraham said.

"Husband."

Anna frowned. Brandy said *husband* as if it were a cuss word.

Brandy picked up Jude and grabbed Hazel's hand. "Tell him I'm not here."

Anna frowned even harder. It was a sin to lie, and probably a double sin on Thanksgiving. She liked Brandy, but she couldn't lie for her.

Apparently, Abraham could. "You were never here."

Hazel started whining the minute Brandy pulled her off the chair. "I want jam," she said.

Anna was pleased. Most of her family hated her huckleberry raisin jelly. Hazel obviously had good taste.

"We'll come right back," Brandy said.

Unfortunately, Hazel caught sight of the husband coming up the porch steps. He was impossibly thin, with a day's growth of whiskers on his chin and a completely inadequate coat. "Daddy!" she squealed, yanking her hand from Brandy's grasp. She bolted to the front door, threw it open, and catapulted herself into the man's arms.

Ach, vell, at least now, nobody would have to lie.

CHAPTER 5

*B*randy's husband smiled and lifted Hazel into his embrace. "Hey, Hazy. Where's your mom?"

Abraham folded his arms and stood in the doorway like an immovable brick wall. "You're not welcome here," he said. He held out his hands to Hazel. "Come on, sweetie. Let's get you some more jam."

The husband narrowed his eyes and pulled Hazel closer. "Who are you?"

"A friend of your wife's. I don't know what you did, but she doesn't want to see you. If you know what's good for you, you'll release Hazel, turn around, and go back to where you came from."

"Release Hazel?" The man sounded absolutely apoplectic. "How dare you? I'm no danger to anyone, not the least my own daughter."

"Be that as it may," Abraham said, "you need to go right now."

The man did his best to look past Abraham into the house. "Brandy, I'm not mad. Let me come in. I just want to talk."

"Oh," Brandy said, her face turning a muted shade of red.

"Now you want to talk? You didn't want to talk last night. You didn't want to talk three weeks ago. You didn't want to talk last summer."

"Brandy, can I just come in? Hazel is freezing out here."

Brandy charged past Abraham like an angry bull, snatched Hazel from her husband's arms, and hissed at him. "How dare you use my daughter as a bargaining chip? How dare you? That's a new low, even for you, Kyle."

Hazel put her hands on either side of Brandy's face. "Mommy, don't be mad at Daddy. He's my bestie."

Brandy pulled in a deep breath and seemed to gather all her anger back inside herself. "Of course, baby. I'm sorry." She set Hazel on her feet. "Let's go back inside and finish dinner. There's pie."

Hazel pointed to Kyle, the husband. "Can Daddy come?"

Anna knew how hard it was to resist a wide-eyed child, and Brandy probably felt guilty for separating Hazel from her father, no matter how justified she was.

"No. He has to go."

"I don't have to go anywhere," Kyle said. He was obviously not above manipulating his daughter for his own purposes. Anna disliked him already, and not just for Brandy's sake.

Hazel turned to Abraham who was still standing in the doorway. "Please, Mr. Abbaham. Let my daddy come in."

Abraham hesitated, obviously trying to resist those big brown eyes and that quivering chin. He glanced at Brandy and nodded. "I'm sorry, Hazel. He can't come in."

Kyle spread his arms in surrender. "Look, Brandy, your car is dead. I'm your ride home. Think about the kids."

Hazel began to cry and pulled on her mother's hand. "Please let him come in."

Brandy finally relented. "Okay. He can come in, as long as it's okay with Anna and Felty."

Anna was tempted to put her foot down and keep Kyle out

in the cold, but Brandy was thinking of the children and what a terrible scene there would be if she barred Kyle from the house. It was really rather brave. And if things got out of hand for whatever reason, Abraham looked like he'd be good in a fight. Felty wasn't young, but he had been trained in hand-to-hand combat in the war and could probably still throw a punch —not that he'd ever do it. The Amish were pacifists. Thank *Derr Herr*, Abraham didn't seem to be a pacifist.

Brandy led Hazel into the house, and Abraham stepped aside so that Kyle could just barely squeeze past him. Abraham shut the door and stood in front of it with his arms folded across his chest, glaring. Kyle pretended Abraham wasn't there, though it was clear he was keenly aware of the big man.

"It smells good in here," Kyle said.

Was he hoping for a piece of pie? Because his behavior hadn't earned him anything but a swift kick in the pants.

Felty motioned to the sofa in the living room. "Kyle, why don't you go sit in there and get warm while we finish our Thanksgiving dinner?"

Anna wasn't sure what Felty was thinking. Dinner was ruined. Surely nobody wanted to finish anything, what with Irene and John fighting, Vernon taking up more than his fair share of space, and Brandy's husband sucking all the joy out of the room.

"Come sit by me, Daddy," Hazel said, patting the chair where Abraham had been.

Kyle sort of slouched his way to the chair. He had to know how unwelcome he was. He'd used his daughter to get what he wanted. At least he had the decency to look sheepish.

Anna pointed to the broom closet. "Abraham, there's a folding chair in there if you'd like to sit too."

Looking very satisfied with himself, Abraham pulled out a folding chair and set it up right next to Kyle. Kyle scooted as close as he could to Hazel.

For the children's sake, Anna felt the need to act as normal and as cheerful as possible. She took a bite of turkey. It was delicious. "Now, what were we talking about?" Her stomach dropped to her toes when she realized that Irene had been chastising John for being insensitive. Maybe she should change the subject.

To Anna's surprise, Brandy seemed eager to pick up the conversation. She eyed Kyle. "We were talking about husbands who don't care about their wives' feelings."

Kyle sneered at her. "Oh, you want to talk now? I thought you didn't want to talk."

Abraham laid a firm hand on Kyle's shoulder. From where Hazel was sitting, it probably looked like a little tap. "You should mind your manners."

Brandy's voice shook. "Four months ago, a certain husband decided he wanted to make a YouTube channel and paid some guy ten thousand dollars to get it going. *Without telling his wife.*"

Anna was appalled. She wasn't familiar with YouTube, but ten thousand dollars was a lot of money to keep secret. "He didn't tell his wife?"

"Then three weeks ago, he paid almost fifty thousand dollars for a fancy new truck, again without telling his wife. *She* has an old Chevy with bald tires and no air conditioning. His wife has to get another job just to pay the rent while he sits home and dreams of being a YouTube star."

Kyle stuck out his bottom lip. "It takes a while to build up a following, but soon I'll be making more than enough to pay all the bills and buy the house of our dreams."

Brandy folded her arms. "Be sure to drop me a text when that happens."

Hazel's eyes widened in distress as the tension between her parents increased.

Anna cleared her throat. "Irene, would you take Hazel and Jude to my bedroom and see if you can spot any birds out the window? There are also some toys in the bottom of my chest of drawers."

Irene glanced at John and turned up her nose. "I'd be happy to. Please take the pies out of the oven when the timer rings."

Vernon's ear perked up at the mention of pie. "I call the first piece."

Irene led the children out of the room, and Anna was *froh* Irene had gone willingly. Taking the children away probably should have been Anna's job as the grandmother, but she wouldn't miss this conversation for the world. The gossip was just too juicy.

John, on the other hand, didn't seem to care about Kyle and his spending habits. He jumped to his feet. "I'll go help Irene."

Hmm. John was a bright young man with a promising future of marital bliss ahead of him.

Abraham stood and moved to Hazel's chair, so he was between Kyle and Brandy. He jabbed a finger at Kyle's chest. "You are a sorry excuse for a husband."

Kyle reared back. "I didn't come here to be insulted."

"Why did you come?" Brandy snapped.

"I was worried about you. It was foolish to try to drive all the way to your mom's on those tires."

Brandy rolled her eyes. "If only I had the money for a new set."

Kyle growled under his breath. "I knew you were headed to your mom's, and I followed the GPS tracker on your car."

Brandy's face turned red. "You put a tracker on my car?"

"It's a clunker. I wanted to be able to find you if it ever broke down. I'm a better husband than you think I am."

Abraham sat back and studied Kyle's face. "But you weren't concerned enough to buy her a reliable car. You could buy three for the price of that new truck."

Kyle pouted with his whole body. "I need that truck for my YouTube channel." His expression brightened. "It's called 'The Man in the Blue Truck.' Sometimes I sit in my truck and shoot the breeze. Other times I tell funny stories about my kids. Sometimes I offer tips on camping, hunting, or car maintenance."

Brandy rested her elbow on the table and propped her chin in her hand. "Do you see how ironic my life is, Abraham?"

Anna couldn't remember what *ironic* meant, but it seemed that a guy who knew about car maintenance should probably help his wife with her car.

Kyle leaned forward so he had a good view of Brandy. "When I found your car in the snowbank, I came up the hill, figuring someone had helped you or at least knew where you were. I was worried sick."

"I didn't think you'd care if I was gone."

"Of course I care. You'll see. I'm gonna buy you the biggest house in town and the fanciest car at the dealership."

"I don't want a fancy car," Brandy said. "I just want to be able to pay the rent and the utility bill. I want a partner, not another child. I'm done carrying this burden alone, Kyle. I'm just done."

"Please come home, Brandy. You hate living with your mom, and the kids need a father."

Brandy picked at the food on her plate. "At least at my mom's house, I don't have to worry if the electricity will go out or the water will be shut off."

Kyle winced. "Please come home." He reached over Abraham and took Brandy's hand in both of his. She stiffened. "I promise, *promise*, I'll do better. I'll buy you some new tires and put them on myself." When she didn't respond, he said, "I can make putting new tires on your car into a YouTube tutorial and post it on my channel."

Brandy drew her brows together in disbelief, and her lips

curled into a faint, unhappy smile. "That's a great idea. Maybe it will go viral."

Kyle didn't seem to recognize the despair in her voice. "Yes! Yes, that's what I'm talking about. All I need is one video to go viral, and it creates a chain reaction. We'll be able to buy anything we want. We'll be able to hire a housekeeper. We'll be able to pay a nanny to watch Jude and Hazel."

Anna could see the defeat and despair in Brandy's eyes, but to her credit, she spoke kindly, keeping her voice mild and her tone unemotional. "I wish you the best, Kyle, I really do. But I'm not coming home. I've been living on promises and 'wait-and-sees' for months. I won't do it anymore."

"But I promise, Brandy. I promise with all my heart. You just need to have faith in me. I can do anything if you have faith in me."

Brandy sighed and looked at Kyle with pity in her eyes. "I'm sorry, Kyle. I don't have faith in you anymore."

"What about the kids? Hazel will never forgive you if you leave me."

Anna held her breath. Kyle was grasping at straws now, but Hazel was his strongest argument.

Brandy nodded. "Maybe, but I hope someday she'll understand that I did it for her."

Kyle opened and closed his mouth like a fish out of water. "But . . ."

Abraham stood and pulled Kyle with him. "It's time for you to go."

"You can't tell me what to do," Kyle hissed.

Abraham was as composed as an owl eyeing his prey. "This is what we're going to do. The children will come out to say goodbye, and you are going to exit gracefully without upsetting or manipulating them in any way. You will not try to contact Brandy until she contacts you. If you want to prove your change of heart, you'll have Brandy's car towed to the nearest station and buy her four new tires. But I don't really care if you do that as long as you go away and let us finish our Thanksgiving dinner in peace."

As if on cue, the timer for the pies rang. Anna jumped from her chair and removed them from the oven. Irene had carved three stars into the top crust of each pie and sprinkled each with sugar and cinnamon. They looked delicious and smelled even better.

Vernon stood and hovered around Anna at the stove. "I called first piece."

"*Ach*, Vernon, go sit down. They have to cool before we slice them." Anna neglected to add that she had never agreed to let Vernon have the first piece. Abraham would get the first piece and every piece he wanted thereafter. If he wanted a whole pie to himself, Anna would not say no. For sure and certain, *Derr Herr* had led him here today. He claimed he wasn't an angel, but Anna wasn't so sure.

Irene and John brought the children into the great room where Kyle said goodbye with Abraham looking over his shoulder. Anna felt so bad for Kyle, she went to her closet and pulled out a beautiful blue scarf she had knitted in case of an emergency. She called him back just as he was walking out the door. "Kyle, I have a gift for you." Surprise popped all over his face as she looped it around his neck and tied it snuggly under his chin. "My scarves have been known to save lives," she said.

Brandy didn't even look at her husband as he donned his coat and went out the door. To everyone's surprise, he picked up the shovel propped against the railing and shoveled the porch steps before jumping into his truck. His fancy truck rumbled to life a few seconds later, and the sound soon faded to nothing.

Anna wrapped her arms around Brandy. "It will be okay, dear. God has a way of making everything work together for our good.

"I really do love him," Brandy whispered, glancing at her children.

"Of course you do," Anna said.

"He's not a horrible guy. He's kind to me and the children, and he's not addicted to anything. Have I made a huge mistake?"

"It's perfectly reasonable to expect Kyle to be a true husband, someone you and your children can count on. Sometimes you have to take a step back to move forward."

Brandy caught her breath. "That's exactly what I've done, though I've never been able to articulate it before. That makes me feel better about my decision. It hasn't been easy. Nothing has been easy."

"Nothing worth having is ever easy."

"I don't know how I'm going to get to Green Bay tonight."

"We have a lovely little room in our barn with two beds and a woodstove. You're welcome to stay the night. Most service stations will be open in the morning."

"Thank you. I'll think about it." Brandy smiled at Abraham. "I'm so glad you were here. Kyle wouldn't have been so cooperative if it had just been me and a bunch of Amish people." She glanced at Anna. "No offense."

"None taken, dear," Anna said. "We Amish like our reputation as adamant pacifists, even if it means people think they can walk all over us."

Abraham huffed out a breath. "I'm pretty good at helping other people fix their lives. I'm a complete failure with my own."

Brandy led her children back to the table. "I don't believe it for a minute. You were my knight in shining armor."

Abraham's expression was all mushy as he studied Brandy's face. "I have a daughter about your age. I hope someone would stand up for her like I stood up for you." His gaze fell. "I wasn't ever there for her."

Pain flicked across Brandy's face. "Do you want to tell me about her?"

Abraham sank into the chair next to Hazel, as if he'd aged ten years in five minutes. "Her name is Annie."

Anna's eyebrows shot upward. She was sure she'd never see another Thanksgiving quite as exciting as this one. Irene was still glaring at John, despite the potholder. Abraham had defended Brandy but had apparently abandoned his daughter. Kyle had bought a fifty-thousand-dollar truck but had also shoveled the snow from Anna's porch. Vernon was still sitting at her table, unwelcome as ever, eating the last of the buttered noodles and two more biscuits. And Abraham's daughter was named Annie. There were entirely too many Annies in the world. How could she ever keep track? It was the most bizarre, exciting, interesting Thanksgiving ever.

Irene and John sat down at the table again, though Irene was still reluctant to even look at him. Anna decided she should serve the pie quickly before someone else drove up the hill. With the way things were going, it would probably be a platoon of lost soldiers, and she'd have to break out the Cream of Wheat. It was about all she had left to serve. She gave Abraham the first and biggest piece. Vernon got the last piece, and Anna only had to give him the stink eye twice before he stopped complaining and waited patiently for his turn.

"Where is your daughter now?" Felty said.

Thank *Derr Herr*, Felty had asked. Anna shouldn't always be the one to pry into other people's business.

Abraham poked at his pie with his fork, looking at it as if it held the secret to being a *gute* father. "She's in Ohio." He cleared his throat and glanced at Anna. "She's Amish."

"Amish?" Anna could tell Felty was trying not to sound astonished.

Abraham's face turned bright red. "The truth is, I used to be Amish."

"You used to be Amish?"

"I grew up in Ohio and almost left the community for good during *rumschpringa*. But I came back, got married, and had two kids before I realized I just couldn't do it. I was so tired. Tired of breaking my back on the farm for a few dollars a day. Tired of the rules. Tired of never being good enough for my wife." He looked up and searched Anna's face. "I'm sorry, Anna, Felty. I'm not worthy to sit at your table."

Felty pointed to the ceiling. "Only God can judge that."

"My son Abraham was twelve years old when I left. Annie was five. I told myself it was for their own good. Better to not have a father than one who was miserable and depressed. But I was fooling myself. I abandoned my kids, and there's not a day goes by that I don't regret it. I went to Montana and worked on a ranch, doing harder work for less money than working my own farm. I wrote to Abraham and Annie every week for three years. They never wrote back. That might have been their mother's doing. After three years, I wrote and asked my wife if I could come back, but she told me they were all much happier without me, and I believed it." He looked at Brandy. "Like you are probably happier without . . ." He trailed off. Hazel was staring at him intently.

"Maybe," Brandy said, her voice cracking. "Maybe not. How can anyone know for sure?"

"I drifted for a while, then found a good job working the oil fields in North Dakota. I've been gone for twenty years. Haven't heard from my kids for seventeen of those years. I have a cousin in Ohio who writes to me on and off, said my wife left the church and ran off with an *Englischer* after Annie got married last month."

Anna frowned. "*Ach*, that's too bad." She cleared her throat. "I mean, it's too bad that your wife ran off but nice that Annie got married."

He slumped his shoulders. "The kids have been abandoned

57

twice." His hands shook as he picked up his glass and took a drink. "Three weeks ago, I reached out to Annie. Didn't hear back. My cousin wrote that Abraham had moved to Bonduel, Wisconsin, and sent me an address that turned out to be wrong. That's how I ended up here."

"You're trying to find him?"

"I just . . . I need to ask forgiveness, and I want to give him the opportunity to throw me out of his house." He swiped his hand across his mouth. "I don't deserve nothing better."

John, who'd been gazing longingly at Irene, snapped his head around. "Abraham Schwartz?"

"Yes. That's me and my son."

"I know Abraham Schwartz!" John got so animated, he bumped his glass with his hand, and it spilled all over Anna's tablecloth. "He moved into the old Johnson place last summer. He's a wonderful-nice man. He's got four kids and one on the way."

Abraham's face turned pale. "You . . . you know him? You know where he lives?"

"Well, sure. He's in my district."

A glimmer of hopeful terror flashed in Abraham's eyes. "Can you take me there after the snow stops?"

Anna was ashamed of herself. She should keep better track of all the neighbors. A matchmaker's job was too important to just glide through the day without a care in the world, as if people didn't need to be matched, as if there weren't urgent connections to be made and gossip to spread.

Vell. This day had been her wake-up call. She would never be so negligent again.

"I would be happy to take you there." John went back to gazing longingly at Irene. "Irene, would you like to come with me?"

Irene, on the other hand, hadn't stopped glaring at John

58

since she'd accused him of ruining Thanksgiving. "No," she said, as if turning down a plate of worms for dessert.

John tried for a smile and failed miserably. For sure and certain, he didn't want to make Irene angrier than she already was. "Can we go somewhere privately and talk?"

Irene lifted her chin. "Everybody already knows our business." She motioned toward Abraham and Brandy. "Go ahead and say what you want to say."

John's eyes darted back and forth between Anna and Irene, but Anna didn't know what he was expecting from her. She couldn't help him, not even if she had a queen-size knitted blanket in her special drawer. Irene was immovable. He'd dug his own hole. He'd have to get himself out of it.

He pulled Anna's pink potholder out of his pocket and handed it to Irene. Anna held her breath. This might be the biggest test of her potholders' power yet.

"I love you more than anything, Irene," he said, "but I haven't shown it in the past couple of weeks, and I'm sorry. I got so excited about Pennsylvania that I didn't even pause to consider your feelings. I was being selfish not to ask your opinion or explain why I was thinking of going to Pennsylvania." He took a deep breath and closed his eyes. "I'm not going to Pennsylvania. I'll start baptism classes in January so we can be married next fall. But only if you still want to marry me. I don't blame you'd rather be done with me."

Anna studied John's face. He didn't seem to be bluffing. Then again, Anna wasn't very good at discerning if someone was bluffing. It was why she was so bad at board games.

The lines around Irene's mouth relaxed, but there was still a deep divot between her eyebrows that looked as if it was etched there.

John stared at Irene with a forlorn, puppy-dog look on his face. He certainly seemed sincere. "If you still want to go to Milwaukee, I'll be waiting for you if you decide to come back."

"*If?*" Irene snorted. "What a thing to say! Of course I'll come back."

This moment called for a little reverse psychiatristry. "You never know, Irene. I hear Milwaukee is a really fun town. And that beer isn't going to make itself."

Felty poured himself a glass of milk. "It has lots of great license plates if you like to play the license plate game."

Irene eyed John. "You would give up Pennsylvania for me?"

John nodded. "I already have. You are more important than a trip to Pennsylvania. I just haven't given you any reason to believe in me."

"I will always believe in you." She grabbed his arm. Irene probably didn't realize it, but that gesture opened up a happily ever after for them. You didn't reach out for someone like that unless you wanted to hold on to him forever. "I should probably insist you go. It would be good for us. For our future." She frowned. "But I really, really don't want you to go."

"I didn't think it through very well," John said. "I can't stand the thought of being away from you for that long. Andrew Petersheim is a wonderful-*gute* carpenter. It wonders me if he would let me be his apprentice."

Irene's eyes lit up like a propane lantern. "I'm sure he would." She slid her hand into John's. "I wasn't really serious about Milwaukee. I said that because I wanted to hurt you like you had hurt me."

Anna laced her fingers together and nodded wisely. "Hurt people hurt people."

John's smile was wider than the Mississippi River. "I love you, Irene."

"And I love you. Just try not to be so dense once we're married."

Vernon licked his plate and set it down in front of Anna. "I'll have another piece of pie."

There was a quarter of a pie left, but Anna hated the

thought of wasting it on Vernon. Of course, giving him another piece was the neighborly, Christian thing to do, but Anna wanted to save it for the people who'd actually been invited to Thanksgiving dinner.

Ach.

Vernon was the *only* person in the room who had actually been invited to dinner.

She cut Vernon a sliver of a piece and set it on his plate. He eyed it in disappointment. "Can I have a bigger one?"

"Now, Vernon, we need to save the rest for everyone else."

"But I'm still hungry."

Anna's neighborliness had been stretched as far as it would go. "You can have a bowl of Cream of Wheat."

"With or without lumps?"

Ach, du lieva! If she gave the wrong answer, she'd have to cook Vernon a bowl of Cream of Wheat. And there was no place for Cream of Wheat at Thanksgiving dinner. "Which way do you like it?"

"Without lumps, of course."

Phew! She had never made Cream of Wheat without lumps. "I'm sorry, Vernon. You'll have to make your own."

He opened his mouth to protest, but before he could say anything, another vehicle crawled up the hill. This was the strangest Thanksgiving Day in the history of Thanksgiving Days, even stranger than the day her *bruder* Isaac set the house on fire when he tried to deep-fat fry a frozen turkey. It was why Anna kept a fire extinguisher in every room of the house.

"It's the Tuttles," Felty said. Nothing ruffled Felty's feathers, except maybe Vernon Schmucker, but even *he* sounded surprised. The Tuttles were Anna and Felty's nearest neighbors. They lived down the hill and a half mile to the east.

Anna would have known Fred Tuttle's truck anywhere. It was fire-engine red with wide hips and an elongated cab that could fit at least five passengers. Anna squinted into the snowstorm. There were more than five passengers in Fred's truck today. Surely there wasn't a seatbelt for everyone. Fred wasn't usually so foolhardy.

Fred and Mabel were very nice neighbors, Englischers in their sixties with six children and twenty-one grandchildren. Mabel was a devoted wife, but even she thought Fred's truck was a little fancy for rural Wisconsin.

Fred jumped out of the truck, wrapped his arms around himself, and lowered his head as he ran for the house. The man didn't wear a coat or a beanie or a scarf. He was not dressed for the weather, but when you could get in your truck and turn on the heater, maybe a heavy winter coat wasn't so important.

Felty jumped to his feet and opened the door. "Fred, what brings you here?"

Fred stepped quickly into the house and closed the door. His eyes twinkled as he looked around the table. His gaze landed on Abraham, and he smiled so hard, Anna could count all his teeth. "You're here! I was hoping with all my heart you were here."

"I'm here," Abraham said, returning Fred's contagious smile.

Fred opened the door and motioned to the group crammed into his truck. "Earlier, you seemed so unhappy about not being able to find Abraham Schwartz. After you left our house, Mabel and I decided we wouldn't enjoy our Thanksgiving dinner until we found him for you. I drove around to my Amish friends in the area until I found someone who knew him. Then I went to his house and brought him here."

Abraham leaped to his feet and backed away from the front door. "You . . . brought Abraham here?"

"Sure. With his whole family."

Abraham scrubbed his fingers through his hair in agitation. "I rehearsed a speech and everything, but I'm not ready." He crossed the great room and headed toward Anna and Felty's bedroom. "I'm not ready."

"Abraham," Brandy said. "It's going to be okay. I'll vouch for you."

"Nobody can vouch for me. I'm a horrible person. My son will be disappointed and angry. I've got to get out of here."

It was too late. A tall young man stomped quickly into the house followed by Mabel Tuttle, a petite and pretty Amish woman, and four Amish children, the youngest probably no older than three. The young man had his father's light blue eyes, a short, dark beard, and an earnest, determined look on his face. He paused momentarily as his gaze traveled around the room until his eyes landed on Abraham, whose head was bowed and shoulders rounded as if he hoped Abraham Junior wouldn't see him.

In three long and powerful strides, Junior crossed the distance between them and snatched Abraham into a forceful hug that would have made any grizzly bear proud. Tears streamed down Junior's cheeks as great sobs wracked his body. *"Mein fater. Mein fater."*

Abraham's eyes nearly popped out of his head before he clapped his thick arms around his son and wept into his shoulder.

CHAPTER 6

*R*eally, most likely, the strangest, best, happiest Thanksgiving Day ever. If Vernon hadn't been there, it would have been the perfect day.

Vernon was the only person still sitting at the table, still eating. He had finished off the chow-chow, buttered noodles, macaroni and cheese, turkey, rolls, and even the huckleberry raisin jelly. He hadn't touched the five-alarm chili, but he had pretty much consumed the rest of the Thanksgiving feast. He was as voracious as a vacuum cleaner. Anna was *froh* she'd hidden the rest of the pie. Vernon couldn't have possibly appreciated it.

Abraham sat on the edge of the sofa with his three-year-old granddaughter Becky Sue and his five-year-old grandson Benuel perched on his knees, while Abraham Junior and his *fraa*, Mary Etta, sat next to him, all of them chattering merrily about the weather and Thanksgiving and the miracle of family. Junior's two oldest children, Rachel and Leroy, sat on the floor entertaining Jude and Hazel, while Brandy, John, Irene, the Tuttles, Felty, and Anna gathered with them in the great room.

Abraham Junior, whom his *fraa* called Abe, was of a

solemn, earnest disposition, but it was plain as day that he was full of love for *Gotte* and his family. He had the look of goodness about him. Anna could always take the measure of a man by "the look."

As obvious as it was that Abe Junior had forgiven his *fater* for past transgressions, Abraham had asked his forgiveness at least half a dozen times before Abe Junior begged him to stop. "We have so much catching up to do, *Dat*," Abe Junior said. "Let's only talk of *gute* things and happy memories. We don't have to replay past mistakes."

Anna loved him already. She'd have to knit potholders and scarves for the entire family.

Abe Junior and Mary Etta told everyone about their family, how they had moved to Bonduel because the land was much cheaper in Wisconsin. "My *schwester* Annie was published, and I thought Mamm was planning to move to Bonduel with us after Annie's wedding. But she had already fallen in love with an *Englischer*. A week after Annie tied the knot, Mamm married the *Englischer* and moved to Milwaukee."

"I hear they make *gute* beer there," Anna said, trying to look on the bright side.

Abe's mouth twitched upward. "*Jah*. I hear that too. *Mamm* lived alone for twenty years. I can't judge her decision. All I can do is love her and hope she's happy."

Abraham pressed his lips together. "I'm sorry, Abe. I failed all of you miserably."

Abe sighed. "*Dat*, I have forgiven you."

"But how?"

Abe shook his head. "Annie doesn't remember you as well. She forgave you long ago. It wasn't so easy for me. At first, I was very bitter. At twelve years old, I couldn't understand why you would abandon me. I thought if you'd loved me more, you wouldn't have left."

Abraham opened his mouth to speak, and Abe held up a

hand to stop him. "On the day I married Mary Etta, I found dozens of letters you had written to me and Annie hidden at the bottom of one of *Mamm*'s bedroom drawers. I read every one." He blinked some moisture from his eyes. "I knew you loved me, even if I couldn't understand why you'd left. For sure and certain, I was glad to get those letters. I prayed for grace to replace my pain, and *Gotte* said, 'Be still and know that I am *Gotte*.' So I waited on Him. Once I had children of my own, He created a space in my heart for forgiveness."

Abe ruffled little Benuel's golden hair. "One fall afternoon, I was tilling my field, preparing it for winter, while Leroy and Rachel played next to me, building miniature cities and towers out of dirt clods. Suddenly, one grasshopper after another leapt from the ground, and *die kinner* started chasing them. Rachel squealed at me to help her catch a grasshopper, and we spent the next hour frolicking in the field. The pure joy of being with my children overwhelmed me. It was a perfect day. As I stood there laughing at Leroy's attempt to catch three grasshoppers at once, a devastating sense of loss stole my breath. But it wasn't *my* loss, *Dat*. It was yours. I mourned that you had missed out on countless joyful and wonder-filled experiences that could have blessed your life and filled it with happiness. I mourned that you had missed out on being with your children, that you had missed out on giving and receiving their love. I mourned that you hadn't seen me grow into a man. I couldn't help but think there must have been a gaping hole in your life, and it made me sad for you."

"There has always been a gaping hole," Abraham said.

"I had more love for you than I had ever felt in my entire life, *Dat*. That love saved me. It was a gift from *Gotte*."

Anna felt the tears on her cheeks before she even realized she was crying. Couldn't this feeling go on forever?

For sure and certain, Abraham Junior and his family and the Tuttles hadn't eaten Thanksgiving dinner yet, and Anna very much wanted them to stay. But what in the world would she feed them? She had a pot of inedible chili, seven boxes of Cream of Wheat, and a fourth of an apple pie. But through the years, Anna had learned that *Gotte* would always provide a way if she just had enough faith. She spread her hands wide. "Won't you all stay for Thanksgiving dinner?"

Fred Tuttle eyed the table of dirty dishes. "But haven't you already eaten?"

"Yes, but can you ever eat too much on Thanksgiving?"

"Always," Felty said.

Anna tapped her chin. "*Vell*, we celebrate Second Christmas. Why can't we celebrate Second Thanksgiving? If we wait a few hours, it will be time to eat again." She neglected to mention there would be nothing but Cream of Wheat, but there would be plenty of time to break the bad news. Why ruin Second Thanksgiving prematurely?

When Mary Etta grinned, her nose crinkled and her freckles danced. "I put a turkey in the oven right before we came here." She looked out the window. "It's stopped snowing. Mr. Tuttle, could I impose on you to drive me home? I could fetch the turkey and the stuffing and all my other Thanksgiving fixings and bring them here."

Mary Etta was the dearest girl in the whole world. Anna was very sad they'd only known each other for an hour. Anna thought her smile might fly off her face. "That would be *wunderbarr*."

Mabel Tuttle put her arm around her husband. "We were planning on a small, quiet meal at home with our cat and the football games. If you'll have us, I can fetch our ham and my famous yam casserole."

Felty slapped his knee. "Now it's a party."

"We can use the rest of my Thanksgiving care package if there's a need," Brandy said.

Fred looked at Brandy. "Was that your car stuck in the snowbank at the bottom of the hill?"

Brandy nodded.

"Well, I hope the man in the blue truck is someone you know. He just towed your car away."

Brandy's expression was like a sunrise. "He did?"

"Yep. Saw him as we were coming up the hill."

Brandy didn't say anything, but she tightened her arms around Jude and blinked back what Anna assumed were happy tears.

Fred jangled his keys. "I'm ready to make a food run. Who's coming with me?"

John and Irene seemed very cozy, huddled together in the corner of the great room, whispering to each other as if they were the only two people in the world. Irene looked up when she heard the keys. "I can make another batch of biscuits."

Anna remembered her fall canning projects. "I have three bottles of pickled kitchen scraps on the shelf just waiting for a special occasion!"

Irene's smile froze in place. "*Appeditlich, Mammi.*"

It would be the best Second Thanksgiving ever. Abraham had reunited with family, Abe had a forgiving heart, and Brandy was forging a new and hopeful path. Kyle might even come around in the end. Mabel had a ham, Mary Etta had a turkey, and Anna didn't have to break out the Cream of Wheat. Best of all, John and Irene were back together. Anna would be accused of pride if she said it out loud, but she truly was the best matchmaker in the world, and it wasn't even close. Her grandchildren were blessed to have such a careful *mammi*, who knitted potholders, canned huckleberry raisin jelly, and found them suitable matches, all at no charge.

Irene stood and pulled John with her. "I should go and apologize to my *mamm* for being snippy, and John needs to explain things to his family, but we want to come back and eat with you, if that's okay."

"It's more than okay," Anna said. "It wouldn't be Second Thanksgiving without you. My one regret is that I only have a quarter of an apple pie to divide amongst us."

Brandy pointed to Vernon and made a face. "He ate it," she whispered.

How had Vernon found her pie? She'd hidden it so well. Who would have guessed anyone would be persistent enough to look underneath the garbage can liner? Vernon was the most aggravating person Anna had ever met.

Oh, *sis yuscht*! She had unwittingly invited *everyone* to Second Thanksgiving, even Vernon. Why hadn't she waited until he'd gone to the bathroom?

Mary Etta giggled. "I got a little carried away and made five pies. It's too many for our family, but not too many for all of us. I'll bring them with the turkey."

Vernon looked up from his plate. "I call the first piece."

Jah, it would have been a perfect day except for Vernon Schmucker.

And he would get the first piece over Anna's dead body.

MOM'S APPLE PIE

Foolproof Pie Crust

3 c. sifted flour
1 T. sugar
2 t. salt
1 ¼ c. vegetable shortening
1 egg
½ c. water
1 T. vinegar

Combine flour, sugar and salt in bowl. Cut in the shortening with a pastry blender. Beat the egg and mix the water and vinegar with the egg. Sprinkle the egg mixture a little at a time over the flour mixture, tossing lightly until all the particles are moistened. Mold into a ball and chill. Return to room temperature before rolling out. Makes three pie crusts.

Mom's Apple Pie

Pastry for 2-crust pie
2 lbs. tart apples (7 to 10 depending on the size)
1 ½ T. lime juice
3 T. flour
¾ c. sugar
Dash of salt
1 t. cinnamon
3 T. butter
Canned milk
1 T. sugar
1 T. cinnamon

Prepare the pastry and refrigerate 30-40 minutes before rolling out. Line pie plate with pastry.

Peel apples; slice. Place in the pie shell. Sprinkle with lime juice, flour, sugar, salt, and 1 t. cinnamon. Dot with butter.

Cover with top crust, brushing edges of lower crust with cold water before pressing together. Flute. Cut slits in top of pie to allow steam to escape, or decorate with pastry cut-outs.

Mix 1 T. of sugar and 1 T. of cinnamon together. Brush top crust with canned milk. Sprinkle with sugar-cinnamon mixture.

Bake at 375°F about 1 hour, until nicely browned. Put a cookie sheet under pie pan while baking in case the pie drips.

ABOUT THE AUTHOR

Jennifer Beckstrand is the USA Today Bestselling author of clean romantic comedies, sweet historical Westerns, and Amish romances. Her popular books include *Dandelion Meadows*, *The Matchmakers of Huckleberry Hill* series, *The Honeybee Sisters* series, *The Amish Quiltmaker* series, and *Cowboys of the Butterfly Ranch* series. Jennifer is a two-time RWA RITA® Award finalist, a Carol Award® finalist, and a #1 Amazon bestselling Amish author. Find out more about Jennifer and her books at https://www.jenniferbeckstrand.com/.

The Matchmakers of Huckleberry Hill are at it again! Anna and Felty Helmuth have raised thirteen children of their own and now they're out to make matches for all their grandchildren. https://amzn.to/40EmDzm

HELPING HANDS

MINDY STEELE

ACKNOWLEDGMENTS

To the brave women out there who keep on keeping on, and to those blessed encouragers beside them all the way.

CHAPTER 1

$\mathcal{I}$t was the sound of laughter that had driven her to sudden tears this time. That deep, slow laugh always made thirty-one-year-old Beth Graber feel like the most blessed bride in all of Cherry Grove, Kentucky.

From behind the counter of Graber's Bent and Dent, she glanced down the aisle where the two men stood near a large window, the sun piercing in after days of storms and cloudy skies darkening everything. From the moment she caught the sun rising outside her kitchen window, she felt *Gott* Himself had sent it to lift the darkness around her. So much so, she'd even smiled at Mary Alice Yoder, who only visited her store for discount canned tomatoes, soap, and to spy on all the comings and goings of others.

Still, despite the tall, lean figure blotting out much of the lighting, Andrew wasn't there. Her late husband's dark brows weren't lifting above his perfect straight nose and lips she had kissed a hundred times. Those hands slipping into two front pockets didn't belong to the father of her four *kinner*.

Her Andrew was gone, buried now over seven months ago in the community cemetery. It was hard to accept, even now, as nothing of their normal everyday comings and goings remained. Anything of her former life faded into the backdrop of what was now.

When the second man turned, catching her staring, Beth sucked in her breath. Just the sight of Paul Lengacher, the local undertaker, sent a sudden flood of fresh grief skidding over her.

Placing a hand on her growing middle, Beth left the register and hurried out the side door. She shouldn't leave Andrew's twin fourteen-year-old siblings, Stephen and Rachel, to see over the store alone. Rachel being so terribly shy and Stephen easily distracted would only risk the store losing more money than it had. *Privacy.* That's what she needed right now.

Andrew had always overseen the books and ordering supplies. He made all the deals with local merchants for damaged goods that filled most of the shelves. *He* was the very heart and soul of the store, not her. Beth didn't even enjoy spending more than an hour in the store when she had duties of her own, seeing over their house and children. Paul Lengacher was another reminder that she was alone with stacks of mounting bills and *kinner* to raise.

Widows were kept by the church, but Beth was now the sole owner of a business. The seventeen acres of pasture and hay, the three-story house and barn had been paid for, thanks to a husband who knew how to save and invest and spend money correctly. She had no reason to bend the wallets of their community.

However, Beth was receiving more help than she figured any widow ever did, from the Pencil Grabers, a nickname many called Andrew's lot to acknowledge them amongst the many other Graber families in the community. Alma Graber referred to them as *helping hands*. Her mother-in-law had taken on the task of organizing everything. Down to who made hay and, when she couldn't come, which of Andrew's unwed siblings would keep watch over Beth's *kinner*, despite Christina being a child of twelve now.

If Beth wasn't mistaken, Christina was equally put out by all the helping hands. Beth and her children were plenty capable of doing their own laundry and readying their own meals, but Alma wasn't convinced. It had been Beth's fault, spending those first weeks in bed nursing tears that refused to dry up after Andrew's death.

Andrew's family had been plenty kind, and she didn't dare complain, but few moments alone with her girls was taking a toll. Christina had become more stern, while Beth Ann was more contrary. Tracy was either nursing a headache or trying to find excuses to skip out on her chores. Little Lisa had gone from a sweet child to one who had taken up disappearing acts. Beth missed being the mother she had been before Andrew's fall. If only her extended family understood that she'd shed her long bouts of grief.

She said nothing, simply carried on. That came from generation after generation of wearing a false veneer of gladness and of forged smiles and hidden suffering.

Beth's chest squeezed even tighter. She wanted life to be as it was. She wanted her husband to come in for supper soon. Perhaps she would always carry the ache to see him once more. She knew she shouldn't, and those last words between them, "See ya for supper," would remain etched in her heart for the rest of her days.

If only wants became realities. She cried more lonely tears. At least her younger girls enjoyed spending time with their many *aentis* and cousins. Tracy and Beth Ann had created a game over who would surprise them with a visit each day. *Jah*, instead of feeling overwhelmed by the constant helpers, Beth should be grateful that she hadn't been alone for a single moment in the last seven months. Who knows what else she might mess up.

Sounds of laughter pulled her gaze toward the house where her sister-in-law, Della, was currently seeing over Beth's home. Hopefully, Della hadn't seen Beth sneaking out the side door. It wasn't good for her girls, or others for that matter, to see tears still coming so easily. But grief was a powerful force, its death grip on her heart ever so tight.

Slipping around the corner, she found a shadowy corner at the end of the concrete walkway between the store and storage building, which held the overflow of dwindling supplies, and let the tears fall as they had on her pillow again last night. *Jah*, it was best to put as much distance between her and the undertaker as possible.

Those first three weeks, Beth's parents had helped out. Her sisters, Trina and Lucinda, had visited, and they still wrote or phoned at least once a week. They understood her grief. They let her cry. She glanced toward the house again, where the sounds of little Lisa's squeals echoed inside the large three-story home, and Beth's heart shuddered even more, causing the tears to come even harder now. Thankfully, she could find dark places to hide. How would she explain another run of tears to their questioning hearts?

Her girls. They were all she had left, yet they felt so far away from her now. It was her duty to teach Beth Ann how to do dishes and Tracy to mend a loose stitch.

Cradling her middle once more, Beth felt the sting of loss all over. Andrew would never know this *boppli*. Her *boppli* would come into the world fatherless.

"Oh, Andrew. I know I should be grateful, but why did you have to go? Our *kinner* need you."

Closing her eyes, the memory of death brought back a vivid picture. The wet, sleeting snow that cold December day had been fitting. The weeping of her girls matched that of the cold winds coming out of the east, bending the cedars to bow their heads. Black umbrellas dotted the grounds of their community cemetery. Underneath, the black-clad family and friends of their Old Amish community stood equally hurt by a life cut short.

Bishop Graber had delivered the common words and kind ones that Beth felt helped eldest Christine after losing her *daed*, even as the plain wooden box was laid reverently in the earth.

Women had served ham, cheese, and homemade bread sandwiches before the service. Tidied up young *kinner* after the long day. Their caring hearts, as was custom, were appreciated, as well as the flood of dishes that followed afterwards. But in the end, Beth, too, had to let go of her husband, once the rich chocolate Kentucky earth covered what was no longer hers, but *Gott*'s. She remembered well the urge to pull the dirt away and find him happy to see her.

The Lord giveth, and the Lord taketh away.

Gott's will took Andrew for reasons Beth would never know. A test of faith is trusting *Gott*'s final say, her mother had said. But why Andrew? Beth continued to question many times in her heart, but only twice to her mother. Andrew'd had much life left in him yet. The keeper of many things, a father to their children, a brother to his siblings, and devoted to helping anyone in the community if the need arose. So why would *Gott* take him? Why would *Gott* leave her to figure out how to sew up this gigantic hole he left behind?

"Beth?"

Beth's eyes flew open, and she quickly wiped her face dry before turning. Paul stood there, slightly bent from years of heavy-lifting, a look of terrible regret over his weather-wrinkled features. "If me stopping in causes you hurt, then . . ."

Beth quickly collected herself. "*Nee*, Paul." She waved a hand. She stepped closer, but not so much he could see the tears birthed by his presence. She couldn't afford to lose any customers.

"It's a hard day, is all." What more could she say?

"*Jah*, I reckon there will be more of those." He shifted his weight to his other leg. "I'm not one many want to chat with, after . . ."

After losing a loved one. She knew the words Paul had failed to deliver. Beth imagined it so, but Paul's duty was as important as a deacon or bishop. He served his community, gave his time for others at the worst of times. During a family's deepest grief, he saw over the dead from the funeral home to the grave. The frown lines buried deep within his face had been earned in sacrifice. Smiling was not appropriate for his job.

"I should get back inside to see over the customers," she said, not knowing what to say and desperate to get away from another awkward conversation involving becoming a widow.

"No rush. A walk always does my *fraa* well. Lester has been helping those young folks with the store since you ran out."

Beth bit her lip at the suggestion riddled with fact. She didn't run, did she? How embarrassing. If Paul and Lester noticed, did the twins? If Alma was further disappointed in Beth's weak constitution, it would only earn her more Graber helpers in her everyday routine.

"Don't fret. Lester knows his way around," Paul further added, as if that somehow made it sound better that a practical stranger was running her store.

"He may run the machine shop, but he's seen over a few shops before." Paul looked around, putting both hands in his pockets. "Hiring help is *goot, jah*?" He lifted bushy brows, but thankfully, said nothing of her remarrying, as was their way, to have a husband see over such things.

"I . . ."

"You have hay yet to sell, and that barn roof needs repairing after that last storm. Shelves are getting thin, too. I reckon Lester can see to ordering more supplies before they go bare."

84

"He has his own work," Beth reminded him. Why did everyone think they knew what was best for her?

"His shop isn't open every day. Give it some thought. I'll send my eldest over soon to see to those steps. Likely Andrew didn't use a good wood sealer." Paul's forward-speaking tongue was another reason Beth preferred avoiding him.

Paul's gaze shifted to the barn again. An Amish barn was the heart of any farm, and after one storm after another in her life, it would need tending to soon enough.

"Robert will see to the barn. He knows what's expected of him, and Lester will offer up his help too. It is our way," Paul repeated as if Beth had suddenly forgotten the very core of their community.

Before Paul limped away, Beth didn't have time to share that she was plenty capable of figuring out what supplies to order. Then again, in seven months, she hadn't even given it a thought, instead replenishing stock with supplies Andrew had stored up in the shed.

New steps would be nice, she considered, then quickly shook off the thought. She needed to get back inside before folks thought her so mad with grief they'd have her visiting Dok Stella for something bitter to drink. Or worse, they might think to have her visit Esther from the neighboring district, who offered strange treatments and counseling for all things unspoken. *Nee*, Beth had to straighten her shoulders and take over what life she had left.

Inside, Beth found Lester standing behind her register, ringing up Linda Shetler. Now the minister's *fraa* would think Beth incapable of ringing up her own sales.

"Hiya, Beth. School will be here before we know it." Linda wiped a sleeve along one side of her face to erase the evidence that it was only July, nearly eight more weeks before the new school year.

"*Jah*, they do enjoy it." Beth quickly stepped up and shot

Lester a look. Taken aback momentarily, Beth noted that his eyes weren't dark at all, but as blue as a midsummer sky. His sandy hair was in need of a trimming, and his beard much tamer than Andrew's had been.

Lester lifted one brow and locked gazes with her. She hadn't noticed how tall Lester was until now. Standing incredibly close, she pursed her lips despite how wonderful he smelled on a ninety-degree summer day.

"Excuse me," she muttered. She could tend to her own customers.

After one awkward minute, Lester nodded and stepped away from the register, and Beth turned back to Linda, who was smiling at the awkward exchange.

"It's wonderfully hot today, is it not?" The Amish loved talking about the weather.

"*Jah*, Alma tells me your *kinner* have a sweet tooth. I'd be happy to bake a batch of my Madhouse Cookies."

"This is *verra* kind of you, but they have been getting their share of sweets lately, and the sugar does not run out until late in the day."

"I do have a liking for sugary things myself." Linda chuckled. "It's a wonder Alma allows for such."

Beth winced at the comment. Alma's dominant ways were noted by most within the community, but Beth didn't like that others thought Alma decided on her *kinners'* snacks!

"Lisa already has more energy than most three-year-olds. Alma sends a different girl each day just to keep up with Lisa, but madhouse cookies sound tempting to me."

Linda laughed heartily and bagged her own things as Beth rang them up. "I remember well how much energy it takes to keep up with one that age. Joe was a chore for both John and me. I will certainly send over a batch, and I won't tell a soul if you hide them just for yourself." She winked.

After handing back Linda's change, newlywed Oneida

Miller stepped to the counter with three dented cans of kidney beans, a new broom head, and a spool of thread that was far too green for any dresses worn in the Old Order community.

"It is a fine day, is it not?" Oneida was short with rounded hips and lovely blue eyes behind thin-framed glasses. Having never married until the age of fifty-two, she'd found none other than stern ole Arlen Miller to be the one for her. Beth had always wondered what Arlen had said to convince Oneida to marry. They were as opposite as oil and water. Yet, one didn't see either of them without smiles happily planted on their lips these days. Proof that love joined together even the strangest of pairs.

"The sunshine is a blessing today for sure."

"We need the rain as we need the sun, but I, too, am glad to see one of them go." Oneida smiled. "Will you be signing up for school lunches this year?"

More talk of school had Beth suddenly contemplating new dresses for her girls. It was late July, which meant five more weeks before the first day of school. The first Monday after Labor Day. With three girls attending, Beth would do her part.

"Of course. Christina and Beth Ann are excited to return." Not Tracy. Beth's ten-year-old didn't like school, though her grades never reflected her disinterest.

"I volunteer, though I have never been blessed with *kinner* of my own."

"How kind of you." Beth accepted two ten-dollar bills and opened the register to make change.

"I was wondering if you plan on ordering more Midas flour. It makes the best cakes, and the Wickey's store charges more than what you normally do."

"Oh." Beth should probably find out where Andew ordered flour from soon. "I can make a note of it."

"Arlen and I have been hoping you and the girls would *komm* for supper soon. Friday, perhaps?" Oneida lifted a brow.

On Fridays, Alma always paid her a visit, and Beth knew she'd not get away anytime soon after closing the store. Like clockwork, Alma always insisted on lingering into the evening, expressing her thoughts of what was best. What Alma thought was best was often rearranging Beth's kitchen to match her own. It had taken three hours last week for Beth to put everything back to normal.

"I do have plans for Friday, but soon we would be happy to *komm. Danke.*"

"Okay, then. You have a blessed day, Beth Graber."

By the time Beth finished up ringing out a few more customers, Lester was gone. That was good. The last thing Beth needed was another person stepping in and taking over her life, and if there was one thing Paul was wrong about, it was that Andrew's brother Robert would mend the barn. That one was not like the rest of the Pencil Grabers. Robert kept his distance.

CHAPTER 2

*W*hen the clock struck four, Beth locked the door of the Bent and Dent and aimed for the house. Inside, she found Christina at the stove mashing boiled potatoes. The steam only added to the dreary look of her.

"Don't add too much butter, or it will be soup," Della instructed.

On her hip, three-year-old Lisa sucked her thumb. She'd clearly just woken from a nap much too late in the day; she wouldn't go down easy tonight. The soft *kapp* for her head was missing, exposing four tiny blonde braids that took nearly half an hour to thread together.

Tracy and Beth Ann were busy cleaning up crayons, coloring pages, and books from the family table. Beth noted right away they'd read the newest Benji story and tried not to frown. Oh, how she wished to read to her own *kinner* as she once did.

Her children had Beth's light hair and blue eyes. Andrew had never once complained they favored her likeness. Instead, he praised being blessed with each one.

Seeing her, Beth Ann dropped her armload, scattering

crayons onto the wooden kitchen floor and ran into Beth's arms. Beth Ann was missing one front tooth, which made her smiles more fetching, and her words produced a light spray of spit when she was excited.

"Della let us have apple cake for a snack today."

"How sweet of her." Beth shot Della a grateful smile.

"She's bringing baby ducks for us next time." Tracy readjusted the stack of books in her arms and blinked a few times.

Beth hoped she wasn't experiencing another headache. None of the remedies she'd tried so far had helped very much, since the changing seasons often contributed to them.

"We can't know if that is tomorrow or next week," Tracy added. The stains on her dress looked as if she had been rolling around in the grass.

Because you never know who will be here from this day to the next, Beth wanted to say but nodded instead. Beth Ann loved all animals, especially her little flock of chickens they were all immensely grateful for. How would they afford to feed more than the livestock already in their care?

"Stephen and Rachel are readying the buggy. I can finish up here." Beth set down her own stack of books on the counter. Unless she wanted more help, it was best she try and make heads or tails of Andrew's bookkeeping.

"Robert asked that I give this to you." Della reached into her pocket and handed over a white envelope.

Beth felt the stack of bills tucked inside right away. This wasn't the first gift of this kind that Andrew's *bruder* had sent but not delivered to her. She'd open it later. Hopefully, this time, Robert had penned a few words to explain why he had kept to himself.

"It's not necessary for him to continue sending these," Beth remarked, before pocketing the envelope in her own pocket.

90

"He wants to help. It's surely hard for you since Andrew's death."

It was hard, but harder not knowing what to do from one day to the next. "His help as well as yours is much appreciated, but he has yet to visit or say two words to me," Beth whispered. "I've yet to lay eyes on him outside of Sunday church." Even then, Robert avoided Beth and her girls as if they carried a deadly disease.

Della lowered her head. At only twenty-five, she'd lived a sheltered life among her large family and had only begun courting Val Beechy. She was just beginning to understand the powers of love and loss.

"Robert blames himself. I heard Mamm and Lavina talking about it."

Beth blinked hearing that. It did explain why certain members of the Graber lot clung to her hips, while others, like Freeman, Robert, and Lavina, avoided them when possible. *Jah*, losing a *bruder* had taken a toll.

Robert owned his own construction business and with their *bruder* Freeman and Tim traveling with a few of the young folk, Robert had asked Andrew, who seldom did such work, for help that cold winter's morning. The warmth of the day before, mingled with the frigid temperatures overnight, made repairing a roof more dangerous than at other times. It was the ice, some said, that caused Andrew to slip to his death. It was the cold of that season that still sent chills through Beth's heart and hands even now in the heart of summer.

"It hurts him to think that if he had never asked, then . . ." Della sucked back a run of tears, shaking her head.

"*Danke,* Della, for all you do for your nieces. I couldn't manage without you." Beth watched the appreciation lift her sister-in-law's sorrowful expression immediately.

After bidding Della and the twins so-long, Beth saw the table set and each child seated. She might not have cooked the meal, but she'd be sharing it with them alone. These scant hours in the evening were all Beth had to look forward to each day, and she'd not waste a single minute of them worrying over the helpers, if Midas flour was hard to find, or if the store would be open a month from now.

Supper consisted of thin mashed potatoes, leftover chicken, fresh beans from the garden with bacon grease to flavor them, and cornbread that Beth was sure Della forgot to add any sugar to.

When Beth lowered her head before they ate, she remembered to be thankful there was plenty on the table for her girls to eat and that she had plenty of honey stocked up to make any slice of cornbread taste edible.

They ate happily as talk of ducks took over the majority of the conversation. By the time Beth finished ironing the day's laundry and seeing the *kinner* had baths, she happily sat and listened as each girl shared her version of the day. It was a gift to see an ordinary day through the lives of children.

"And Beth Ann cried because Della didn't know she doesn't like raisins." Christina frowned. "I told *Mammi* Graber, but she forgot to tell Della. Everyone else knows Beth Ann doesn't like raisins."

Christina's lips pruned.

"Everyone cannot know everything," Beth said to her eldest. "It was kind of Della to bake something for you. That's what we need to remember." Beth pulled Beth Ann onto her lap. "And you can always pick them out."

"*Nee, Mammi* says good girls eat food made for them, and we can't be picky because some *kinner* don't get any food at all."

Which led Beth to the topic of being thankful for our food, even with raisins in it. While the girls sat on the couch, Beth read from Psalms. She'd always found some of her favorite verses within those pages. Andrew never let an evening fade without reading to them. She'd hold on to this last familiar thread of what remained.

Taking up Lisa, Beth instructed the girls to head up to bed. She soon came to tuck each of them in once Lisa had her sippy cup of milk and was rocked to sleep. Her three-year-old would soon face another change. Not being the youngest for long, Beth wanted to breathe in each of these little moments as she could with her.

Once little Lisa faded into a deeper sleep, Beth laid her little girl in the bedroom nearby. She didn't mind that Lisa had been more clingy and had fussed to sleep with her, or when Tracy got up in the night and slipped under the covers next to them. In truth, Beth loved the nearness of her girls, waking in the night to the sounds of them sleeping beside her. Sleeping alone after all these years had proved harder than she'd expected.

After checking on the older children, Beth climbed the stairs to the second floor. Behind the first door, Tracy lay on her side, her shoulder rising and falling beneath her nightgown. Beth thought to pull the light cover over her, but the humid night made for a miserable sleep as it was.

In the next room, Beth Ann lay on her back, mouth open and a hint of a smile on her lips. She was likely dreaming of ducks. Beth smiled. How strong her children were. Smiles came so easily to them despite being fatherless. If only Beth had their strength and the ability to sleep through the night without shedding a single tear.

At the next door, she pressed her ear to the wood. All was well in Christina's room. Poor girl. She was falling asleep much more quickly these days, since taking on more responsibility as eldest.

Slipping back into the kitchen, Beth readied herself a cup of chamomile tea and sat at the large oak table. Before her, she spread out all the folders and ledgers she'd found in Andrew's desk. It was time to figure out how her husband had run the store and had kept everything from falling apart.

The first book contained handwritten names of community members at the top of each page. The evidence of numbers and dates revealed that this was likely how much each person owed the store. Andrew understood hard times fell on folks at the worst times, and being as they were blessed with more than their share, he didn't mind giving credit to those in need. He had a big heart.

Beth skimmed over the dozens of pages before taking up a sheet of paper and adding up all the debts. Once she'd totaled them, she leaned back in her chair and shook her head in shock. If everyone paid what they owed, then surely, it was more than enough to order new supplies for the store.

But where do I order supplies? Next, she found a small notebook with business cards taped to the pages. Businesses Beth had never gone to, much less heard of. Tossing that aside, she picked up a hardbound book that contained dates and numbers, which Beth could only assume were totals for each day's end. Did Andrew keep this record for the tax lady up the street? Should she have been totaling her day's earnings all these months?

A fast-racing chill ran up her spine and into her fingertips, completely consuming her. If only she had tried figuring this all out sooner. What if she had to pay money she didn't have?

Beth never cared much for business. It was Andrew who loved his work while Beth saw to the house and *kinner*. If only he had insisted on sharing more with her. If she had listened more closely when he spoke of his days, her stomach wouldn't be in so many knots. How would she collect funds from overdue accounts without stirring hard feelings? Where did she purchase Midas flour?

Her head started to spin. Beth was overwhelmed with seeing over duties as foreign to her as speaking French, and she longed for the everyday rhythm of being a wife and mother. Perhaps Paul's idea of hiring help wasn't such a bad thought after all. Surely, someone knew more about running a store than she did.

Suddenly, Beth thought of Lester and his quiet demeanor and drawing blue eyes. Paul had talked him up. Beth had been one of the community members who happily accepted Lester on the day of his baptism when he joined the church. Folks tended to gossip, and though Lester may have gained his forgiveness from the community after leaving for years and returning with a *sohn* and no *fraa*, forgiving was not forgetting. *Nee*, if forgetting was that easy, Beth wouldn't have been so stuck in grief that she might have lost her last link to supporting her family.

Setting all the books aside, Beth yawned. She had never been the best at math or understanding such things. She never had to. From the cradle, she had been expected to learn how to properly run a household.

She stepped outside into the warm night air and strolled barefoot over the side yard under the growing moonlight. Her feet were swelling more in the warmer season than she recalled with her other girls. Her rounded middle was only growing. Another six weeks perhaps. That was all the time she had to figure out how to order supplies, update books for the store, and begin sewing dresses for the *boppli*. She also needed to figure out how to collect debts owed her. Oh, but how could she speak to community members about wanting paid when so many of them had been there to help her after her husband's death?

"Oh Andrew, why did I not listen to you more? I have no idea what I'm doing, and I certainly can't go asking for money from folks. I had no idea I was to keep numbers down each day, and now I very well may have lost everything you worked so very hard for."

He never answered, telling her all was well, and once Beth shed her nightly tears and shared her concerns with her husband, she aimed for the house. That's when she saw the rectangle of white lying on the concrete walkway near the store. How had she not seen it before?

Picking up the notecard, Beth flipped it over. In the top right corner was a colorful picture of a robin. In someone's handwriting, she read, "Community is like a worn coat. The longer it's worn, the harder it is to take off." She smiled at the old adage she'd heard at least a dozen times since her childhood. Then, she read the second line.

"When thou pass through waters, I will be with thee; and through the rivers, they shall not overflow." It was signed Isaiah, but Beth knew it was Isaiah of the Bible, not either of the Isaiahs she knew from the community.

It was far too warm for a coat, and Beth wasn't wading or swimming in rivers, but the reminder that no matter how many times she felt as if she were drowning, she wasn't alone, and the verse delivered a sense of calm over her current worries.

Whoever lost the card while visiting her store today had no idea how much those words might bring a more peaceful sleep to her tonight.

CHAPTER 3

*T*he first Friday in August, Beth stepped out of the house as the sun rose over Sugar Mountain and Alma's buggy pulled into the drive.

"You need rock hauled in. One more rain, and we will all be swimming in a muddy road." These were Alma's first words as she tethered her horse, a high-stepping gelding with four white hooves and a coat as black as a starless night. She was a minister's *fraa* with wide hips, having borne almost two dozen *bopplin*, a long body, and dark brows that gathered permanently as if disapproving. Beth admired her strength, yet feared her mother-in-law at the same time.

"*Mei* Joan was coming to help in the store so we could see to putting beans up, but Daisy and little Matt were feverish this morning. I thought it best she see over her own today."

Joan was one of Alma's first set of twins, and Joan and her husband, Jason, ran a produce shed on the other end of Cherry Grove. Beth didn't like to think Alma was pushing her married daughters with *kinner* of their own into becoming helpers as well.

Alma didn't see her own as those-in-need, only Beth. It was

Beth's fault she hadn't even thought about canning beans yet. Her mind being torn between so many decisions, she'd hemmed and hawed as if deciding on her favorite cheese when there were over a dozen she liked. Surely Alma thought her inept. Beth had always thought so, though Andrew declared such thoughts untrue. No matter what , Alma had always given gentle advice over the years, and even in the wake of losing her eldest child, she could grieve and move on. A true example of strength and the steadfast faith that carried their bloodlines for centuries. Beth had none of that strength.

"The *kinner* and I will put beans up tomorrow. I can see to the store alone today," Beth told her. In fact, Beth was sure she could handle the store much more easily with Christina and Tracy at her side. "The *kinner* are finishing their breakfast now, and Christina will see to the dishes."

"They are accustomed to late meals for sure." Alma clucked her tongue. "Surely, they remembered to gather eggs first."

Alma simply couldn't accept Beth's way of doing things. She certainly wouldn't agree with eating breakfast before chores, whereas Beth felt a full meal always made for a better start to the day.

"I'll see to your horse before unlocking the store." Beth reached up to work the first buckle when Alma stopped her.

"*Nee*, you are in no condition for such. I've been seeing to my own horse for years."

Biting her lip at the insult that Alma didn't think Beth capable despite her hitching her own buggy these days, Beth ducked her head and went to begin her day at the store.

Fridays were busy days, especially with two upcoming weddings on the horizon. Ignoring the sweat dampening her dress, Beth went to work. Thankfully, the day went by swiftly. Oneida visited a second time, claiming she'd need extra chocolate chips, though Beth was certain she had purchased three bags just days ago. Oneida also extended a second invitation for supper. Evenings were the only hours Beth cherished her girls alone, yet she didn't like hurting Oneida's feelings and promised they would share supper soon.

When Beth locked up the store at four, she caught the strong stench of green beans cooking and groaned most unladylike. Alma must have noted the many weeds taking over Beth's garden.

Stepping inside the house, Beth first noticed a basket of bug-ridden kale and fat Roma tomatoes on the counter. Jars of beans lined both countertops. Alma had already gone through the picking, washing, snapping, and canning. Beth felt a sorrowful tug. She loved working in her garden, canning up all the healthy vegetables she grew, but with the store and difficulty bending for long minutes, it was a wonder she'd picked the first tomato.

"Forty-nine quarts ain't bad for a day's work," Alma greeted, her kapp askew and tendrils of dark hair sticking to her face. "Though some were tough from the lack of watering, and you won't be getting more than a mess yet from how sorrowful those plants look, but I'm sure Christina and Tracy are plenty old enough to see to the chore of stretching them out a little longer."

Beth said nothing, only nodded. Alma was right. Her garden had suffered from the lack of watering and weeding this year.

"Fran mentioned you no longer carry large bags of sugar. Such a staple should be stocked in the store, and Kara is still wondering if you'll be stocking her newest batch of pickles." Alma moved to the table, giving it a final polish. *Jah*, Fridays her mother-in-law made a habit of addressing every issue on her mind before leaving.

"I'd be happy to," Beth commented, though she was plenty

happy to help sell Kara's pickles and had mentioned such to Kara herself already during the last gathering.

"I'm sure you are aware that Tracy could use an eye appointment. Those headaches may not be the changing weather at all. Did you know she squints when coloring or practicing her letters?"

Beth glanced at her daughter as she raked bean tips into a bucket that would be gifted to Beth Ann's chickens. Beth hadn't noticed, but the longer she stood awkwardly watching her mother-in-law move about her kitchen as easily as she did her own, Beth realized Alma could be right. Hadn't Trina needed glasses when it became hard for her to read smaller print?

What a terrible mother Beth was. No wonder Alma saw over so much of her life. Being a widow was not only a hardship, but now Beth was struggling with knowing her own *kinner*.

"Della tells me you have been seeing to the books. I know what a chore that can be. Amos would be glad to see to the chore for you."

Her father-in-law had enough of his own work already. Beth couldn't ask him to see to her business and his. "It's no trouble. You all have done so much."

"*Jah*, but it is what family does," Alma said with a softer smile, the lines of her face reminding Beth how much it meant for her to live by those words.

"*Mammi* made us dresses." Beth Ann held up a pretty powder-blue dress for Beth to admire.

"She made dresses for all three of us," Christina remarked.

"School is but a few weeks away. They need new dresses for sure."

Beth reached into her deep well of patience. Alma meant well, a woman well-versed in seeing over her lot on a daily basis, but Beth had sewn every stitch her children had ever worn. "Alma, I do appreciate all you do, but me and the girls can sew our own dresses. Christina enjoys sewing, and it's time Tracy learns."

"*Ach*, what is a grandmother who doesn't have time to sew a few dresses?"

When Alma left, Beth tried not to let Alma's words from earlier bother her. She readied a simple supper of ham sandwiches and chips for the girls. Alma's canning all day had warmed the house more than what was comfortable. Why her mother-in-law insisted on canning in the large kitchen when the summer kitchen had ample room was a mystery, but surely, Alma had a good reason for it. Just as she did for sewing her grandchildren new school dresses.

Once the children were asleep, Beth went to the porch out of habit when she ached to share her thoughts with someone. A starless sky and low clouds moved overhead. "I had no idea Tracy had trouble with her vision," Beth informed her late husband, in hopes he could hear her. In hopes he would forgive her shortcomings.

"But we have forty-nine jars of beans to eat." *Try to be positive.* "Oh, how I wish you hadn't fallen that day. I miss talking to you and you talking back." Andrew had been a fine talker. He'd never met a stranger, her *daed* had always said. "I'll see to making Tracy an appointment, but I wish you could tell me what is best to do about the store." Some problems had easy remedies, while others required more than her knowledge allowed.

After a few moments of nothing but the sounds of frog song and cicadas singing, Beth let out a sigh. The dead didn't speak, and direction didn't reveal itself in the clouds.

"*When you can't figure out what to do, just do what is in front of you,*" *Mamm* had always told her.

So that's what Beth would do.

Looking about her, Beth looked down at her flower bed. Marigolds were such beautiful flowers, normally. Perhaps there was life in them yet. She slowly got to her knees to deadhead the drying flowers along the back walkway. She was doing what was in front of her until she figured out what to do next. Before reaching the end, she found the card tucked in between two plants as if it had fallen from someone's pocket. This one with a cardinal on the top right-hand corner.

"For our light affliction, which is but for a moment, worketh for us a far more exceeding and eternal weight of glory;"

Beth clutched the blue material to her chest and sucked in a slow breath. The handwriting was slightly slanted, delicately penned. The second line read, "Keep on keeping on." It was signed "Corinthians," and Beth was starting to suspect they weren't lost cards after all, but notes of encouragement from someone.

What choice did she have but to keep going? She appreciated the reminder that no matter how hard things seemed to be, there was hope for tomorrow, and the message remained in her heart as she drifted off to sleep that night.

CHAPTER 4

*C*hristina was plenty capable of driving the pony cart to school, but it was the first day for her little Beth Ann. Beth refused to miss walking her inside the large two-story schoolhouse, even if Beth Ann had visited plenty on days scholars brought younger siblings to school. Beth didn't even mind the stares of a few other hovering parents, who watched as she waddled up the steps of the schoolhouse, giving Beth Ann a final kiss on the cheek and Tracy and Christina a so-long before leaving.

Beth had insisted that she had no need of help today, and thankfully Alma hadn't sent another sister-in-law, but working with Lisa underfoot had proved harder than Beth expected. Every time Beth turned to help a customer, Lisa disappeared, sneaking out of the store through one of the three exits to play on the sidewalk.

At noon, Beth decided to close the store and see to Lisa's lunch. Banana and peanut butter sandwiches were Lisa's favorite these days, and Beth made herself one as well. Collecting laundry and giving her floors a quick polish while Lisa played with her animal picture cards, Beth finally sat down and gave her aching back a rest. If Dok Stella, the local herbal *doktor*, who had taken on delivering *bopplin* as well, had calculated correctly, Beth was over her expected time, but Beth Ann had been almost two weeks late, so Beth felt no need for concern yet.

She had sifted through the collection of business cards Andrew kept in alphabetical order and made a list of potential places she hoped she could purchase flour and sugar from. She'd call and inquire more after supper. At one-forty-five, she harnessed Bones, their buggy horse (Christina had named him years ago on account of his being so skinny when Andrew bought him that the horse had resembled a bag of bones), and loaded Lisa in the seat beside her. Cherry Grove Schoolhouse was only three miles away.

First days didn't always go without hitches. Beth sat waiting, along with a few older siblings and Lester Milford, who insisted on parking next to her, where a long line of shade trees kept the sun from burning them as they waited for the school doors to open.

Under a hot September sun, wearing the traditional black most widows wore, Beth tried not to sweat buckets, then decided it mattered not. She certainly wasn't hoping Lester noticed her at all.

Tired from her many escapes, Lisa slept heavily in the back, while the hot wind blew through the treetops. Beth smiled over her shoulder. Her youngest was fearless and full of adventure.

"I remember when John Lewis could sleep that hard." Lester's low chuckle startled Beth.

Beth looked over as he stared at her child. "She had a busy day helping at the store."

Lester's rolled-up sleeves revealed a man who worked hard with his hands. She quickly averted her gaze.

"Paul said you may be hiring help soon." His black gelding

swatted at flies, refusing to stand still. "I could help unless you're set on hiring out."

"I've plenty of help," Beth said sarcastically and exited her buggy. It was becoming harder to do now, but she managed not to get tied-up in her skirts. How much longer would it take for dismissal? In the three miles getting here, surely it was now past two.

"Have I offended you somehow?" His face pinched sorrowfully.

"Not at all." She needed to work on her people skills. Then again, she knew from dealing with customers alone over the last eight months, it was not people she had such a problem with. If only the helpers of Cherry Grove weren't such a sore spot for her.

"Beth, you are a widow, expecting, and we all need help."

"I know what I am, as does everyone." She rolled her eyes.

"It was just an offer." He lifted a hand in defense. "I'd extend the same to anyone in your . . . situation, but I'm sure you'd be more comfortable hiring on one of the Pencil lot."

"I don't plan to hire anyone." How would she pay for it? "In case you didn't notice, the store isn't thriving." She ran the bottom of her left flip-flop over the gravel to loosen whatever sticky mess she'd stepped in. Great, now she was hot, tired, and smelly. So why was Lester Milford looking at her as if she were the only blooming rose in a winter garden?

"*Jah*, the shelves did look thinner than on my last visit."

"And thinner they'll get, I imagine. Andrew never talked up the important parts of the store." He only shared who'd come by and who shared something that tickled his funny bone. "I've no idea where he ordered anything, and the supply shed is nearly bare!"

"I see."

He couldn't see. Not from her standpoint anyhow. Perhaps she shouldn't be sharing such private things with him, but how many folks must she encounter to remind her of her shortcomings?

"No one thinks I can do anything, and they may be right, but I'm trying!" Perhaps it was the high temperatures of the day or the list of retailers in her pocket she had to deal with that was making her cranky.

"Of course you are. Folks want to help. If I had half the folks helping me when times got hard, I would have faired a bit different, though I'm not complaining. I enjoy my work, and John Lewis and I do well enough."

Beth stared at him. Was that why he left all those years ago? It was none of her concern. "I appreciate the offer, really. It's just . . ."

"What?"

"No, never mind. It's hard to explain." She waved him off. Was Teacher Kevin keeping the *kinner* all evening?

"Try me," Lester said, drawing her attention back to him.

Lester leaned against her buggy . . . waiting. It had been some time since anyone cared to hear her thoughts. As wonderful as Andrew was, he seldom asked about her day or if she worried over something.

Taking a deep breath, Beth couldn't help but say what was on her mind at that exact moment. "It's not my fault Andrew went and helped Robert. He knew nothing about fixing roofs. He's left me to figure all of this out alone. I keep trying, then someone tells me I'm doing it wrong, or best try it this way. I just want to do one thing without a fuss. Is it too much to ask? I can sew my *kinners'* dresses and cook them suppers and see to my own garden!"

"I see." Lester took a step back.

Clearly, he had never met an angry Amish widow before. "I'm sorry, I didn't mean . . ."

"It's good to have help, but too much help can be . . . too much."

"Exactly."

"Don't blame him for leaving, Beth. Folks leave. Either by choice or *naet*, but Andrew went with *Gott*."

How could she be so selfish? Lester's story was one no one knew, but many speculated. John Lewis's mamm wasn't taken up. *Gott's* will hadn't pulled her from her family. She left. At least that was the rumor. "I'm sorry, Lester. That wasn't *verra* kind of me to say."

"I hope you always speak the truth with me, Beth. We all have a journey to travel, and some are not as easily paved as others." He added, "My offer stands. I can't spare more than a few hours a week while John Lewis is at school and when I don't have many customers of *mei* own. But I can help."

"What of the food pantry? It's a wonder you have any time for yourself, much less to help others."

"I make time for what is important," he said flatly. Something in the way he said it made Beth suddenly feel important. A silly thought. Lester was just being kind. That was all.

"I work mostly when John Lewis sleeps. I get to wind my own clock." He grinned. "As far as the food pantry, I pick up the delivery every other Saturday. Folks come and get what they want, leave what they can afford in a jar. I leave the building unlocked. It's none of my concern who enters inside or how much they take, and any donations I split between my driver and the community fund."

Beth admired that, as she knew firsthand what it felt like to be the center of sympathies. Maybe Lester wasn't the rebel most thought him to be. His past had been forgiven, whatever it was. She need not shed a light on it.

Sensing Beth was contemplating his proposal, he continued. "It doesn't take away from my work or learning how to make Mamm's pie crust, which John Lewis insisted I learn, and . . ." He scratched his chin.

Though he wasn't married, Lester wore the beard of a married man. She barely remembered what he looked like as a *youngie*. Her eyes from the age of fifteen had been solely on Andrew. If she had paid attention to Lester, she would have noticed how his eyes twinkled when he was trying to be funny. Beth almost smiled, but stopped herself. It wasn't proper to smile at another man or to notice how his eyes sparkled.

"If I'm seeing over these things for you and keeping my mind sharp, you'd have more time to pick your own garden."

He'd heard her every word. Beth wasn't sure if she was impressed or embarrassed. His words brought her head up and her gaze landing on his once more. "I fear the kind of help I need is more than any five men could figure out, since I've yet to keep a record of sales." She'd not subject him or anyone to her terrible mistake.

Lester crossed his arms, his brows perplexed in the silence between them, but his eyes never left hers as if all the answers were right there. Beth slowed her breathing.

"Well, your register has receipts. Did you keep them?"

He was thinking, Beth. He was not looking at you in that way. "*Jah*, and I have rolls and rolls of them in a shoe box under the counter, but how can that…"

The sound of over forty scholars spilling out of the schoolhouse drew both of their attention. Beth turned to greet her children and smiled when she caught sight of Tracy running ahead of the flock. Little John Lewis was the spitting image of his father. His short legs did well to keep up with Beth Ann's longer ones, but Beth could see her daughter was taking it slow, so he could keep up.

"Mamm, John Lewis is the same as me, but he's a boy." Beth Ann said, bringing a smile to both Beth and Lester's faces. It seemed her little animal lover had made fast friends. The little boy was missing his two front teeth. *Perhaps they had plenty in common*, she mused.

"Sounds like you both had a good first day." Lester sat and patted them both on the head.

"Would have been better if Teacher Kevin didn't think to give out homework to us older ones." Catherine rolled her eyes. Surely, something could bring a smile to her face, but Beth feared that maybe nothing would for some time yet.

"*Jah*, but the more work you do today, the smarter you will be, so you'll work less later," Lester said, earning him a half shrug from Beth's eldest.

"I messed up my words, but Teacher Lydia said I spelled them all correctly, I just was too sloppy."

Beth went to help Tracy into the buggy, but Lester stepped forward, lifting her high into the air. She gave a happy squeal, and he deposited her in the back seat.

"Who's next?"

"Me! Me!" Beth Ann was not about to let Tracy out-squeal her, but no matter the eyes drawn their way, Beth appreciated Lester's playfulness. Her children had been robbed of such innocent moments as these.

"You shouldn't be lifting," he muttered before stepping away so Christina could get in. "I'll stop by on Friday, and we can look over those books."

"Yah!!!" Beth Ann bounced. "Can John Lewis *komm*? I have to show him Penny and Roo!"

"Her chickens," Beth shared.

"Of course. I'd like to meet them too."

That evening after chores had been finished, Beth began a pot of potato soup and grilled cheese sandwiches and tried not to think about Lester Milford and how he had made her girls laugh and wormed his way into seeing her out of her current troubles. *Mudder* always said laughter and *kinner* were good medicine. Beth wondered what her *mamm* would say about Lester Milford.

"I grabbed the mail," Christina said, dropping the stack

onto the counter before setting the table. It was late in the evening and the girls were already in bed before Beth thought to leaf through the stack that consisted of a water bill, some junk mail, and a letter from Lucinda.

She ripped open the envelope, desperate for the connection she had missed since her last visit. Lucinda had been only a few years younger, but she loved her teaching job so much she refused to marry any of the men who had asked her so far. Beth remembered well how stubborn Lucinda could be as a child, but as a woman, she admired that independence more now.

Beth,

I'm coming soon. It took some doing, but Martha Hershberger, you remember her, agreed to taking my place through the fall. I'm staying until Thanksgiving. Be there in a few days. I'll be with you soon, sister.

Lucinda

Beth cried her first tears of relief as she set the letter down. Lucinda was coming. Beth wasn't going to be alone.

CHAPTER 5

*B*eth's flip-flops slapped the concrete floor. Her feet had started swelling in July, and she only suffered wearing proper shoes when it was absolutely necessary.

While two *Englisch* customers browsed the dented canned food section, Beth added to the list of supplies needed to keep the store running that she had worked up last evening.

The counter was dotted with milk-based products from the Raber farm. Beth had tried the aloe-and-goat-milk soap and found it a favorite of hers. There was honey, also from the Raber farm, lip balms, jars of honey with chunks of the honeycomb included, and little pocket storybooks for *kinner*. The plantain salve containers came from Dok Stella and did wonders for stings and bug bites. Beth always kept it on hand, considering gnats and mosquitoes traveled great lengths to nip at Christina in the warmer months.

She was busy in her work when the sound of someone entering drew her attention to the door. Despite Lester mentioning he would come today, Beth had no intentions of giving it further attention.

"Hiya." His kind blue eyes didn't hide the fact that she was the size of a haus.

"Hiya," she said, suddenly flushing. "I was just working up a list of necessities for the store."

"You could have waited, and I would have helped you. You look tired."

"Linda delivered Madhouse cookies to the girls last night. I don't know what she puts in those"—*everything including potato chips*, Beth wanted to say—"but Lisa was awake long into the night before settling."

"John Lewis gets his share of cookies from *Mamm*, but only on nights he wants to sleep over." Lester chuckled.

"I hadn't thought of that," Beth teased.

"It's a wonder you sleep at all with so many looking to sweeten your *kinner* up."

"Well, I put my foot down this morning. No more sugar except for special occasions."

"I reckon that went well." He laughed again, causing the air around her to lighten.

"There were protests, but I'm the *mamm*. At least until Christina informed me I have dessert duty for the school next week."

"Well, don't look to me for help. I've failed at making an edible pie crust." Lester smiled and suddenly Beth's head spun. Maybe she was overdoing it. She'd drink more water. That's what she'd do.

"Doesn't Lavina run a donut shop?" His tone remained even.

Beth liked that he didn't try to sound as if he was telling her what to do like most did, and it was true that her sister-in-law owned a donut-and-coffee stand at the local Amish market. Why hadn't Beth thought of it sooner?

"I could close the store Saturday and take the girls. Make it a day out for them." What a brilliant idea. Beth suddenly felt a pinch of excitement looking forward to tomorrow. What fun it would be spending the day with her girls.

"I bet little Beth Ann would like that," he said with a gentle smile that spoke of his already cemented affections for her daughter. "They have stuffed ducks at one booth, and Christina might like the candle shop. I reckon young *maedels* still like that sort of thing."

"They do, but so do big girls. You have an answer for everything, don't you?"

"Nee, I'm puzzled yet why you can't sew dresses on your own, and I have no idea why I have one pant leg longer than the other." He looked at his trouser legs, which were clearly uneven.

"One of the hems has worked loose," she said. It was a simple bachelor mistake.

"Oh," Lester replied, his cheeks turning a warm shade of cherry blossom.

It had been over nine months since her husband's death, leaving her on this journey alone. She'd never thought she'd laugh again, but suddenly Beth found herself laughing out loud. She quickly slapped a hand over her mouth. She had no business laughing with another man. No business at all.

"Beth, it's *goot* to laugh. It can be healing, and you really have a nice laugh." His blue eyes stared down at her in understanding.

Was that true? Did laughter bring forth healing? *Nee*, she pushed off the thought. "Let me show you to Andrew's office." Beth turned to Lisa who was pouting most determinedly under the register counter for not being allowed to eat a sucker today. "Want to see Lester into the little office?"

Even with her *mamm's* higher-pitched chipper voice, Lisa didn't budge. Her folded little arms were clearly squeezing her little body tightly in defiance.

"She can stay here and mind the store." Lester peeked

around the corner. "Or . . ."—his voice drew both Beth and Lisa's gaze—"she can show me which way to go, so I don't get lost."

"I know the way." Lisa bounced to her feet, happy to help Lester, causing Beth to shoot them both a displeased look.

The small office was a cramped section of the building without any windows and stuffed with boxes of old receipts and invoices collected over the years. Beth stood in front of the old metal desk Andrew had purchased at a yard sale years ago when they first opened the store. It seemed like an eternity now, yet it had only been seven years.

"I laid everything out this morning." Beth dropped her list of necessities on top. "I already mentioned I had no idea I was to keep track of everything. It's probably a waste of time, and the tax folks will take everything."

"It doesn't work like that." Lester rounded the desk and gave the ledgers a quick scan. "Plus, there is forgiveness in not knowing, just as there is in making mistakes. Did Andrew allow for folks to charge?" Lester's brows gathered sharply when he opened the yellow notebook.

"*Jah*, and some still do."

Lisa plopped down on a box her size and watched them. If she thought her silence would earn her sweets, she was sorely mistaken. It had been months since Beth had given the office any attention, and she had yet to sweep or dust. She pulled Lisa to her feet before she got much dirtier.

"Beth, until I have time to go over all of this and find which vendors are already used to working with the store, I think it best not to let folks have things for free."

"What if they really need those things?" She had no head for business if it included insisting on folks paying old charges.

"We can hang a sign up saying NO CREDIT, and folks won't ask you. But you can't give away things you don't actually own."

"It's my store." Lester was making no sense at all.

"It's my *mutter*'s store!" Lisa folded her arms again and gave Lester one of her sharp looks, which wasn't sharp at all on her adorable little features.

"It is your store too, Lisa," Lester told her with soft eyes and lifted her up. "Only three and already a business owner. You'll be the talk of the community."

Lisa liked that, though she had no idea what being a business owner really meant.

"A community you all depend on." He turned to Beth. "Each time you buy something to sell, you have to earn that money back before you can collect extra from the sale price. If you don't have any money ahead, then you have none to give out."

It made perfect sense, which only made Beth feel even more silly for not thinking of such a basic mathematical problem.

"There you are," Alma stepped into the doorway, beads of sweat running along her dark hairline and down the sides of her long face. With the older girls now in school, Beth had convinced Alma she had no reason to burden anyone. Thankfully, Alma said nothing to that, but here she stood once more, on a Friday.

Alma looked at Beth as if she had been searching for her for hours. Then she noticed Lester holding her granddaughter, and her frown deepened. "What is this?"

Sensing her unease, Lester set Lisa back on her feet.

"Lester offered to look over the books. Paul Lengacher thought it a good idea." Perhaps she shouldn't have mentioned it was Paul's idea. Beth was trying to demonstrate her ability to do more to her mother-in-law.

"Did he now?" Alma continued to stare.

It was then Lisa thought to reach for Lester's hand. Without a thought, he accepted it, and Beth's heart almost melted. Lisa didn't take to others quickly. Let alone those outside the family.

"Beth worries she's not doing a fine job, but from what I can see, she is. She has a few matters of placing orders yet, and I suggested she hang a sign so folks will stop shopping on credit. Until I update everything, folks really shouldn't be borrowing from her."

Clearly taken back seeing another man with her granddaughter, Alma inhaled a long breath and lifted her chin before releasing it. "I agree. Makes good business sense. Folks have no business borrowing from a widow in her predicament anyhow. I would have mentioned it if I had known she was doing so."

Beth tried not to frown, but Alma needed to know Beth wasn't the one behind all the forgotten charge accounts. "Andrew let them do that. I just didn't change anything."

At the mention of Andrew's name, Alma stilled. "Well, I just wanted to drop by and let you know Tracy is in the house getting a drink of water and will be in here when she's done. Didn't make sense returning her to school today."

"Tracy? Is she ill?" Beth gathered the side of her dress in her hand and started for the door. Now why didn't Teacher Kevin call her?

"*Nee*, I took her to the eye doctor. It was just as I said. Those headaches stem from poor eyesight, but no trouble in it. She thinks herself already smarter for having them."

"She has glasses?" Beth's voice faded to a soft murmur.

"*Jah*. Amos and I saw over it, but I must go on now. My driver hates waiting, and I have much to do before supper." Alma gave Lester and Lisa one last glance before marching back into the front of the store and out the door.

With one hand on her middle, Beth dropped into the chair and tried to collect herself. She'd not cry in front of Lisa or

Lester. She would not, but it was another milestone in her daughter's life that she hadn't been a part of. How scared Tracy must have been to go through the exam without her.

"You didn't know?"

Beth shook her head. "Alma does what she thinks is best, but . . ."

"But you didn't know. Even my own *mamm* knows feeding John Lewis cookies before supper is as far as she should go. You should have been with her."

How right. Beth knew that.

"Beth, you have such a soft heart, but you need to grow your spine."

She did, and hearing Lester say such only confirmed that she had allowed others to help her with what came easily instead of what came hard.

"Will you watch Lisa for a short bit?" Beth stood and made her way out the door without giving Lester time to answer. Hopefully, she'd catch Alma before she got into the van.

SPIRITS LIFTED, the weight of uncertainty vanished, Beth breezed through picking the last tomatoes in the garden. After thanking John and Alma for going to great pains to be with her and the *kinner*, Beth assured them that she could manage her home without them. Alma said nothing as her husband reminded Beth they were only a rock skip away.

As Tracy helped set tomatoes on the foldout tables in the basement, Beth recalled how Lester had said nothing either, despite his eyes revealing how he wished to know what transpired between Beth and her extended family. Instead, he gathered up her list, Andrew's ledgers, and bid Beth goodbye.

After a meal of bacon and tomato sandwiches, Christina's

favorite cheese-flavored potato chips, and oatmeal hand pies, she and her girls sang as they tidied up the kitchen.

She was just finishing Lisa's bath when she heard the knock on the door. As if they'd never had company before, the rest of her girls were already greeting whoever had arrived in the kitchen. Wrapping Lisa in a towel, Beth helped her youngest down the steps and into the kitchen. A squeal of delight erupted from Beth at the sight of Lucinda at the counter eating one of her oatmeal hand pies. Proof her girls had inherited their sweet tooth from her more than Beth, who often hankered for salty flavors.

Lucinda bore the same matching light hair and blue eyes, but she stood a good half foot taller and had always been far more athletic than Beth when they were young.

"What are you doing here so soon? I thought you'd be coming in a few days." Beth handed Lisa wrapped in a towel over to Christina and enveloped her sister in a hug.

"Surprise!"

Lucinda's full mouth didn't distract Beth one bit from squeezing her sister more tightly.

"*Mamm* says she feels your time coming, and we can't have you doing it alone."

Precious *Mamm* and Lucinda. They always knew the right time to show up. Beth hadn't had much time to consider her *boppli*'s upcoming birth. If she had, no doubt she would have fretted over the fact that she would bring a child into the world with only Dok Stella at her side.

"Let me get a better look of you all," Lucinda said, giving each girl her full attention. "Christina is nearly as tall as me."

"Mamm says I'm as *goot* at volleyball as you too." Christina snickered, and Beth's heart burst seeing the fast smile on her face.

"We shall see," Lucinda challenged. That was Beth's

nearest sister, always up for the next challenge. After fussing over the girls, Lucinda insisted on seeing each of them to bed, giving Tracy a few longer minutes of time before returning downstairs, where Beth had readied a pot of coffee, Lucinda's preferred choice, no matter the time of day. Beth made tea for herself. It would be a long night catching up.

"I can't believe you're here." Beth lowered herself into a seat next to Lucinda.

"I don't know why. You know how I want to be first holding your little one." Lucinda stretched her long arms as her smile widened. "That Tracy looks adorable in glasses, but don't think she won't be spiking her own volleyballs soon enough."

"Don't remind me." Beth added a healthy dose of milk and three spoonfuls of sugar to Lucinda's cup.

"I feel like the pesky little sister since you'll be with me until Thanksgiving. You'll need the wages."

"I have fewer needs, and more dresses than I can wear in a week!" Lucinda rarely was serious, a product of being a teacher who often induced joy in her students. "*Mamm* worries you are the one in need of money. That's why I'll be helping out while you rest up before you never sleep again. I'm so excited to meet another little girl. You're the same as when you had Christina and Beth Ann."

"What if it's a boy?"

The room grew quiet.

"Then I will finally have someone who might challenge me at basketball."

Beth sobbed out a laugh. Lucinda placed a hand over Beth's.

"Andrew would be happy to know it, though he never minded his lot of females."

"He didn't." Beth smiled into her cup.

"*Gott* and your family are with you. I cannot know what

you are thinking, and if *Daed* wasn't feeling so poorly, *Mamm* would be here with something wise to say."

"She would say, Beth . . ."

"Keep doing the next thing," they finished together and laughed.

CHAPTER 6

*P*erhaps it had been the cool night air inducing a fine sleep, or having her sister sleeping in the same house as her, but Beth felt unusually happy and full of energy. The sun had yet to climb over the nearest hill as she stood beneath the wash line. She'd been up for hours, happily scrubbing cupboards and washing towels.

She hung the whites on the wheel line, pushed clothes over the yard, high towards the barn loft. Knots of worry lifted from between her shoulders. Her overexuberance of feel-good was hopeful. Lester had come up with a few solutions for the store. He assured her not all was lost, that mistakes could be amended. She paused, clipping a plastic clothespin, and felt a pang of guilt. She should not be attracted to Lester Milford. She hadn't been a widow a full year, and soon she'd bear another *boppli*. What silliness was coming over her this morning, thinking he was interested in her. What betrayal to even want him to be.

"I hope you don't mind I sought help," she muttered to the breeze, always hoping Andrew would say something in return. Of course, life and death were so far apart, it didn't work that way. She knew that, but it didn't stop her from speaking her thoughts. Did he know her thoughts had been swimming lately about Lester? Beth hoped not. Though she knew Andrew would expect her to remarry, giving their *kinner* a *daed*, she also knew her heart was not ready to set aside the life they'd had together.

Pushing the empty four-wheel laundry cart toward the back door, Beth heard the sound of hooves clip-clopping on the pavement nearby. Someone up and going even earlier than she was.

Before reaching for the door, she saw it. Another encouragement card, this one with a tiny wren in the upper corner. Her smile bloomed immediately. The encouragement cards delighted her. That's what Beth was calling them as they kept popping up in unexpected places on various days of the week. After the first two, she no longer felt they were lost cards, but purposefully placed. Until Andrew, Beth never thought such gifts were so sweet.

He Makes All Things New Again.

Jah, He did. Like special friends with encouraging words and sunrises that waited for you before arriving.

But who was leaving them?

Someone who obviously shopped at the store as her extended family never came regularly. But she had so many supportive patrons and friends within the community. Her giver could be any one of them.

Slipping the card into her apron pocket, Beth pushed the wash cart inside. Was it Alma's driver? Driver Dan was known for his quiet charities and kind heart, but he wasn't there that hot Monday evening when she'd discovered the first card.

It certainly wasn't Paul Lengacher. She made a face. He was kind, in an eerie sort of way, but he'd never pen words when he could speak them aloud.

She'd figure it out, the mystery of the encouragement cards.

Beth was just plating scrambled eggs with shredded cheese when the first pain radiated across her middle.

"You look much more ready for the day than me." Lucinda stepped into the kitchen, a sleeping Lisa on her hip. Her dark blonde hair was still in a long braid, and her powder blue dress, wrinkled.

Beth grinned. Sharing a bed with Tracy all night was not for the weak. Tracy had been known to move around often through the night.

"Beth Ann is still searching for her socks, but the rest will be down in a minute. *Shew*, I had no idea Tracy needed glasses. She talked all night about how they made her smarter." Lucinda filled glasses with milk and helped Lisa into a chair.

"She fancies being a top scholar." Another pain, this time a little sharper, caused Beth to wince. She had birthed four times already and knew right away that labor was starting. Hopefully, she'd get the girls off to school before alarming them.

"Are you okay?" Lucinda asked, noting Beth's pinched expression.

"I am. Let's get the girls ready, and we will talk."

"*Ach*, no need to. I can see it all over your face," Lucinda whispered.

"I don't want to worry them, but you can go call Dok Stella as soon as the girls leave for school."

Lucinda's smile bloomed. Of course, every new hope of life brought forth smiles and anticipation, but Beth now realized she'd be spending her day, and possibly her night, working harder than she had in some time. Hindsight told her perhaps it would have been better to remain in bed longer, not washing towels and waiting for the sun to wake.

Once the *kinner* were off to school, Lucinda did as asked and phoned the Dok. Beth told her it could be hours yet, but she was plenty grateful Dok Stella insisted on coming over right away as this time she was much further along than in the past.

In the room she once shared with her husband, Beth bore a son only six hours later.

A son.

Oh, how the heart could ache and fill with joy at the same time.

"He's healthy and has lots of hair," Dok Stella said, handing him back over to Beth after weighing him and giving him a detailed inspection. "And won't the girls be surprised when they get home!"

"Beth Ann will think we bought him at the market. She still thinks *bopplin* come with price tags." Lucinda chuckled. "I'll go fetch Lisa. I left her napping despite how loud you got," Lucinda teased.

It wasn't the teasing, or the precious beautiful little boy with dark hair and eyes in her arms that caused the tears to start coming, but once they did, Beth couldn't will them to stop.

"She may need a few more minutes before that," Dok Stella instructed. "The body needs time to adjust, and bonding is very important."

Lucinda nodded as if she understood, collected any linens in need of washing, and slipped out of Beth's room.

"Now, sweet Beth. This may be part of it for a few days, but don't you worry. I brought red clover tea and a few herbs that will do you right without upsetting this little one's tummy."

"He has a son," Beth muttered and looked to the Dok with watery eyes and shaking arms. "Andrew always wanted a son. Though he never told me, I knew. He will never lay eyes on his son."

Dok Stella's face shifted to understanding as she placed a hand on Beth's hair, caressing it in long strokes while a terrible ache burned through Beth's chest. Sitting on the edge of the bed, the dok must have known how Beth needed the contact, the understanding, as she sat quietly while Beth's tears fell in sheets down her face.

"*Gott*'s will is too much to try and understand," Dok Stella finally spoke. "Your body has been through so many changes since your husband died, but don't you let what you cannot know be what hurts your heart now. You shared four beautiful *kinner* together. You have sorrows, *jah*, but you will find joy again."

Beth wiped at her wet face. "That is kind of you to say."

"Well," Dok Stella smiled, "It was John, not me, but never think Andrew is missing what is unknown to him or feel bad for it. He lived his days until *Gott* called him home. You have your cry and you mourn what aches inside of you, but Beth Graber, you do have a *sohn*. A healthy and strong son who will love you all the days of your life."

In the following days, Beth resigned herself to following Dok Stella's advice and let Lucinda see over the store. They both agreed to only opening the store on Mondays and Saturdays. Introducing a *bruder* to a house full of girls came with varied reactions. Beth Ann was thrilled to have a little *bruder*. Christina thought Beth had broken the tradition of an all-girl home, but when she thought eyes weren't looking, her tender heart and arms held little Andrew with complete affection. She'd even insisted she was better at changing him than Lucinda, who did so too quickly and not with gentleness. Tracy was simply overjoyed to hold him and stare into his little face for long stretches. Then there was Lisa, who was still curious if *bruders* could be returned to the store and swapped with *schwestern*.

Last night, Beth dreamed of Andrew. They were young, holding hands, and dreaming of the family they hoped to have one day. With the excitement of a new *boppli*, it had been nearly a week since she'd longed for a vision of him in her dreams.

Caught somewhere between day and night, Beth ventured outside, a restlessness inside her. The crickets sang in haste, and cicadas protested from the cedars. The sky was crowded with stars, pale at this hour as sunrise crept toward the horizon while an overly warm September wind pushed through.

"Thank you, Andrew," If he could hear her, it no longer mattered. Speaking to him came as natural as breathing. If it was unnatural, then she was too, for she might always look up and share a part of her day with him.

"He's the most precious gift you have ever given me. Christina thinks him to have the look of you. Your family has come, taking turns meeting him." With a sympathetic heart, Beth recalled the moment Alma met little Andrew, turning the strong woman into a pool of quiet tears, which none pretended to notice. Alma saw firsthand that the *sohn* mirrored the father. "Tracy helped Kara with the mac and cheese for supper. It was the highlight of her day, but the glasses have made a difference. No headaches."

As the sun rose, Beth wanted to tend to the laundry. Lucinda had been doing much of the housework with the girls' help and seeing over the store a few hours at a time.

"I can do that," Lucinda said, stepping into the basement where the ringer washer's gas-powered motor hummed.

"I feel ready to do it."

"Dok said don't overdo."

"It's been days. I feel fine, I assure you."

Lucinda stared at her as if to be certain. "The *kinner* will be up soon. I should see to breakfast and making lunches." Lucinda paused before leaving. "I reckon you could fit into your old dresses again. Much like *mamm* when you were born, you barely look like a new *mamm*." Lucinda, being the eldest, had such memories of what their mother looked like during those times, whereas Beth and Trina were only a year apart and couldn't remember.

"The black is what is expected."

"It's not a steadfast rule."

True, though women had done so after losing loved ones for generations. "It's proper though," Beth reminded her.

"*Jah*, for a one in mourning, but how can grief be set by days or weeks or a full year? I reckon you will always have an ache for Andrew. You shared a life together, but at least put on something that doesn't look like a blanket over your head."

"I did nearly put on my blue dress today," Beth admitted, but only to her sister. What would folks think of her if she harbored such thoughts?

"You will always love and miss him, but a time will come when it hurts less and each memory is just a treasure to look upon. Not something you should hurt over."

"Danke, Lucinda." Beth shot her a thankful look. "I'm glad you're here, and you have plenty of wisdom yourself," Beth said. Letting the laundry sit for now, she followed Lucinda upstairs to help ready breakfast for the *kinner*.

"Hopefully, I can open the store full time again soon. Folks will be wondering if I plan to." Beth flipped bacon as it sizzled on the stove. Over the last few days, she'd heard cars and buggies pull into the gravel lane, aiming for the store. Surely she needed to get back to work before what little finances she had left from Robert ran dry.

"Folks are happy enough, as we didn't close the store at all," Lucinda said in a matter-of-fact tone as she distributed plates around the table.

"We?" Alma was Beth's first thought. The woman had the capability of handling not only her household, but that of everyone else's as well. Most likely she hired one of her unwed *kinner*. Beth narrowed her brows worriedly. How could she afford help when there was still so much to pay for?

"Lester Milford, that fella you hired on, is seeing over it on days I'm here with you. I hear he's unwed or widowed. Got a fine look to him too." Lucinda grinned cunningly over one shoulder as she collected glasses.

"I didn't hire him," Beth informed her sister.

"Oh, *vell*, even better!"

How was that better? It was one thing that Lester agreed to make sense out of Andrew's recordkeeping. It was another that he was running the store.

"He's asked me at least a dozen times already how you and little Andrew are." Lucinda set a basket of eggs on the counter next to Beth before spreading jelly on slices of thick yeast bread.

"He taught Christina to run the register and how to write down receipt sales. She saves us both a lot of time going through all those rounds of sales. Yesterday, I caught him helping Tracy with her multiplication tables as he stocked shelves. I reckon it's all in good hands, *schwester*."

Something in Beth's chest squeezed. Lester did seem like he knew what he was doing, but he had his own life to see over. If anyone knew of the winding ways of living a life without a helpmate, she knew.

Beth wanted to march over there right now and insist he close the store, but there was no way she'd let him see her so soon after little Andrew. What choice did she have?

"You all have played a fast trick on me." Beth aimed a fork in her sister's direction. "I've only been gone a few days!"

"He's that good, *schwester*."

Forcing herself to focus on breakfast and not on Lester Milford, Beth cracked a dozen eggs into the hot skillet. She added a pinch of salt and pepper and gave the concoction a few stirs.

"I know now is not the time to mention it, but . . ."

Lucinda was going to mention it, nonetheless.

"Andrew would want you to be happy again."

Beth stilled. She knew what her sister was saying, but

thankfully, the sound of her girls coming down the stairs stopped Beth from replying. She simply had mixed thoughts about it. Happiness was having her family all together, not being the only parent to her *kinner*. It hadn't been a year yet. What kind of person thought to stop mourning and start thinking of her future so soon?

CHAPTER 7

*T*he first October Church services were to be held at her in-laws' home. Beth ironed her Sunday covering and all the *kapps* required for a household of girls. She decided on the robin egg blue dress Lucinda insisted on, tired of being the poor widow watched with sympathetic expressions or pitiful stares.

Christina had polished all their shoes, reminding Beth that she would soon need new laces.

She packed her carry-on bag with a small container of goldfish and another filled with small graham cracker pieces, and tucked two small cubby dolls inside with extra wipes for Beth Ann and Lisa, more than for little Andrew.

The morning was brisk with the air hinting of autumn and sparse fog dotting the lower-lying parts of the community. The leaves were still green but hung wearily in the damp air that lingered from overnight rains. The goldenrod was picturesque. The maples were turning scarlet and pumpkin.

Their buggy fell in line with two other open buggies on the narrow country lane. Passing homes with soybean fields near harvest and fencing that ran for miles, Beth took in the cadence of horses finding a common stepping.

Minister Graber's home was a vast three stories with two adjacent homes attached by walkways and eves from his most recently married *kinner*.

"I always enjoy how pretty the hills and valleys are here," Lucinda commented. Dressed in a perfect shade of bold blue and white apron front, she sat tall in the seat next to Beth, holding little Andrew as they followed the nearest buggy into the wide drive.

"You could move here," Beth suggested. Oh, how she wished Lucinda would come to live with her. Then she wouldn't feel so lonely.

"I cannot leave my scholars. It's a wonder they haven't sent out someone to fetch me back yet. I'm *goot* at teaching and adore each of my students."

"I know, but it would be nice to keep you a little longer." Beth followed the Bontrager's, giving Mel time to park before she nervously tackled backing into the neighboring spot. She didn't like being responsible for parking with so many buggies taking up the space. Andrew always handled that chore, but she had been given some practice since that cold January day.

"That's *goot*," Christina called out while looking over her shoulder to see they weren't too close to the drop in earth.

Beth let up on the horse's reins slightly, and Bones immediately went to stomping his feet and swishing his tail as if horseflies had already targeted him, instead of freshly laid gravel underhoof making him uneasy.

"You're getting better, *jah*." Christina bounced out of the buggy and quickly helped Beth Ann and Tracy. Once Beth had climbed out, Lucinda eased little Andrew into Beth's arms. How content he was, even after riding on the uneven gravel roads of Furrows Creek.

Of all the changes pressed upon her after Andrew's death, seeing to the horse and driving, hitching, and unhitching reddened Beth's face. Christina had more practice, but Beth was determined to see over her family the best she could.

Beth reached under the seat for the halter to buckle to the bridle, but Bones didn't want to end his fine stroll this morning and gave his head a disapproving shake. Beth tightened her hold and prayed that none watched her struggle.

"I'll see to him."

A voice forced her to pivot. There stood Lester. Beth's breath caught momentarily at the sight of him dressed in his Sunday best. He had been the quiet hero behind making life better for her and her children. His eyes held hers for longer than proper, and her heart skidded for a few beats. Beth quickly turned her gaze on young John Lewis, a motherless child with eyes that mimicked oceans.

"Hello, John."

"It's John Lewis. Not John. Not Lewis," he said firmly with light brows knitted together.

"I'm afraid *Onkel* Luke and *Onkel* Leon have made a game out of stirring him over two names."

"Well, I think John Lewis is a fine name. Like . . . Beth Ann."

"I told him as much," Lester smiled, then looked at Lucinda holding her son. "He is a looker, Beth. *You* have a fine *sohn*."

It wasn't compliments she fished for, but Beth smiled brightly to see Lester pleased as he looked down on her son, who could sleep through an earthquake. "*Danke*," Beth whispered, offering him the lead rope.

"It's a boy, which means we ain't got all girls now," Tracy said, pushing her glasses up higher on her nose. She'd already managed to gain a few scratches on them, and Beth made a mental note to see to getting a second pair.

"Now what is wrong with boys?" Lester teased and bent to Tracy's level.

"I like boys!" Beth Ann chimed in, not to be left out.

"So do I," Lester replied. "*Gott* makes both male and female to help one another out. So we all go together even if you outnumber us."

"Well, Andrew is our only boy, so he's already outnumbered." Tracy smiled.

"Since our *daed* is dead, he will have to be our helper, since we ain't got any more boys left," Beth Ann added, causing all the adults to tense.

"Well, *Gott* knows what we need and when. Andrew will grow to be a fine helper if your *mamm* raises him as she has you four, but don't think of him to do all the work. I've learned women—I mean, girls—are as capable as we are." Lester nodded toward Christina, who bloomed at his words.

"You can help," Beth Ann said. "You and John Lewis are boys. You could help us 'til he's bigger."

"Lester already helps," Lucinda put in. "He's fixed the books and shelves for the store and ordered supplies and all. Why, he even sought to help your *mamm* collect a few debts recently."

"What are debts?"

Beth's eyes went wide as she stared at Lester.

"We can talk about all that later. Ah, I have plenty of good news to share, but not on the Lord's Day."

"What was I thinking?" Lucinda faked a look of astonishment. "Beth often tells me I need a calendar to carry around in *mei* pocket to keep track of days and a roll of duct tape to remind me to keep silent."

Beth had mentioned duct tape but never a calendar. Lucinda had announced what Lester was doing behind Beth's back on purpose. Yet, Beth didn't feel angry. She was simply shocked to know he had done so much in such little time.

"Why don't you and John Lewis *komm* to supper Monday. I have yet to get to know your *sohn*, and Beth Ann would love to show him her chickens."

Lester looked to Beth, who still had her mouth hanging open as she stared at Lucinda. What a terrible trickster.

"You can speak of such things on a Monday, can you not? Beth makes the best pecan pies you've ever eaten, too."

"If that's alright with you."

What could she say when Lester looked at her as if he could lift all her burden and worries with one arm? Beth nodded.

Beth quickly set aside the encounter with Lester as little Andrew was soon the center of attention in his grandparents' home. Quite the fuss was displayed at his growth in a few short weeks and the likeness to his father. Glances of sympathy and regret held eyes and tongues. There was simply no right or wrong way to state the obvious.

Alma took him up and disappeared as Beth saw her *kinner* to a seat. If Beth wasn't mistaken, her mother-in-law's somber expression this morning held watery eyes once more.

Glancing toward the men, Beth's gaze skimmed over to her many brothers-in-law. She had no idea what it was like to have such a large family, yet Andrew had introduced and made her a part of their lot. The Graber cousins alone took up more benches than most.

When her eyes collided with Robert's, Beth didn't turn away. She thought of Della's comment, the guilt Robert possibly nursed all these months. Offering a tender half smile, she hoped he understood she found no blame in him. No reason to hoard anger for his needing his *bruder*'s help.

Robert turned, whispered something into Lester's ear, and disappeared out the back. Oh dear, had he taken offense at her appreciation? Did the very sight of her force his feet to flee?

Lester sat with John Lewis at his hip. The pair did

everything together, she mused. Although it made no sense because no man would have her heart again, looking at Lester, she felt the tug nonetheless.

He was a good foot taller than her, whereas Andrew had been closer to her level. Lester had sandy hair and blue eyes, Andrew's were dark. Nothing about Lester should appeal to her, but she kept staring.

It wasn't until Minister Shetler began the long sermon that Alma appeared again. Andrew's soft cries had grown rather testy. Even a grandmother knew it was time to eat.

Beth slipped out of the barn and into the main house to nurse her son in private. What a beautiful connection, the bonds knitted between a mother and a child.

After services, Beth worked alongside Kara, setting out pickled beets and end-of-the-garden pickles, which contained bits of carrots, cauliflower, beans, and cucumbers, to go with the rest of mixtures of cheeses and meats and loaves of bread common at the fellowship meal.

When Kara mentioned Robert's abrupt leaving earlier, Beth knew it was her doing.

"I don't know why he caused a scene and at *Daed*'s house at that," Kara went on.

"I fear it was my fault."

"How so?" Kara cocked her head Beth's direction, a perplexed look on her face.

"He has been kind to us, sending envelopes of money through Della, yet he hasn't spoken a word to me since. I worry he can't stand to see me or the *kinner* with his *bruder* gone."

"It's true," Kara said, not one to take the long way around an issue, but to march through it head on. She was much like Alma in that way, and Beth admired her forwardness most days.

"Seeing you without Andrew near is strange. You have always been a pair. Perhaps Robert feels much the same." Kara turned to Beth, whose face had turned ghostly pale. "I'm sorry. It's not my meaning to hurt you. It's hard seeing how sad you are, what your *kinner* lost, and having our hearts sad too. We should all do better in that."

"*Nee*, you lost a *bruder*. Andrew was eldest, much like Christina. Beth Ann and Tracy rely on her for many things."

"*Jah*, and Andrew was reliable. He was an extra set of eyes for our parents, that's for sure. Not sure Iyla cared much for his overly brotherly ways when she first started helping at the furniture shop."

Beth remembered well how Andrew fretted over his siblings, insisting they follow his advice, which few rarely did. "He did insert himself more than most *bruders* do."

"Lavina and he butted heads plenty. Freeman as well."

"He fretted over them. He prayed so hard for Lavina's situation. Once he even sent out letters, trying to find Ruben. And I know he tried talking to Freeman about his faith on many occasions."

"He loved us, and loved all of you, deeply."

"He did," Beth's throat grew thick, but thankfully, tears didn't come as she talked of her late husband.

"We were all blessed to have him for as long as we did. But, Beth, know that none of us feel you should mourn him for the rest of your days."

"It's been easier of late. Little Andrew gives me much to be thankful for."

"*Mamm* says you have much going on with the store and *kinner*."

Beth stiffened. Would Kara think Lester's helping somehow wrong?

"Perhaps you should think about remarrying. Andrew would not want you facing everything alone, and the *kinner* need a father and a mother who can see to their needs each day."

Beth bit the inside of her lip to keep from blurting out how much she had been thinking more about her *kinner*'s future, but the thought of remarrying was not something she was ready to consider. Andrew was her husband, even still.

"*Mamm* thinks once your *schwester* leaves, we should all start pitching in once more."

Beth could see how much Kara hoped that wasn't true, as she had her own family to care for.

"I appreciate the help, but I don't see the need any longer."

"*Mamm* says you should hire help." Kara stared at her intently.

"I—I . . ." What could she say? Soon, Lester would have things to rights once more, and Beth would be back running a store and a house.

"It is your store, is it not?" Kara lifted a brow.

"It is," Beth replied.

"Then I will be certain to remind *Mamm* that you have taken care of things."

Beth thanked Kara for her understanding. Knowing the Pencil Grabers were all ready to give her more breathing room did wonders for Beth's heart. Knowing they were there if a need arose gave assurances to her future.

It was on the buggy seat when they readied to go home. The notecard had two small finches facing each other and words handwritten from the book of Hebrews. "Let our conversation be without covetousness, and be content with such things as ye have for He hath said, I will never leave thee, nor forsake thee."

Then in smaller print, she read: "It is the actions of a man that reveals his heart."

Folks were only starting to leave. They gathered in clusters of *youngies* to old men. Her eyes found Lester right away. When he smiled, she knew the encouragement cards had to have come from him. Since the day his laugh had caught her attention, he'd been there, quickly doing what he could. His actions, and now his words of encouragement, were dangerously close to a confession of his heart.

Trouble was, despite the attraction and utter appreciation, was she ready to start all over again?

CHAPTER 8

*M*onday, Lester and John Lewis arrived promptly at six as Lucinda insisted they should. As they all sat at the family table, Christina shifted her gaze from Lester to Beth. Christina was old enough to have thoughts of her own, and Beth could see the way her brows moved. A few thoughts were currently running through her head at seeing another man at the head of the family table.

Tracy bumped over her glass of water, and her cheeks bloomed beet red from the embarrassment. Lester smiled her way, used his own napkin to soak up the mess, and poured her a fresh glass as he continued to talk about John Lewis's new pony cart. Beth appreciated his way of drawing the attention away from Tracy, who embarrassed easily. Tracy's shoulders relaxed, and she resumed eating, proving his ways worked wonderfully.

Beth Ann's blue eyes were sparkling and pretty as she continued to push more food on John Lewis's plate. "*Mamm* makes the best creamed corn," she boasted this time.

Little Lisa munched on her brown-sugared carrots, sat on

her knees, and sang to her fork in soft tones as if nothing abnormal was happening at all.

It couldn't be ignored. Having Lester there made Beth a little nervous too. After Lester entertained the children with stories of growing up in a house of all boys, he encouraged Beth's girls to share a little about growing up in a house full of girls. Beth and Lucinda laughed as they tidied the kitchen, sharing a few stories of their own. Like the time Lucinda cut four inches of Beth's hair because Beth had gotten bubble gum stuck in it.

After slices of pecan pie were eaten, they all played UNO, a card game that Beth had never played before, but after winning two hands, decided she liked. The outside grew dark earlier this time of year, but after chasing chickens into the coop before the sun set, Beth Ann and John Lewis succumbed to exhaustion.

"I'll see to getting the *kinner* down this evening. You and Lester have much to talk about, I reckon."

It was at least an hour past the *kinner*'s normal bedtime, yet Beth didn't want Lester and his son to leave. It was nice having a man in the house once more and hearing sounds of laughter. And as Lisa sat on Lester's lap, her eyes drifting closed while sucking her thumb, Beth wasn't alone in enjoying Lester's presence.

"I might just have the right-sized pocket to keep this one. She's wonderfully quiet." Lester's long lashes swooped down slowly and back up, emphasizing the depths of his beautiful eyes.

"Because she's worn out." Lucinda picked Lisa up and gave Beth a sly grin. "If you spend more time here, you'll find she's one you need to keep two eyes on for she often wanders off."

After seeing her girls had brushed their teeth and put on their gowns, Beth told each of her girls good night. When she stepped back into the dimly lit room downstairs, her breath caught. Lester sat in the rocker by the window, little Andrew in his arms. It was a picture she had been deprived of since her *sohn* came into the world, and for a moment she lingered in the doorway.

"It wonders me if *bopplin* know how blessed they are to be loved by so many, cradled from the worries of getting up early to open their shop." Lester smiled and stood, handing over her son.

Beth wondered if Lester was capable of loving little Andrew as he loved John Lewis, then realized the thought was a silly one, considering his kindness was as transparent as her newly washed windows.

"We should leave now and let you get some rest before he wakes to eat soon."

She didn't want him to go, wishing he would offer to sit on the couch and tell her more stories of his childhood until she too drifted off to sleep.

"That's up to you."

He stood close, his eyes holding hers in a quiet connection that breathed by the beats of the clock on the kitchen wall.

"We should talk about the store I reckon. If it's not too late?" Lester asked, a hint of a grin on his lips.

"Jah, the store." Beth snapped back to present.

"Would you like to sit with me on the porch? It's not too cold yet."

Beth's hands trembled in the simple request. It had been over a decade since a man had asked her that. She put little Andrew in his crib, then laid a soft blanket over John Lewis on the couch, before stepping into the kitchen where Lester was already warming water to make them each a cup of tea. Andrew had never been much for knowing his way around the kitchen. Perhaps being a bachelor for so long earned you knowledge that married men had no need of learning.

"I'll get us another slice of pie." Beth quickly plated two

slices and set them on the table. Lester went straight to business, and though that was the reason for his sharing a meal with her family this evening, part of her wished he wanted to get to know her more.

"It was harder to talk to the Martin's about their bill than anyone. Who would have thought they were such sticklers for not paying debts?"

All in all, Lester had not only collected most of the money owed to the store, but he'd worked with a professional to see, come tax season, Beth wouldn't lose the store. He had his own life and business and charities, and yet, made time to save hers.

"I don't know what to say. You've done so much to help us."

"You have a wonderful family, Beth. I'm glad to help. You don't have to say anything. I'm glad I was in the store that day, and Paul suggested it."

The undertaker. A cold shiver moved up Beth's arms.

"You've done a fine job, Beth. Seeing over your children and all of this. I hope you know that."

"I've had no choice, but I've also had help."

"*Jah*, and I'm glad you see that now. I'm sure having in-laws can be a thorn at times, but they care for you yet." Lester's eyes lowered. "I feel if they hadn't helped, you could have managed." At the sound of the tea kettle hissing, he poured hot water over two tea bags and added the right amount of sugar to both cups before setting one in front of her.

"I know Alma means well, but since you spoke to her, I see more and more of what it takes to keep your farm running."

The shadow of his well-maintained beard added to his ruggedness, which was quite appealing, yet Beth was discovering Lester had a soft side that appealed to her more. "I've thought to maybe sell the pastures, yet feel it best to hold on to for the *kinner* now. Alma cried when she met little Andrew the first time. I know he reminds her of her firstborn."

"She has her own grief to handle. Perhaps helping you was her way of dealing with that."

"I see that now. Oh, what a terrible daughter I've been to her."

"Andrew was her son, but you are still her daughter. Losing those we care about is never easy, but we must keep on keeping on."

Beth felt his words parallel with her mother's and found his wisdom sound. So how did a man capable of so much, find himself unwed with a child? Beth was eager to learn more about the man who was making her stomach flutter and hands tremble.

"Do you still grieve for John Lewis's *mamm*?" Beth jerked up in her seat. "I'm sorry. That was too personal."

"*Nee*, you may ask me anything, Beth. How else will I ever get to know you?" If Lester saw how his comment surprised her, he didn't show it.

"Faith was the prettiest woman I'd ever met." Lester looked up from his cup and smiled again. "Well, at least when I was a teenager."

"The moment I laid eyes on her, I was smitten. Lewis tried to sway me from talking to her, but I thought he'd had his time flirting with a life among the *Englisch*. Why shouldn't I have mine?"

So Faith was *Englisch*. Beth was beginning to understand a little more clearly. "I've heard our newest minister was quite the rabble-rouser when he was a *youngie*."

"He was indeed." Lester shook his head. "Don't tell a soul, but he even got a tattoo." Lester chuckled. "Yet, despite knowing losses of his own, he turned his life around and ministers to the wayward youth."

Lewis Milford had become a widower young and with no children of his own. It was no secret he focused on helping others who questioned their faith or found themselves in troubled spots.

"Not long after befriending Faith, I saw someone had left bruises on her arms. It didn't take long to learn she'd not had loving parents like I did."

"That's terrible." Beth had been blessed with wonderful parents and siblings. She couldn't imagine growing up in a home less than the one she knew. "Is that why you left like you did?"

"*Jah*, I thought if we ran off and married, they'd not come looking for her, and she'd be safe. Then my *bruder* Leon showed up. He meant well and was hoping I'd come home, but again, I was stubborn. I know now that putting my faith in her and not . . . my faith, was the wrong choice. Her folks did find us, so I hurried us to Illinois. I found a community starting up there, yet, Faith wasn't happy."

Lester stared into his cup, his own tragic memories holding his gaze. Beth ached to reach out, hold his hand as he shared this personal part of himself with her. Instead, she remained in her seat, both hands wrapped around her own cup.

"I'm sorry."

"It's hard to leave your upbringing. Even for the *Englisch*. I woke up one morning to John Lewis crying. Faith wasn't much of a morning person, and I'd never gotten used to late nights, so I thought little of it. I went to make his bottle when I found the note."

"Oh, Lester," Beth instantly reached out and placed a comforting hand over his. Lester had his own losses to carry.

"Even after all I've seen and done, I returned and am thankful I was welcomed back into the fold."

"Thankfully so."

"She didn't want to marry me, so . . ." His face darkened, carrying a sadness that stemmed from rejection, from being stripped away from the person you loved; not part of *Gott*'s design. "I should have seen it coming. I've waited for her to return, for John Lewis more than me now."

"She might yet."

"*Nee*, she left a note saying she didn't want to be a mother. She had papers made up and notarized giving me full custody of John Lewis. Faith doesn't like looking back, and her ties to family are thin threads. The thing is, I set aside that part of me. The part that wanted love for myself. John Lewis has been my sole focus, along with finding forgiveness for putting both of us in the situation I did."

Love crossed fences, and it jumped oceans. Beth couldn't blame him for following it down the wrong path. Many young folk thought they knew what was best, letting their hearts lead their heads. She shivered to think that in just a few more years, Christina would be old enough to go to gatherings herself.

"I came home when Lewis lost his *fraa*, I and couldn't leave again. Lewis and Luke and *Daed* have been a great support. *Mamm* fusses over John Lewis." His eyes smiled before his lips.

"She is a fine fusser. I think you both have that in common." His eyes glinted as he turned to her.

"I do well for us and have plenty to spill over to help the community."

"The free food pantry."

"*Jah*, why not? We can never know when it may be us who needs it. Well"—Lester leaned forward and said—"that's my story, now tell me yours."

Beth spoke of the first time she saw Andrew at the community youth gathering. She was only fifteen, barely old enough to even consider courting. But he spoke to her anyhow, and she never forgot a single syllable until he was finally permitted to court her. Lester listened intently as she spoke of her wedding day and when Christina was born. All the wonderful memories she'd collected didn't change the way he was looking at her now.

"You have so many wonderful memories to hold on to. I know folks have thoughts about us."

"I'm sorry if Lucinda has made you feel . . ."

"*Nee*, your *schwester* only wants the best for you as do we all, but I would be lying if I didn't say that I'd like to get to know you better."

"I like to get to know you better too, but . . ." Beth pulled her lower lip between her teeth. Her growing affection for Lester was not the same as years of loving memories with Andrew. How could she decide?

"But your heart isn't ready, and I know that. It doesn't mean we can't be friends. I have been known to have plenty of patience no matter what *mei bruders* ever tell you about me." He placed his other hand over hers, cupping it between both hands.

"*Danke* for understanding."

"Thank you for not thinking I was a complete fool when I was young."

"How can I, when you have John Lewis? *Kinner* are a gift, a blessing, and it's sad Faith will never know that."

"It is. Beth, I care for you, for our friendship, and I don't want to rush you or your *kinner* into anything, but I have hopes that someday we may become more than just friends."

"Someday?"

"Let's take it slow. I have my own fears. I worry about John Lewis. He's never had what your *kinner* have."

"A *mamm*," she whispered. What a terrible thought, a child with no *mamm*. Beth ached to go straight into the next room and sweep the little boy into her arms and cradle him just as Lester had little Lisa and Beth Ann. But broken hearts needed time for healing. Even little hearts that didn't even know healing was required.

"I don't want to replace your late husband, and you are not

responsible for being everything John Lewis has not had, but in time, I'd like to see where this is going between us."

Beth couldn't believe her ears. Lester's affections were shared, but his concerns too. A younger Beth would not have recognized the gift, but the older one cherished his understanding.

"You are the most honest and wonderful man I've ever known, Lester Milford. I look forward to getting to know you and John Lewis better too."

Beth smiled at him across the table, knowing that no matter how long it took, he'd be there for her and her *kinner*. That John Lewis might experience more love than before and that one day, they'd be ready to take the next steps to becoming a second-chance family. As awful as that once sounded to her ears, Beth's heart was thankful *Gott* gave second chances.

After Lester left, Beth nursed little Andrew while the wind blew the wooden chimes outside into a sweet slow melody that blended with sounds of crickets. She didn't realize tears were falling on little Andrew's dark downy hair. Just like his father, her heart whispered as she took in the straight little nose, dark knowing eyes, and long fingers that held a perfect reminder of his father. Here in her arms lay Andrew's gift to her. He always did give the best gifts. She smiled.

Life went on, she found. It moved right along. She could stay in a past that only brought tears, or choose to keep on keeping on. Lester's words were now stenciled on her heart.

"I love you Andrew. I will always love you."

CHAPTER 9

*B*eth paid for a driver on Saturday and went to Lester's shop. After inviting Lester to Sunday supper, which they both agreed was a good start for two people just getting to know one another, she offered to take John Lewis with them to the market today. Beth wasn't sure who was more excited, John Lewis or Beth Ann, as he climbed in the back seat, nearest little Beth Ann.

Driver Dan had stern rules about anyone riding in his van. First being his seatbelt rule, which many objected to, but Beth didn't mind his extra measures of safety, even if they made one feel more trapped than safe. Little Andrew slept, cradled in the carrier secured beside her while Lucinda chatted from the front seat.

"I can't believe I've been here all this time, and you've yet to mention a market nearby," Lucinda quipped over one shoulder.

"Lester's *bruder* owns it. He suggested we pick up donuts for the school *kinner*. I missed my turn with snacks when little Andrew decided to *komm*. I wanted to do something extra special to make up for it."

"Lester, huh." Lucinda winked. "I knew it."

"Shh." Beth quieted her in hopes the *kinner* didn't hear over Christina reading the newest Billy and Blaze book in the back. "We are *freinden.*"

"Bet he wishes you were more than that."

"Lucinda! What a thing to say. You speak far too boldly, *schwester.*"

"I speak the truth, and who's to say little Andrew's new carrier is not the first of many gifts to *komm* your way." She winked again.

Beth frowned and focused out the window. She had no idea who left the carrier on her back porch Friday afternoon, but even she felt Lester was the giver once more.

The Amish Market in the neighboring district of Miller's Creek was a large building filled with various booths of local Amish merchants. Outside, the Troyers sold produce and apples. They owned one of the largest orchards on this side of Pleasants County, and much of the focus was apple-themed.

"Can we go see the book section? Barbara Bontrager says they have a big selection," Christina asked.

"*Jah*, but hold Beth Ann's hand so she doesn't touch anything."

"I'll follow them while you and Andrew fetch donuts," Lucinda offered, reaching down to take Lisa's and John Lewis's hands, in case they, too, forgot to keep their hands to themselves.

As soon as she entered, Beth was greeted with the strong aromas of cooked beef, pickles, and scented candles. It was a wonder anyone could work all day under such an array of smells without getting ill.

"Hiya, Beth," Hannah Troyer greeted. Her dark red hair parted perfectly down the middle as she stood supporting a growing middle. If memory served Beth correctly, Hannah already had two sets of twins. All girls.

"I see you have brought your newest to come visit. What a handsome fella you are," Hannah crooned.

"I have hope yet Leon will have at least one son soon," she touched her midsection. "I hope you plan to attend Addie's wedding on Thursday."

"I hope to as well," was all Beth could say, and quickly made her way to Lavina's little corner coffee and donut shop.

The brightly colored sign made Beth smile. Lavina had always been a wonderful baker, her lot in life. Having a husband walk out without a word had to be more of a hardship than Beth had had to endure this last year. Beth was beginning to understand how right Lester was. For as difficult as it was to walk through life as a widow, she wasn't the only one walking a journey riddled with hardship. Perhaps Beth could have reached out more to Lavina when her husband abandoned her. Andrew had been stern about his sister's situation, claiming men didn't leave without cause, but after hearing Lester's confession, Beth was coming to realize that one could never know what led a person astray.

"Beth?" Lavina said, surprised. Andrew's sister was the epitome of an Amish *fraa*. Her dress was the perfect shade of blue, and her kapp always looked freshly ironed.

"I thought we were long due for a visit." Beth angled Andrew's carrier so Lavina could peek at him. "This all looks . . ."

"*Jah*, Ina had some ideas to brighten everything up."

"She does have a good eye for things,"

"She does." Lavina motioned toward an empty picnic table nearby where customers could eat their sweets. "Let's sit so I can swoon over this one."

Lavina held Andrew, taking in the look of him with motherly eyes. "It's good to see you out and dressed in more color than usual."

Beth felt her face warm as she looked down at her bold blue dress.

"Don't fret. I think it's *goot* you are feeling well enough."

"I admire how well you did what you had to after. . ." Beth refused to say Lavina's husband's name and upset her. "I clearly didn't do as well."

"It's no contest. Life is different for each of us, and I had plenty of help." Lavina chuckled. "*Mamm* would send Joah and Ina over all the time to see I was eating and the *kinner* were well. *Mudder* would have been running my donut shop if not for the scents from the candle shop causing headaches."

"It has some varied aromas for sure," Beth put in.

"*Jah*, Leon and Hannah are hoping to add ventilation soon, but it's harvest season." Andrew stretched, and Lavina marveled at how tiny he was.

"She invited me to the wedding, yet how can I attend such alone?"

"You are never alone. You have five *kinner* and the Pencil Grabers!" Lavina chuckled. "You'll never find a moment of quiet for the rest of your days, Beth Graber."

Beth laughed out loud. It was true that the growing lot gave one little space for self, which now Beth found she appreciated more and more.

"I hear you hired on help. I think it's a fine idea, giving you time to be a *mamm*."

"I didn't hire on yet. Lucinda helps, and Lester Milford does when he can. He knows business much better than me. I was never one for numbers, and Andrew never thought I needed to learn much about running the store."

"*Nee*, Andrew thought it was not proper." Lavina's lips pinched recalling how many times Andrew insisted Lavina was not doing proper by her *kinner* with opening a donut shop to support them instead of finding a husband.

"He was set in his ways for sure and certain."

"Men forget we can't be left completely in the dark. You never know when knowing the ins and outs of business or trimming hooves may fall upon our shoulders."

Lavina smiled up at her as if Beth spoke profound wisdom. Beth knew nothing profound and little that was wise, but appreciated Lavina's smile.

"Some think you have grown sweet on Lester Milford," Lavina abruptly said.

Beth reached out when Andrew started to fuss, bringing him close to her chest. "We are *freinden*."

"*Freinden* are nice to have. Did you know that Lewis, his *bruder*, used to leave boxes of groceries on my porch?" Lavina shook her head and smiled.

Beth didn't, and she was certain Lewis had never shared it with Andrew.

"He doesn't know I know, but Roman caught a peek of him one time." Roman was only seven, and like his *mamm*, a quiet sort. "We are blessed to have those around us who see our needs and aim to fill them. I will always miss Andrew, as you do, but we must trust *Gott* knows what is best for us. He led me to take a simple recipe and support my family without a *mann*. He's given me three fine *kinner*, who think me the finest baker in Kentucky." She laughed. "I pray you find the peace that I have and that someday love finds you again."

Beth wiped a stubborn tear from her eyes and stood. "I should go. Lucinda and the *kinner* are looking at the book section and probably have ten books already picked out for her to pay for."

"Don't leave without taking donuts home," Lavina insisted.

"Oh, I have snack duty next week and thought the scholars would love donuts instead of my usual cookies or granola bars."

"What a fine idea, but there are forty-two students!"

"*Jah*, and I'm prepared to tip well if you help me carry them to Driver Dan's van." Beth smiled.

CHAPTER 10

*T*he Pencil Grabers did everything together, which included taking turns hosting special gatherings. Thanksgiving was a day spent with family, but with twenty-one *kinner* and twenty-nine *grosskinner*, it was enough to drive the next woman in line to madness. Seeing as all the married couples had a turn, it had come back to the beginning.

Alma.

The patriarch had years of practice feeding her large family, but even with help from her married and unmarried daughters, Beth could see this particular holiday was weighing heavy on her emotions in the absence of her eldest.

Everyone anticipated feasting on turkey and mashed potatoes smothered in Lavina's gravy. Alma barked orders, as was common, and everyone scuttled to obey to see the table perfectly set.

Three foldup tables and church benches weren't nearly enough to seat everyone, so grown *kinner* happily reserved seats in the nearby room that, during most months of the year, formed Alma's summer kitchen.

Beth watched as her mother-in-law moved between

stovetop and table. Beth did her part, seeing a homemade salad dressing stirred and bottled. The noon hour wasn't permitted to arrive until Alma declared it, but under her watchful eyes and years of experience, water was poured and heads bowed when the clock chimed. Beth felt an extra measure of thanks needed to be given. This last year had been the hardest she'd lived, and yet, without the helping hands of the Pencil Graber lot, Beth would have been lost.

Breathing in the aromas of a brined turkey stuffed with celery, onions, and sage, basted every half hour, Alma waved off any compliments. "It's the same way my own *mamm* did it," she'd spout, never one to find compliments proper or expected.

Plates filled and hearts warmed as chatter went from the weather to who was on what team for afternoon basketball, another Graber tradition during gatherings. Beth savored the fine meal while anticipating the vast array of pies waiting to be served.

They were partway through the meal when Andrew found his own appetite being ignored. Beth slipped into Alma and John's room to quietly nurse him.

A stack of notecards sat with tiny birds in the corners. "Enoch has a fine hand. When he isn't building birdhouses or working at the furniture shop, he likes to make those."

Alma stood in the doorway, her soiled apron and straight shoulders the epitome of the mother she was to all around her.

"It was you. You left those for me to find."

"I don't coddle my *kinner*, Beth."

That was true.

"Yet, I don't like seeing them suffer or lost. I've been handed a blessed life." She glanced over her shoulder, where laughter mingled with the clacking of forks. "More blessed than most for certain, so I don't know any other way but to see a job done. Lavina tells me I've overstepped, but I had only meant to help. You are . . . were Andrew's fraa. How could I not set aside my own in your time of need?"

"Oh Alma. I've been selfish, not seeing what a gift you truly are to me. *Danke*. From the whole of my heart, *danke* for words you left me. They helped more than you know. *Danke* for being you."

Beth reached out, despite Alma's insistence on not being overly affectionate, and hugged her mother-in-law. It wasn't just the help at the store or how Tracy's new glasses had truly made a difference. It wasn't how Lester arrived just in time to help her out of a financial downfall and become someone important in her life. It was the helping hands of so many that revealed that no matter what life pressed down on you with, it also lifted. It was emotional support, and physical help. It was kind blue eyes that were hopeful yet patient, and little *kinner* smiling with missing front teeth. Beth would keep on keeping on, and was thankful for doing so.

AMISH MADHOUSE COOKIES

Cookie Ingredients

1 c. unsalted butter
1 c sugar
2/3 c brown sugar
1 T light corn syrup
1 lg egg
1/2 t vanilla extract
1 1/3 c all-purpose flour
1/2 t baking powder
1/4 t baking soda
1 t kosher salt
1 1/2 c chocolate chips
1/3 c old-fashioned rolled oats
2 c potato chips
1 c mini pretzels

Combine the butter, sugars, and corn syrup in the bowl and cream together for 2 to 3 minutes. Add the egg and vanilla, and beat before slowly adding flour, baking powder, baking soda, and salt. Mix just until the dough comes together. Gently fold in chocolate chips, oats, potato chips and pretzels. Be careful not to over mix or break too many of the pretzels or potato chips.

Spoon out onto greased cookie sheets at least 3 to 4 inches apart and pat the tops of the cookie dough domes flat. Wrap the sheet pan tightly in plastic wrap and refrigerate for at least 1 hour. Do not bake your cookies from room temperature—they will not bake properly.

Bake at 375°F for 15 to 16 minutes.

ABOUT THE AUTHOR

Raised in Kentucky timber country, Mindy Steele is a bestselling author who writes in favor of her rural surroundings. She's the winner of the 2022 & 2024 Reader's Choice Award. Steele lives in northeastern Kentucky with her husband, Mike. They have five grown children, eleven grandchildren, and many wonderful neighbors. Read more about Mindy and her books at https://mindysteele.com/.

Her Daniel's Daughters series: Becoming Amish wasn't the same as being born Amish. https://a.co/d/eOyIqZk

SEASONS OF THE HEART

TRACY FREDRYCHOWSKI

CHAPTER 1

October – Sugarcreek, Ohio

*T*he fall air was laced with the sweet tang of apples and cinnamon as Patricia Wengerd stepped into the bustling warmth of the harvest community dinner. Copper pots of apple butter bubbled over open flames, sending wisps of spiced steam into the cool afternoon sky. She adjusted her sweater against the October chill, her eyes sweeping across the crowd of families gathered around tables laden with pies, roasted meats, and freshly baked bread.

Patricia had been in Sugarcreek, Ohio, helping her *schwester* with her new *boppli* for the past few months. Now, with only a few days left before she returned to Willow Springs, Pennsylvania, her plans were jumbled. She was eager to be home, yet a pang of uncertainty tugged at her. Her special friend, Albert Troyer's letters had grown sparse and dull, the words dry as last year's corn husks. She couldn't help but wonder if the connection they'd once shared had withered away in her absence.

But tonight wasn't for worrying. Tonight was for a bit of

fun and saying goodbye to some of the people she had met during her stay. She stepped into the line forming at the buffet table, savoring the sight of pumpkin pies and platters of fried chicken. Her stomach rumbled at the smell of warm apple cider donuts, a childhood favorite.

Ahead, she spotted the last donut sitting golden and tempting on a platter. She reached for it just as another hand darted in, brushing hers.

"*Ach*, sorry—" Patricia started, looking up, and her words caught in her throat.

The man standing opposite her was tall, his muscular frame filling out a light purple shirt that highlighted the deep tan of his forearms. A straw hat perched slightly askew on his head, and dark curls peeked out from beneath its brim. His eyes, as warm and rich as the apple butter simmering nearby, crinkled in a smile.

"It seems we've both got the same good taste." His hand lingered a moment too long against hers before he pulled it back, leaving Patricia's skin tingling.

She flushed, suddenly aware of her own plain dress and the smudge of flour on her apron from helping with baking earlier that day. "*Ach*, maybe I shouldn't be so quick to grab the last one," she said, trying to steady her voice. "You can have it."

He chuckled, shaking his head. "*Nee*, I wouldn't dare take a donut from a lady, especially one who looks like she's had a hand in making them."

Patricia raised an eyebrow. "How did you know?"

He pointed to her apron with a grin. "Just a wild guess."

Patricia couldn't help but smile. "Well, maybe we should split it then. Fair is fair."

"I like the way you think," he said, breaking the donut in half and handing her the larger piece. "I'm David, by the way. David Schrock."

"Patricia Wengerd," she replied, brushing her fingers lightly against his as she took the piece.

As they stood there, the chatter and laughter of the crowd seemed to fade, leaving only the crackling of the fire outside and the soft rustling of falling leaves. Patricia brushed the crumbs of her half-donut from her fingers, suddenly aware of the crowded barn as she and David turned in unison. Long wooden tables stretched across the space, packed with families and friends laughing, eating, and swapping stories. Lanterns hanging from the rafters illuminated the hay bales that lined the walls.

Patricia's eyes swept the barn, searching for a sitting spot. Across the room, near the door, she spotted a vacant hay bale. David saw it at the same time.

"Well"—David flashed a quick grin—"do you mind sharing?"

Patricia shook her head, and her cheeks warmed as they both moved toward the stacked hay. With his long strides, David reached it first and leaned back as he balanced his plate on his knee, his hat tilting at a jaunty angle. "How come I haven't seen you here before? Sugarcreek isn't big enough to miss someone like you."

Patricia couldn't help the small smile tugging at her lips. "I'm not from around here. I've been staying with my *schwester*, helping her with her family. I'm returning home to Willow Springs in a few days."

David nodded. "*Ach*, that explains it."

"And you?" Patricia tilted her head in his direction. "Why haven't I seen *you*?"

David's grin turned a little sheepish. "That's fair. I've been working in Wisconsin most of the summer. I only came back to help with the harvest and the holidays. Hoping to head back out West soon."

They sat silently while they cleared their plates. Patricia

raised an eyebrow, her curiosity piqued, as she placed her empty plate on the floor. "Sounds like you're looking forward to returning." Her lips curved into a teasing smile as she leaned forward.

David's eyes sparkled as he placed his empty plate on top of hers, his voice dropping to a playful drawl. "Let's just say I've enjoyed my time in Tomah, Wisconsin."

Patricia leaned back, her smile softening as she studied him. His words rang with confidence, but something about his expression made her wonder if his cocky tone hid a sliver of uncertainty.

"Hmm," she murmured, "sounds like you've got a story there."

"Maybe," he said with a shrug. "But stories are best told over pie. Should I see if there's any left?"

Patricia laughed, shaking her head. "You just don't want me to have the last piece."

As David gathered dessert, Patricia wondered about the man sitting beside her. He carried an air of ease, but his demeanor sparked mystery that tugged at her curiosity. For the first time in a while, her mind drifted away from the uneventful letters coming from Willow Springs.

Patricia watched David from across the room as he maneuvered through the crowd, balancing two plates of pie with the ease of someone used to holding the attention of those around him. The light from the lanterns overhead caught the light purple of his shirt, making him stand out in the sea of more muted colors.

He was nearly halfway back to their makeshift table when two girls stopped him, their heads bobbing as they spoke in hushed whispers. Patricia couldn't make out their words, but the way they hovered close, their smiles coy and giggles muffled behind cupped hands, left little doubt about their intentions.

David's reaction only added to the scene. He smiled back at

them, his countenance one of mild amusement, as if he were used to such interruptions. Though he kept moving, his easy confidence and the girls' lingering observation spoke volumes. Patricia was both entertained and bemused.

So, this is how the girls of Sugarcreek see him, she thought, the corners of her mouth twitching. He carried himself with a certain charm that seemed to draw attention effortlessly. It wasn't arrogance . . . at least not quite . . . but there was an air about him that made the interaction almost comical to watch.

She propped her back against the barn wall, folding her hands in her lap as she considered the scene. It had been years since she'd indulged in such schoolgirl antics, and she was suddenly thankful to be beyond that stage of life. She didn't need the fluttering nerves or coy smiles to shape her future. Her path was already laid out before her, steady and predictable.

Albert. The name settled in her mind like a sturdy fence post, reliable and unmoving. He'd been her special friend for over a year now, and while their relationship hadn't exactly sparked with excitement, it had a quiet steadiness she'd come to appreciate. They were planning to marry next October, and Patricia had envisioned the year ahead complete with courting, simple pleasures, and planning their future together.

Yet, as she watched David with those girls, a dash of something unbidden stirred within her. Curiosity, perhaps. Or maybe it was just the thrill of observing someone so utterly different from Albert. She shook her head, chastising herself for letting her mind wander. David was nothing more than a passing acquaintance, and her life in Willow Springs was already set.

Still, as David finally turned away from the girls and made his way back to their seat, his brazen smile lingering on his lips, Patricia couldn't help but feel a pang of guilt. For a fleeting moment, she'd been captivated by his easy charm, his way of holding attention without even trying.

She straightened in her seat as he approached. *Albert is waiting for me back home,* she reminded herself firmly. *This is just a moment, nothing more.*

Yet, despite her better judgment, she couldn't deny that something about David Schrock had managed to nudge at the cusp of her sensibly planned future, leaving her intrigued—and perhaps just a little unsettled.

Patricia stabbed her fork into the tender crust of her pumpkin pie, savoring the spicy sweetness as she looked over at David. His easy manner had disarmed her, though she couldn't quite shake the memory of the two girls fawning over him.

"So," she began, aiming for casual, "what do you do for a living?"

David leaned back against the wall, chewing a bite of pie before answering. "I work for Schrock Construction. It's a family business, mostly barns, houses, and the like. My older *bruder*, Henry, runs the show when I'm not around."

Patricia froze mid-bite, her fork hovering in the air. "Henry Schrock?" she repeated, her voice tight.

"*Jah*," David said with a nod, taking another forkful of pie. "He lives in Willow Springs. You know him?"

Her heart sank. *Know him?* Henry wasn't just someone she knew . . . he was her bishop. Her *bishop*! And here she was, sitting far too close to his younger *bruder*, chatting over pie at a community dinner while Albert waited faithfully back home.

Her mind raced. If word got back to Bishop Schrock, and it would, if David mentioned this dinner, what would he think? Worse, what would Albert think?

Patricia placed her fork down and offered a strained smile. "Excuse me," she said, standing up as she spotted an empty chair at a nearby table.

David blinked, clearly taken aback. "Wait, what's wrong?"

"Nothing," she said too hastily, smoothing her apron. "I just think—well, maybe it's best if—"

Understanding dawned on his face, and he set his fork down, leaning forward somewhat. David teased. "Let me guess. You're worried because my *bruder* is your bishop."

Patricia didn't answer, but the way she avoided his eyes must have given her away. David's grin turned gentle, his voice low enough that no one else could hear. "Sit back down. There's no harm in two people talking, is there?"

She hesitated, her fingers tightening around the edge of her plate. "I just don't want anyone to misunderstand—"

"Misunderstand what?" he interrupted, his look steady. "That we're two people enjoying a piece of pie at a community dinner? I promise you, my *bruder* won't even know, let alone care."

Something in his voice, in his easy confidence, made her relent. She lowered herself back onto the hay bale, though her cheeks still burned with embarrassment.

"That's better," David's smile returned. "Now, where were we? Oh, right . . . I think I was about to tell you that pumpkin pie is overrated."

Patricia's eyes widened in mock outrage. "*Overrated?* Are you serious?"

With a straight face, he exclaimed, "Completely! Apple pie is superior in every way."

At the same time, they both declared, "Except for pecan pie!"

Their simultaneous outburst made them pause, then burst into laughter. The tension melted away like butter on a hot biscuit, and Patricia became aware of herself smiling despite the knot of worry that had gripped her earlier.

"Well"—David's grin widened— "I guess we can agree on one thing, at least."

Patricia shook her head, her smile lingering as she took another bite of her pie. "I suppose we can."

Though the impact of her connection to the bishop hadn't entirely left her, the lighthearted exchange made the moment feel less daunting. For now, she let herself enjoy the pie . . . and the company.

David inclined forward, his fork idly pushing a stray crumb of pie crust as his eyes lit up with enthusiasm. "Schrock Construction is doing well, but I keep telling my *bruder* and my *datt* there's room to grow. I've got ideas . . . big ones. Like expanding into timber framing for houses, not just barns, or working on larger projects out West."

Patricia tilted her head, intrigued despite herself. "Out West? Like where?"

David's grin widened. "Idaho, Montana." He leaned back against the wall and continued, "Places where the land stretches on forever and the mountains rise like cathedrals. I spent some time out there this summer, working on a ranch project. It was incredible."

She folded her hands in her lap, leaning in a tad. "I've never been farther west than Indiana."

"You're missing out." David's voice filled with wonder. "Idaho and Montana—they're nothing like Ohio or Pennsylvania. The sky's so big, you feel like you're standing at the rim of the world. And the wildlife! I saw elk grazing in the valleys and even a grizzly bear from a safe distance. Yellowstone National Park is like stepping into a storybook. The geysers, the waterfalls, the rivers . . . it's all so untouched. I went fly-fishing in a river so wide and clear, it was like *Gott* Himself had opened the waters just for me."

Patricia sighed as she tried to picture it: David standing in a river with a fly rod in hand, the sun glinting off the water, surrounded by mountains and sky. The image was so vivid, so unlike anything she'd ever experienced, it made her heart ache with longing.

"Fly-fishing?" she asked, her voice soft. "I thought that was just for trout."

"It is." David nodded. "And they're smarter than you'd think. You've got to be patient, study the current, know when to cast and when to wait. But when you hook one . . . well, I'll say there's nothing like it."

Patricia smiled, though her thoughts had drifted elsewhere. She couldn't help but compare David's ambition and sense of adventure to Albert's steady, predictable nature. Albert was a dairy farmer, content to follow the same routines his father and grandfather had before him. She couldn't fault him for that. It was a good, honest living, and she'd always admired his dedication. But Albert had never spoken of dreams or far-off places. He'd never painted a picture of something so grand, it made her chest tighten with wonder.

"Do you think your family will go along with your plans?" she asked, pulling herself back to the present.

David shrugged, though his smile didn't falter. "Maybe. They're practical men, set in their ways, but I think I can show them there's merit in looking beyond what we've always done. It's not about leaving the old ways behind; it's about finding new ways to build something lasting."

Patricia realized she was staring at him, captivated not just by his words but by the quiet confidence behind them. He wasn't boastful or arrogant; he simply believed in what he was doing. It was a belief that radiated from him, filling the small space they shared.

"That's . . . impressive," her voice tinged with awe. "You've done so much already."

David chuckled, rubbing the back of his neck. "Well, I don't know about that, but I've got dreams. And if I've learned anything, it's that the world is so much bigger than we can imagine. Makes me want to do something worthwhile with the time I've been given."

Patricia nodded, though her feelings were tangled. David's words lingered in her mind, stirring something she couldn't quite name. She was certain of one thing: this conversation was opening her eyes to a world far different from the one she'd planned with Albert.

THE EVENING HAD GROWN COOLER, and the chatter of the dinner crowd began to wane as families drifted toward home. Patricia carried their plates to the trash, her mind swirling with images of David's bold dreams and faraway places. She gave him a polite nod as they parted, each heading to their respective tasks. Patricia joined the women in wiping down tables and carrying platters to the kitchen while David disappeared among the men, folding tables and hauling trash bags.

Hours later, as the cleanup dwindled and the air crowded with the smoky scent of burning wood, Patricia was drawn to the glowing bonfire that had been started in the field beside the barn.

The hum of voices floated lightly through the crisp October air, blending with the crackle of the fire. Around the glowing embers, a group of young adults sat or stood in a loose circle, singing familiar hymns in rich, low harmony. The simplicity of the moment filled Patricia's heart as she made her way toward the table of treats, drawn by the warmth of the firelight.

She reached for a peanut butter cup, pausing as another hand met hers at the dish. Her lips parted in surprise as she looked up, once again finding David standing across from her. His expression mirrored her own, though his lips slowly curved into a grin.

"Guess we're making this a habit," he teased, holding her stare for a moment before plucking one of the cups from the dish.

"Maybe so." Patricia's heart skipped a beat. "I didn't expect to see you again tonight."

"Well, I'm not one to pass up a good bonfire. Or a chance to make a perfect s'more." His voice warmed with humor. He gestured toward her hands, now crammed with graham crackers and peanut butter cups. "How about I roast the marshmallows if you keep a good grip on those? Deal?"

She nodded, handing him the bag of marshmallows. "Just don't set them on fire."

David chuckled. "I promise, golden brown perfection every time."

They made their way toward the fire, where David skillfully found two sticks and skewered marshmallows on the ends. Patricia spotted a log close to the flames and moved toward it, but before she could sit, two young women . . . identical in every way down to their matching *kapps* . . . stepped into David's path.

Patricia recognized them from earlier at the dinner. Their voices were hushed, their heads inclined toward him as they spoke, but their intentions were unmistakable. Patricia glanced toward David, expecting him to humor them as he had before, but instead, he only smiled politely and sidestepped around them.

"Excuse me," he said lightly, his manner kind but firm. "I need to get these marshmallows to the fire."

Patricia hid a small smile as David moved to the log where she had already taken a seat. They worked in comfortable silence for a few minutes, the flicker of flames forming long shadows across their faces. When David handed her the first golden-brown marshmallow, Patricia carefully pressed it between the crackers and peanut butter cup, savoring the sticky sweetness as it melted together.

The voices around the fire shifted to a familiar hymn, and after a moment, she quietly joined in. Beside her, David's baritone blended seamlessly with the others, rich and steady. The hymn's simple beauty surrounded them, filling the quiet spaces where words were not needed.

When the song ended, Patricia's eyes skimmed David, who was poking at the fire with his stick. For all his confidence and charm, he seemed at ease here, far from the bold tales of faraway lands. She turned her attention back to the fire, letting the warmth seep into her soul.

The fire had burned down, and the crowd around it had thinned. The low hum of voices singing had given way to scattered conversation and the occasional laugh. Patricia moved to the outskirts of the fire after David left to talk to a group of men near the barn, savoring the quiet while she watched the firelight dance across the remaining faces.

David quickly appeared at her side, his hands tucked into his pockets, his look softer than it had been earlier. "I thought you might have gone."

She smiled softly, glancing at him. "Not yet. I wanted to enjoy the fire a little longer before saying goodbye to Sugarcreek."

David stepped closer, his eyes steady on hers. "I've enjoyed tonight," he admitted, his voice carrying a sincerity that made her heart falter for a beat. "I wasn't expecting it, but I'm glad I met you, Patricia."

She lowered her eyes, her cheeks warming. "I've enjoyed it too."

For a moment, they stood in silence, the only sounds between them the soft pop of the fire and the murmur of the few remaining voices. Then, David leaned in. "Do you have someone special back home?"

Patricia hesitated, her fingers tightening around the fringe of her sweater. "I do. I'm to be married next year. His name is Albert."

David's appearance didn't shift the way she thought it might. Instead, he tilted his head, his eyes searching hers with a quiet intensity. "Albert," he repeated, the name lingering on his tongue as if he were trying it out. Then, after a moment, he smiled. "I have someone waiting for me, too . . . or at least, I hope I do."

His words caught her off guard, especially given the quiet suggestion in his tone earlier. "Then why ask me?"

David's smile grew, but it was tinged with a hint of defiance. "Because life doesn't always go the way we plan. People change. Things change." He shifted, meeting her stare with a seriousness that made her heart flutter. "If somehow, you find yourself single next year . . . and if I do too . . . then maybe, just maybe, we could meet right here. This time next year."

Patricia took a calming breath, his words settling over her like a blanket of autumn leaves. She searched his face for a moment, torn between the sureness of her plans with Albert and the unspoken possibility hinted at in David's words.

Finally, she smiled, her voice a whisper. "And if that doesn't happen?"

David's grin returned, boyish and full of charm. "Then at least we had tonight."

Patricia's smile lingered as she turned her gaze back to the embers. His words left her with more questions than answers. As they stood side by side, neither willing to break the moment, she wondered what the next year might hold and whether life might surprise her after all.

CHAPTER 2

June the following year -
Willow Springs, Pennsylvania

The warm summer breeze carried the sweet scent of ripening strawberries as Patricia knelt between the neat rows of plants at Yoder's Strawberry Acres. Her white bucket was already half full, the berries nestled in a bed of green leaves. Across from her, her best friend, Ellie Beiler, plucked a particularly plump berry, popping it into her mouth with a mischievous grin.

"Ellie!" Patricia scolded, though her smile betrayed her amusement. "If you keep eating them, there won't be any left to take home."

Ellie shrugged, licking the juice from her fingers. "Can you blame me? They're perfect this year."

Patricia shook her head, but her smile faded as her thoughts drifted back to Albert. She ran her thumb over the edge of a berry, her brow furrowing.

Ellie noticed the shift in her expression. "Alright," she said, setting her basket down and sitting cross-legged in the soft dirt. "You're snappy and out of sorts today . . . out with it. What's on your mind?"

Patricia hesitated, glancing toward the nearby stand where families gathered to weigh their baskets and purchase jam. No one seemed close enough to overhear. She sighed and lowered her voice. "It's Albert."

Ellie gave a questioning glance. "What about him? I thought things were all set for October?"

Patricia let out a short laugh, the sound tinged with frustration. "They are. At least, that's what we've planned. But we haven't told our families yet. And now . . ." She trailed off, plucking a berry and tossing it into her basket. "Now I'm not so sure."

Ellie leaned forward, her voice softening. "Not so sure about what?"

Patricia hesitated again, then spoke in a rush. "He left. To work on his uncle's farm in Mill Village. He said it was only for the summer, but before he left, he told me to take this time to think about whether marrying him is really what I want."

Ellie's eyes widened. "He said that?"

Patricia nodded, her fingers fiddling with the hem of her apron. "He's been so aloof lately. It's like he doesn't care anymore. And now he's off working with his uncle, and I'm here, wondering if he even wants to marry me at all."

Ellie frowned, picking at the dirt beneath her nails. "That doesn't sound like the Albert you've always talked about. Do you think he's having doubts?"

Patricia looked up sharply, her voice defensive. "He's the one who asked *me* to think about it. And I have been. A lot. I just—I don't know. He's so steady, so practical, but it's like he's content to just stay the same forever. He doesn't talk about the future, not really. He's happy being a dairy farmer, doing what his father and grandfather did. And I thought I was happy with that too."

"But?" Ellie prompted, her tone gentle.

Patricia's notions wandered back to that autumn night by the bonfire, to David Schrock's tales of Montana, Idaho, and dreams bigger than the rolling hills of Pennsylvania. She shook her head, trying to banish the memory. "But now I don't know if I'm ready to settle into a life where nothing ever changes. I feel guilty for even thinking that way, but it's how I feel."

Ellie reached across the row, resting a hand on Patricia's arm. "You're allowed to have doubts, you know. It's better to face them now than after you're married. But Patricia, do you still love Albert?"

Patricia hesitated, her heart tugging in opposite directions. "I do," she said finally, her voice barely above a whisper. "I think I do. But what if that's not enough?"

Ellie didn't respond right away, her gaze thoughtful. "Maybe this time apart is a chance for you to figure out what you really want . . . for yourself, not just for Albert."

Patricia nodded, though her heart was no closer to an answer. The sweet scent of strawberries surrounded them, but all she could taste was the bitterness of uncertainty. Patricia adjusted her basket of strawberries, brushing dirt from her apron as she moved along the row. The summer sun was warm on her back, but the depth of her earlier conversation with Ellie lingered. She bent to pick another cluster of berries when a familiar voice cut through the stillness.

"Well, well. Look who's working hard enough to impress even the bishop . . . Chatty-Patty herself."

Patricia sighed heavily, her hands stilling as she looked up to see Rudy Kauffman meandering toward her. His easy grin and mischievous eyes were as familiar as the fields around them, and despite her annoyance, she wasn't completely surprised to see him.

"Don't call me that," she said firmly, straightening to face him.

"Why not? It suits you." Rudy rested his hands on his hips, his shirt sleeves rolled up and dirt streaking his forearms. "You're always talking, even if it's just to yourself."

Patricia huffed, picking a berry and placing it in her basket without sparing him another glance. "I'd be talking less if someone wasn't always around to pester me."

Rudy chuckled as he moved the metal row markers to a new spot. "Fair enough. But it's been a while since I've seen you. Been too busy riding in Albert's buggy to chat with your old friend Rudy, *eh*?"

Patricia stiffened, her heart skipping a beat. "I don't know what you're talking about."

"Oh, come on." Rudy's grin widened, though his attitude carried an edge she wasn't expecting. "I've seen you climbing into his buggy after more than a few *singeons*. I'm half expecting to hear an announcement any time now."

Patricia's cheeks flushed, and she focused on picking another strawberry. "That's not any of your business."

His smile faltered, replaced by something sharper. "Maybe not, but it's hard not to notice when someone's always stepping into a buggy with the same fella. Albert must be doing something right to keep your attention."

Her grip on the strawberry tightened, and it seeped juice down her arm before she placed it in her basket. "Albert is a good man," she said evenly, refusing to look at Rudy.

"Is he?" Rudy's pitch was light, but the jealousy lurking beneath it was unmistakable. "Well, he's a lucky one, that's for sure. If it were me—"

"Enough, Rudy," Patricia interrupted, her voice firmer than she intended. She finally looked at him, her annoyance clear. "You can keep your opinions to yourself."

Rudy raised his hands in mock surrender, though his eyes

held a shimmer of something unspoken. "Alright, alright. I'll stop . . . for now."

He stepped closer, lowering his voice as he handed her an empty berry basket. "But just so you know, not everyone's as blind as Albert seems to be. Some of us see you for who you really are."

Patricia blinked, caught off guard by his words. But before she could respond, Rudy flashed his familiar grin and turned away, whistling as he walked back toward the barn.

As she watched him go, Patricia's heart felt as unsettled as her thoughts. Rudy's teasing had always been a part of her life, but today, it left her feeling more exposed than usual, like he had managed to look past the surface and see something she wasn't ready to admit.

Patricia crouched over the next row of strawberries, trying to focus on her picking instead of the lingering irritation from her encounter with Rudy. The sun was climbing higher, making the back of her neck warm, and the faint hum of honeybees filled the air.

Ellie reappeared beside her, her basket swaying as she plopped down on her knees. "What's got your feathers ruffled now?" she asked, a knowing smirk on her face.

Patricia sighed, brushing a strand of hair back under her *kapp*. "Rudy," she muttered, plucking a berry with more force than necessary.

Ellie grinned. "What's he up to this time?"

"Oh, the usual." Patricia rolled her eyes. "Making jokes, calling me names, and acting like a schoolboy who doesn't have a care in the world. You'd think he'd grow up by now."

Ellie leaned in closer, her voice dropping to a murmur. "You know he's always had a big crush on you, right?"

Patricia froze, her hand hovering over the next berry. "What are you talking about?"

Ellie's grin widened. "*Ach*, everyone knew it back in school.

He practically told the whole schoolyard one day. I heard he even warned Albert to watch his step. Said you were like a little *schwester*, and he didn't want anyone messing with you."

Patricia let out a short, dubious laugh. "That's ridiculous."

"Is it?" Ellie teased, raising an eyebrow. "He's always been protective of you, even if he does act like a fool half the time."

Patricia huffed, dropping the berry into her basket. "There isn't one thing about Rudy Kauffman that interests me. He might be easy on the eyes, but his constant joking irritates me to no end. I could never take him seriously."

Ellie lifted her chin, watching Patricia with an amused expression. "You sure about that? Sometimes the ones who make you the maddest are the ones who matter the most."

Patricia shot her a sharp look. "Don't start. I've got enough on my mind without you trying to play matchmaker."

Ellie held up her hands, pretending innocence. "Alright, alright. But if you ask me, there's more to Rudy than you're giving him credit for."

Patricia ignored her, moving down the row as the heat of the day pressed down on them. She tried to shake off Ellie's words, but they lingered, weaving themselves into the corners of her head like a pesky weed she couldn't quite pull free.

Patricia stood and rubbed her lower back before motioning for Ellie to follow her to the stand. As they approached the checkout counter, Patricia's steps faltered a little when she saw Rudy leaning casually against the counter. He was chatting with another customer, his easy grin and familiar teasing manner on full display.

"Of course he's here," Patricia muttered under her breath.

Ellie smirked. "You've got to admire his persistence."

Patricia said nothing, setting her baskets down on the counter with a soft thud. Rudy looked up, his eyes flicking briefly to her before he deliberately turned his attention to another customer.

Ellie raised an eyebrow, nudging Patricia with her elbow. "Looks like he's making you wait."

Patricia folded her arms, trying to ignore the heat rising in her cheeks as Rudy worked his way through the line, his pace maddeningly unhurried. Finally, after what felt like an eternity, he finished with Ellie's basket and turned to Patricia.

"Well," he said, his voice light but his gaze unexpectedly steady. "I didn't think you'd get done so soon, Chatty-Patty."

Patricia bristled at the nickname but held her tongue. "Are you going to weigh my baskets or not?"

Rudy smirked, reaching for the full baskets, but paused as if deciding whether to say more. Then, in a voice lower and softer than she expected, he asked, "Where's Albert? Haven't seen him around lately."

Patricia blinked, caught off guard by the sudden shift in his voice. "He's gone north," she admitted. "Helping his uncle for the summer."

For a moment, Rudy's teasing demeanor faded. The line on his forehead deepened vaguely, and a surge of concern passed through his eyes. "North, huh? That's a long way off."

"He'll be back in a few weeks," Patricia snipped, her voice more defensive than she intended. "And who knows? We might just be making an announcement soon."

She regretted the words the moment they left her mouth. But as she watched Rudy's reaction, something unexpected happened. His shoulders stiffened ever so slightly, and for the briefest moment, his usual confidence faltered. It was subtle, but it was enough for Patricia to wonder if Ellie's words had more truth to them than she wanted to believe.

Rudy recovered quickly, plastering on his familiar grin as he placed her strawberries on the scale. His voice carried an edge of annoyance. "Well . . . I guess congratulations are in order. Albert's a lucky guy."

Patricia nodded, unsure how to respond. She paid for her

berries and turned to leave. As she walked away with Ellie, Rudy's brief sincerity lingered in her thoughts. For all his boyish antics, there was a depth to him she hadn't noticed before . . . or maybe hadn't wanted to notice. And that, more than anything, left her feeling unsettled.

CHAPTER 3

$\mathcal{T}$he screen door creaked as Patricia stepped onto the porch, the warm morning sun doing little to lift the heaviness in her heart. She carried the mail in her hand, flipping through each piece with dwindling hope. Bills, a flyer from the Mercantile, and a letter for her parents. No letter from Albert. Again.

Sinking onto the creaky porch swing, she let the mail rest in her lap as she stared out at the garden, its vibrant greens and yellows mocking her mood. The world seemed alive with summer's abundance, but all Patricia could feel was a dull ache of doubt.

The clip-clop of hooves interrupted her thoughts, and she looked up to see Ellie climbing down from her buggy, her face alight with her usual energy.

"Patricia," Ellie called, waving as she approached. "Why do you look like a wilted daisy sitting there all sullen?"

Patricia let out a soft sigh, brushing sweat from her brow. "No letter from Albert again."

Ellie's cheerful demeanor faltered somewhat, and she took a seat on the swing beside her. "I'm sorry. I know it's hard not to hear from him, especially with everything else weighing on your heart."

Patricia shrugged, though the lump in her throat threatened to grow. "I don't even know why I'm surprised. He told me to use this time to think, didn't he? Maybe he's doing the same."

Ellie frowned, studying her face. "But you're not using this time for anything. You've spent the last few weeks like this . . . waiting for a letter, brooding about what he's thinking. What about what *you* want?"

Patricia blinked, caught off guard by the question. "I don't know what I want. I thought I did, but now . . ." She trailed off, picking at the hem of her apron. "Now it feels like I'm stuck in a place while everything else keeps moving."

Ellie nudged her shoulder kindly. "Well, if you don't know, maybe it's time to try something new. Do something to keep your hands busy and your mind off all this. My mother said she saw a notice at the Mercantile that Kauffman's Fruit and Vegetable Stand is looking for help through the fall. It could be just the thing."

Patricia snorted, crossing her arms. "Oh, joy. Spending the rest of the summer dealing with Rudy's bad jokes. That sounds like a dream come true."

Ellie burst out laughing, the sound ringing through the quiet yard. "*Ach*, you make it sound like he's a tornado tearing through the field."

"He is," Patricia mocked in indignation, though a small smile tugged at her lips. "I can't imagine spending day after day with him teasing me nonstop and calling me Chatty-Patty."

Ellie rested back on the swing, still chuckling. "Maybe it's exactly what you need. A bit of a distraction, some hard work, and, who knows, maybe Rudy's not as bad as you think."

Patricia shook her head, her smile fading as she looked

down at the mail in her lap. "I feel like I don't have room for any more distractions."

"Maybe it's not a distraction," Ellie said quietly. "Maybe it's a chance to see something you've been missing."

Patricia didn't answer, but her thoughts churned as she watched Ellie rise from the swing and head back toward her buggy. The idea of working at Kauffman's Stand occupied her with equal parts dread and curiosity. For now, though, she wasn't ready to decide.

"Joy, joy," she muttered under her breath as she stood and carried the mail inside.

PATRICIA GRIPPED the reins tightly as her buggy rolled to a stop outside the Kauffman farm. The familiar scent of hay and fresh produce filled the air, mingling with the earthy aroma of the fields that stretched out toward the horizon. Her eyes lingered on the weathered barn and the tidy rows of crops beyond the hitching posts.

Her parents' words echoed in her mind. *Sometimes it takes stepping outside your comfort zone to see where* Gott *might lead you.* With a drawn-in breath, Patricia climbed down and secured her buggy, straightening her apron as if it could bolster her courage.

The door to the farmhouse opened, and Rudy's mother, Mariam Kauffman, stepped onto the porch. Her *kapp* framed her kind face, and her hands were dusted with flour. "Patricia! What a surprise to see you here."

Patricia hesitated, her heart thumping as she forced her words out. "I . . . I heard you were looking for help at the stand. I thought I'd see if the position is still open."

Mariam's eyes lit up. "*Ach,* we could certainly use an extra

SEASONS OF THE HEART

pair of hands. But you'll need to talk to Rudy. He's in charge of the stand during the summer."

Patricia's stomach sank. "Rudy?" she repeated, trying to keep the dismay from her voice.

"*Jah*, he's just out back." Mariam gestured toward the barn. "You'll find him near the stand."

Patricia offered a weak smile, murmured her thanks, and trudged in the direction Mariam had pointed. The idea of spending her summer working under Rudy's watchful, and undoubtedly teasing eye, made her want to turn back, but her parents' encouragement pushed her forward.

As she rounded the barn, she saw Rudy unloading a crate of tomatoes onto the stand. He glanced up, his grin quick and familiar. "Well, if it isn't Chatty-Patty!"

Patricia groaned inwardly but pressed on. "I heard you were hiring."

Rudy set the crate down and wiped his hands on his pants, his expression turning thoughtful. "That we are. Are you interested?"

Patricia rolled her eyes. "I'm starting to have second thoughts." She cringed when her words came out so short.

Rudy arched a brow. "How so?"

Ignoring his question, she asked. "I thought you were working at Yoder's."

"Just for a time," he replied. "Saving for something special."

"Something or someone?" Patricia retorted, crossing her arms.

Rudy chuckled and pointed toward a hill just past the farm. "See that spot up there? That's where I want to build my house someday. Working extra jobs helps make it happen a little sooner."

He stepped closer, leaning considerably over her shoulder to gesture toward the hill. "It's not just a house, though. I've got bigger plans. I want to build several greenhouses. Organic produce, flowers, the works. I want to supply the whole area with healthy, local food."

Patricia blinked, caught off guard by the passion in his voice. "You mean, like, for grocery stores and stands?"

"Exactly." Rudy's eyes lit up. "I've been experimenting with some ideas, and it's starting to come together. This stand is just the beginning."

His excitement was infectious, and suddenly she leaned closer, her curiosity piqued. She'd always thought of Rudy as a carefree joker, but something about the way he spoke now felt different . . . an earnestness she hadn't noticed before.

"That sounds . . . ambitious," she admitted.

"It is." Rudy's grin returned. "A little hard work never scared me. What about you? Ready to jump in?"

Patricia hesitated, glancing back toward the barn, then at Rudy. For the first time, she saw him as more than the teasing boy who had annoyed her for years. His dreams were big, his confidence steady. Maybe this job wouldn't be as unbearable as she'd imagined.

"I suppose I could give it a try." Her tone was reluctant, but her lips curved into a small smile.

"Good." Rudy clapped his hands. "Let's get started. And don't worry . . . I won't call you Chatty-Patty in front of the customers. *Much.*"

Patricia sighed, but there was a hint of amusement in her eyes as she followed him behind the counter inside the Farmstand.

PATRICIA ARRANGED a row of ripe tomatoes, her focus sharper than it needed to be. The morning sun was warm, yet no matter how hard she tried, she couldn't shake the prickling awareness of Rudy's presence nearby.

"Hey," Rudy called out from the other end of the stand. His voice had a familiar teasing edge, but it was softer than usual. "You're awful quiet down there."

Patricia glanced up, her brow furrowing. "I'm busy, that's all. You pay me to work, not talk."

"*Jah*, but you hardly talk anymore. Feels like I'm working with a shadow of the girl I used to know."

Her hands were still on the tomatoes as she looked at him, her annoyance flickering to confusion. "What's that supposed to mean?"

Rudy crossed his arms. "You used to talk all the time. Couldn't get you to stop, in fact. But now? You sulk, you scowl, and you barely smile. What happened?"

Patricia bristled, straightening. "Nothing happened. I'm just . . . busy."

"Busy being miserable?" Rudy countered, though there was no malice in his voice. "I don't know . . . you came back from Sugarcreek last year, and something was different. I can't quite put my finger on it, but it's like . . . I don't know. Like you left part of yourself behind."

Her chest tightened, but she forced a laugh. "You're imagining things. I'm the same as I've always been."

Rudy tilted his head, his gaze steady. "I don't think so. You used to laugh at my jokes, even when you pretended not to. Now it's like I'm the only one trying to lighten the air around you."

Patricia's cheeks flushed as she turned back to the tomatoes. "Maybe I've just grown up. Not everyone has the luxury of acting like a carefree schoolboy."

His grin faded, and his voice dropped to a quieter tone. "Maybe I joke because I miss seeing you smile. You've always been quick to brush me off, but at least you used to look happy doing so."

The sincerity in his words sank in, and she fumbled for something to say. "I—I don't know what you're talking about."

"Sure you do." He leaned forward. "You're carrying something, and I don't know if it's Albert being gone or something else, but whatever it is, it's weighing you down."

Patricia's throat tightened. She hated that he was seeing so much more than she wanted to reveal. "It's none of your business."

"Maybe not, but I'd like it to be. At least enough to help you feel like yourself again."

She blinked, startled by the unexpected gentleness in his voice. But before she could respond, Rudy straightened, his teasing smile returning as a customer approached. "Think about it, Chatty—er, I mean, Quiet-Patricia. I'm not always as clueless as I look."

Patricia scowled at the nickname, but as Rudy turned to help the customer, her thoughts churned. For all his joking, he'd struck a chord. And for the first time, she found herself wondering if Rudy Kauffman knew her better than she knew herself.

THE LATE AFTERNOON sun hung low in the sky, adding shadows to the produce stand as Patricia adjusted the rows of cucumbers for what felt like the hundredth time. Each day seemed longer than the last, dragging on with the same monotony. And every day, Albert's unanswered questions in his last letter haunted her.

"Back in a bit," Rudy called as he headed toward the barn to fetch another crate of tomatoes. His easy whistle echoed behind him, leaving Patricia alone with her reflections.

She hesitated, glancing around to ensure no one was watching, then reached into the pocket of her apron. Her fingers brushed against the worn edges of the letter she'd read more times than she could count. Carefully, she unfolded it, the creases deep and familiar.

Albert's words stared back at her, as sharp and unsettling as the first time she'd read them:

Dear Patricia,

We've had a string of warm days here, those late summer ones where the mornings are cool enough for a jacket, but by midday you're wishing for shade. I hope it's been the same by you, and that you're well.

Work with Uncle has been steady. There's always more to learn, but I'm thankful for the chance. Being here, away from home and routine, has given me time to think, about you, about what comes next, and whether we're walking the same path.

I've had a sense that this road I've chosen might not be the one you hoped we'd take together. I don't blame you for that. But it's weighed on me, and I feel I ought to ask straight out: Is this the life you truly want, or the one you feel expected to choose?

Please take time to think on it. Pray about it. I'm doing the same. You know I care for you, but I also want peace for both of us, whatever that may look like.

With respect,

Albert

She sighed, her eyes scanning the words again, searching for some deeper meaning. Each line felt like a puzzle she couldn't quite piece together. *Is this the life you truly want, or the one you feel expected to choose?* The question twisted deep within her heart, forcing her to confront doubts she'd been trying to ignore.

Patricia folded the letter, tucking it back into her pocket as if that might quiet the voice in her head. The truth was, she didn't know how to answer Albert's question. She had always followed the path laid out before her, the one everyone expected. But for the first time, she wondered if her heart was leading her somewhere else.

"Deep in thought again?" Rudy's voice startled her, and she wiped her hands on her apron, composing herself.

"I was just... thinking about something," she said, her voice steady but guarded.

"Must've been something big." Rudy set the crate down and gave her a curious look. "You put the apples in with the tomatoes."

Patricia forced a small smile, deflecting his observation. "Just trying to figure out how to stack tomatoes without them rolling everywhere."

Rudy chuckled, shaking his head. "One day, you'll let someone in on whatever's going on in that head of yours. Until then, I'll just keep guessing."

As he turned back to his work, Patricia pressed her hand against her apron pocket, feeling the edges of the letter through the fabric. She didn't know when . . . or if she'd find the answers Albert was asking for. But one thing was for sure and certain: the seriousness of his words wouldn't leave her anytime soon.

THE SOFT BABBLE of Willow Creek lined the air as Patricia and Ellie strolled along its grassy bank. The sun filtered through the trees, bouncing light on the sparkling water. The walk had been Ellie's idea, an attempt to pull Patricia from her thoughts and into the warm embrace of the summer day.

As they reached a shady spot near the creek, Ellie plopped onto the grass, pulling Patricia down beside her. "You've been quiet again." Ellie propped her chin in her hand. "I can only wait so long before you spill what's rattling around in that head of yours."

Patricia sighed, running her fingers through the blades of grass. "I've decided to let Albert's question sit for now. I can't answer it until I'm sure of what I want."

Ellie nodded. "That's fair. It's a big question. You deserve to take your time."

The creek gurgled gently as they sat in silence for a moment. Finally, Patricia took a cleansing breath. "There's something else I've been thinking about," she admitted, her voice hesitant. "Something I haven't told anyone."

Ellie widened her eyes slightly, intrigued. "Well, now you have to tell me."

Patricia's gaze flicked to the water. "Do you remember the Sugarcreek Harvest Dinner I told you about?"

"Of course." Ellie sat up straighter. "What about it?"

"That's where I met someone . . . David Schrock."

Ellie's eyes widened. "David Schrock? The one from the Schrock family? I've heard of him. Handsome, ambitious, the kind of man who turns heads without even trying."

Patricia nodded, a faint smile tugging at her lips. "We only talked for a little while, but . . . I don't know. Something about him stayed with me. The way he spoke about his dreams, the places he'd seen. It was like he saw the world in a way I never have."

Ellie smirked. "So let me get this straight. You've got Albert, who's steady as a rock but makes you question everything. You've got David, who's barely more than a memory but apparently lives rent-free in your mind. And then . . ."

Ellie trailed off, her eyes landing down the creek. Patricia followed her gaze and froze. There, not far from the shore, stood Rudy, casting his fishing line with an ease that made it look second nature.

Ellie didn't miss the subtle change in Patricia's posture, the way her fingers stilled in the grass. She grinned, leaning closer. "And then there's Rudy."

Patricia blinked, her cheeks warming. "What about him?"

Ellie winked with a lift of her chin. "Don't play coy with me. You lit up like a firefly the second you saw him."

"I did not." Patricia's voice was sharp and unconvincing.

Ellie chuckled, nudging her friend. "You've got three men on your mind, Patricia. Who wouldn't be confused and tied up with strange emotions? Sounds like something straight out of one of those romance books we hide under our beds."

Patricia rolled her eyes, though a reluctant smile tugged at her lips. "This isn't a book, Ellie. It's my life, and it's a mess."

"Maybe." Ellie shrugged, "but it's a pretty good story so far. And I've got to admit, I'm rooting for the guy with the fishing pole."

Patricia shook her head, but her gaze lingered on Rudy as he reeled in his line, the sunlight catching the curve of his smile. As much as she wanted to deny it, Ellie's words left her wondering if her heart already knew where it was headed.

"That's plum crazy," Patricia muttered, shaking her head as she tugged at the blades of grass beneath her fingertips. The gentle hum of Willow Creek filled the pause, but her thoughts buzzed louder.

Ellie tilted her head. "What's crazy? The fact that you've got three men pulling at your heartstrings, or the fact that you're too stubborn to admit it?"

Patricia sighed, leaning closer, her voice dropping to a near whisper. "It's not Rudy I'm thinking about," she admitted, her cheeks warming despite the cool breeze off the creek. "It's David Schrock."

Ellie's eyes widened, and she turned fully to face her friend. "David? Still?"

Patricia nodded, her gaze drifting toward the water. "It's hard to explain . . . but the way he sees things, the way he talks

. . . it's like he knows exactly where he's going and what he wants."

Ellie considered this, her look softening. "And you think you want that too? A life full of dreams and adventures?"

Patricia shrugged, her voice quiet. "I don't know. I thought I knew what I wanted . . . Albert, the farm, a steady life. But after meeting David, it's like . . . I'm questioning everything I thought was enough."

Ellie sat back, studying her with concern. "You're allowed to question things, you know. But don't let a memory cloud your judgment. David might have seemed perfect in the moment, but he's just one man, Patricia. And you hardly know him."

Patricia sighed, pulling her knees to her chest. "I know that. But it's not just him, it's the idea of something more. Something different . . . someplace different than Willow Springs."

Ellie reached over, squeezing her friend's arm tenderly. "That's fair. But don't forget about the people right in front of you. Sometimes, the things we're looking for aren't far away . . . they're just waiting for us to see them."

Patricia glanced down the creek where Rudy stood, his fishing line glinting in the sunlight. She frowned, unsure if Ellie's words were meant to steer her toward him or something entirely different.

"I can't even think about that right now." Patricia's voice was tinged with frustration. "Everything feels like a tangled mess."

Ellie grinned, her teasing flavor returning. "That's what makes it a good story. The best endings come after the biggest messes."

Patricia rolled her eyes, but a faint smile broke through her indecision. As much as she hated to admit it, Ellie wasn't totally wrong.

CHAPTER 4

The Henry Schrock farm looked like a painting come to life as Patricia's *datt* pulled their buggy into the yard. The big maple trees bordering the property were tinged with gold and red, their colors just beginning to creep along the edges of the leaves. A light breeze carried the crisp scent of early autumn, mingling with the faint aroma of bean soup simmering in the farmhouse kitchen.

Patricia climbed down from the buggy, smoothing her apron and adjusting her *kapp* as she followed her parents toward the gathering crowd. The usual hum of Sunday greetings and the clip-clop of hooves surrounded them, but Patricia's steps faltered when she saw him.

Albert stood across the yard near the barn, his posture tall and self-assured as he spoke with a group of men. Patricia's breath quickened. He looked . . . different. His shoulders were broader, his presence commanding in a way that made her chest tighten with equal parts irritation and admiration.

As if sensing her gaze, Albert glanced in her direction. For a brief moment, their eyes met, and he tipped his hat in polite acknowledgment before turning back to his conversation. No smile, no warmth, just a distant, casual gesture.

Patricia's stomach twisted. *He's back and didn't tell me?* The thought burned, sharp and bitter.

"Patricia," Ellie whispered as she stepped beside her. "Is that Albert?"

Patricia nodded tightly, her lips pressing into a scowl. "*Jah.* Apparently, he's back."

Ellie pinched her brow. "And you didn't know? Not a letter, not a word?"

"*Nee.*" Patricia's voice was low and clipped.

Ellie's concern shifted to quiet indignation. "That's not right."

They moved to follow the women into the *haus*, signaling the start of the service, and Patricia followed Ellie inside. As the three-hour sermon stretched endlessly, Patricia's focus slipped every time her mind wandered back to Albert. She sat beside Ellie, her hands folded tightly in her lap, her emotions swirling.

"He didn't even tell me he was coming home," she whispered during a hymn.

Ellie gave her a sidelong glance. "I don't blame you for stewing. I'd be fuming."

After the final prayer, Patricia followed Ellie to the kitchen, joining the women to prepare the meal. She moved mechanically, adding moon pies to a tray, her gaze frequently straying to the window. The yard was alive with activity; children running, men talking near the barn . . . but her eyes searched for one person.

"Looking for someone?" Ellie asked, her tone teasing as she handed Patricia a bowl of peanut butter spread.

Patricia scowled but didn't answer. She couldn't stop herself from glancing out the window again, watching as Albert strode across the yard. His voice, deep and sure, carried faintly through the open window as he laughed at something one of the men said.

Ellie moved closer, smirking. "You could just go talk to him, you know."

"*Nee*, I couldn't. If he wanted to talk, he would've let me know he was here. Instead, he's acting like I don't exist."

Ellie lifted a brow. "Or maybe he's waiting for you to go to him."

Patricia's chest tightened as she resumed filling the bowl with the sticky spread. She wasn't sure what she wanted to say to Albert, or if she even wanted to face him. All she knew was his unexpected return had stirred emotions she wasn't ready to confront.

As the meal preparation continued, Patricia caught herself glancing out the window again. Her heart tugged in conflicting directions, frustration mingling with curiosity. For all her anger, she couldn't deny the strange appeal of the confident, changed man standing just beyond her reach.

RUDY SHIFTED another bench into place, angling it carefully to form a table in the large front room. The hum of voices and the clatter of dishes crowded the space, but his focus was elsewhere.

Patricia stood near the window, her hands working carefully, helping with the noonday meal, but her eyes were glued to the yard outside, specifically, to Albert.

Rudy tightened his grip on the bench, his jaw clenching as he watched her. The wistful look on her face stirred something in him that he couldn't quite put into words . . . an ache that had been growing over the weeks they'd spent working side by side.

He straightened, brushing his hands on his pants as he turned his attention back to his task. It wasn't his place to feel this way. Patricia's heart belonged to Albert, had for as long as he could remember. And yet, he couldn't stop the concerns that crept into his mind.

He glanced at her again, noting the faint crease in her brow, the way her fingers hesitated on the bowl in her hand. She looked troubled, confused, and it only fueled his frustration.

Why did he come back? Rudy thought bitterly. Albert's return had already thrown Patricia into a spiral, undoing the progress she'd made in the past few weeks. For the first time in years, Rudy had seen glimpses of the girl he used to know . . . the one who smiled easily, who laughed at his jokes even when she pretended not to. And now, with just one casual tip of his hat, Albert had brought all that crashing down.

Rudy set the last table into place, wiping the sweat from his brow as he stole another glance at Patricia. His chest tightened as he saw the way her gaze lingered on Albert, who stood near the barn, his posture relaxed as he chatted with the men.

What does she see in him? Rudy wondered, his fists clenching at his sides. He'd always been protective of Patricia, but this was different. It wasn't just about looking out for her anymore. It was about something deeper, something he'd been fighting even more since she started working at the stand.

His heart twisted as he admitted the truth to himself. He wanted more than just to protect her. But what could he do? Patricia's heart wasn't his to claim. She had made her choice, and it wasn't him. Rudy sighed, stepping back to survey his work. The benches were ready, the tables set. And still, his thoughts refused to settle.

As the women began carrying dishes into the room, Rudy caught Patricia's eye for the briefest moment. She looked away quickly, her cheeks flushing as she turned back to setting the tables.

Rudy's chest ached, but he forced a smile, masking the turmoil inside. For now, he would do what he always did . . . stand on the sidelines, ready to help, ready to protect, even if his heart was breaking in the process.

PATRICIA STEPPED OUTSIDE, the soft crunch of her shoes against the gravel barely audible over the sounds of families settling in for the meal. The crisp September air filled her lungs, and she let out a long, steady breath. The confines of the kitchen and her tangled notions about Albert were suffocating, and she needed space to think.

She walked a few steps toward the border of the yard, where the golden edges of the maple trees danced gently in the breeze. Closing her eyes, she tilted her face toward the sun, trying to push away the gnawing unease that had settled in her chest.

"Patricia."

Her eyes flew open at the sound of his voice, and she turned to see Albert approaching, his stride measured and purposeful. For a moment, she was struck again by how different he looked. But the guarded expression on his face brought her back to reality.

"Albert," she said, her voice warily neutral. "I didn't know you were back."

"I got in last night," he replied, stopping a few feet away. He adjusted his hat; his gaze lingered on the ground before meeting hers.

"You could've written and said you were coming home." Patricia's tone was sharper than she intended. "A letter doesn't take much time."

Albert shifted, his hand brushing the brim of his hat. "I didn't think . . . well, I figured I'd see you here."

Patricia folded her arms, her frustration bubbling just beneath the surface. "Well, here I am. What did you want to say?"

Albert hesitated, his shoulders rising and falling in a subtle shrug. "I thought we could talk later."

Her brows knit together. "About what?"

"About us." His voice was stable but lacked warmth.

Patricia's chest tightened at his vague words, but she forced herself to nod. "Alright. I'll be home later."

"Good." Albert gave her a slight, dutiful nod. "I'll see you then."

Without another word, Albert turned and walked away, his figure disappearing back toward the barn with the same quiet confidence that had once drawn her to him. Patricia stood rooted to the spot, her emotions swirling in a storm of confusion and anger.

For a fleeting moment, her mind shifted to David Schrock . . . the way his voice had carried a spark of adventure, his words painting a picture of a life packed with purpose and possibility. Compared to Albert's measured demeanor, David's presence was like a gust of fresh air, unpredictable and exhilarating. The thought only added to her confusion, leaving her questioning everything she thought she wanted.

THE FAMILIAR SOUND of a buggy approaching the *haus* stirred Patricia from her room. She moved quickly, smoothing the creases from her apron as she descended the stairs, anticipation mingling with unease. The solid clop of the horse's hooves drew closer, and she glanced out the window, confirming what she already knew: Albert.

She stepped onto the porch, expecting a familiar invitation for a ride, but Albert stopped her with a raised hand and hastily tethered the buggy to the hitching post. "This won't take long. Let's sit."

Patricia froze for a moment, the abruptness of his words catching her off guard. She followed him to the porch swing and hesitated before sitting down. Albert joined her, leaving a small space between them. The wooden swing creaked as it swayed under their weight.

For a moment, silence stretched between them. Albert bent forward, his elbows resting on his knees, his hat dangling from his hands. Patricia waited, her heart pounding as her mind raced with possible explanations for his unusual demeanor.

Finally, he spoke, his voice firm but devoid of warmth. "I've given this a lot of thought."

Her breath caught in the back of her throat, and she gripped the edge of the swing.

"I don't think we should proceed with our plans," he said, his tone measured. "I'm uncertain about my readiness for marriage and fear that continuing would be unfair to you. You deserve someone fully committed and aligned with your vision for the future."

Patricia's mouth went dry. She stared at him, her mind struggling to process the force of his words. The life they had planned together, the secure, predictable path she thought she was destined to follow, was shattered with a few matter-of-fact sentences.

Albert shifted, glancing at her briefly before standing and placing his hat firmly on his head. "I hope you understand."

She couldn't muster a response; her words felt meaningless.

Albert nodded once; his expression unreadable. "I'll leave you be," he said simply before stepping off the porch and heading back to his buggy.

Patricia remained on the swing, motionless as the sound of hooves faded into the distance. The world she had planned was gone, cut short in a few brief moments. And yet, beneath the shock and heartbreak, a flicker of relief stirred . . . a quiet voice whispering that maybe this was for the best, even if she couldn't yet admit it to herself.

THE *HAUS* WAS SILENT, save for the faint creak of the old beams as the evening wind pressed against the window panes. Patricia lay beneath the patchwork quilt her mother had sewn years ago, its familiar weight a small comfort. The shadows of the swaying maple branches outside danced across her bedroom walls, silvered by the moonlight.

She stared at the ceiling, her thoughts drifting as the events of the day replayed in her mind. Albert's words still echoed, stark and final. And yet, as much as they stung, she couldn't deny the truth in them. He had known what was best for her, even when she hadn't.

Her eyes fluttered closed as she pictured David Schrock. Was he sitting under the same moonlight? Was he in Wisconsin, Montana, or Idaho, living the life he'd described so vividly? Her chest tightened with guilt as the thought lingered. She shouldn't be thinking about David, not now, not after everything with Albert. And yet, his memory pulled at her, tempting her with dreams of a life she'd only glimpsed.

Turning on her side, Patricia pressed her hands together in prayer. The moonlight brushed her face as she whispered into the stillness.

"Lord, I know You closed the door on Albert for a reason, even if I didn't see it at first. Thank you for guiding him to make the choice I couldn't. For that, I'll always be grateful."

She paused, her voice catching as she searched for the right words. "But now, I don't know what to do. I feel lost, like I'm standing in the middle of a path with no idea which way to go. Please, *Gott*, give me a clear sign. Help me see what I'm supposed to do next."

Her fingers tightened, her voice barely above a whisper. "And if David is part of Your plan for me . . . please, show me. Give me a sign, Lord, so I know which path to take."

A tear slipped down her cheek, and she wiped it away swiftly, drawing the quilt tighter around her shoulders. She listened to the soft rustle of leaves outside, waiting for peace and sleep to find her.

As DAWN's first light filtered through the window, Patricia lingered in the delicate space between sleep and wakefulness. In this twilight of consciousness, a dream unfolded with vivid clarity.

She found herself in a bustling barn, the air thick with the murmur of countless voices and the shuffling of feet. Amidst the crowd, a man stood apart, his features obscured by a shadow. He extended his hand toward her, a silent invitation to come closer.

Patricia's heart quickened as she tried to navigate through the gathering, her eyes fixed on the outstretched hand. Yet no matter how she maneuvered, the distance between them remained impossible. The faces around her blurred into vagueness, their presence a barrier she couldn't breach.

Just as the man began to step into the light, illuminating the outline of his form, Patricia's eyes fluttered open. The dream dissolved, leaving her with the haunting impression of a face she couldn't recall.

She lay still, the remnants of the vision lingering in her

mind. The sense of yearning, the frustration of being unable to reach him . . . it all felt so real.

As she rose to face the day, the dream remained with her, a whisper from her subconscious urging her to seek clarity amidst the confusion of her waking life.

CHAPTER 5

The weeks melded together, each day a step further from the sting of Albert's departure. By late October, the Farmstand had transformed into a vibrant display of autumn's bounty: pumpkins, gourds, and a rich array of harvested vegetables. Patricia and Rudy had cultivated a steady stream of returning *Englisch* and Amish customers, finding a comfortable rhythm in their daily work.

One crisp Monday morning, as Patricia arranged a pyramid of pie pumpkins, she noticed Maggie Schrock, the bishop's wife and David's sister-in-law, approaching the stand. Patricia's heart quickened; this was an unexpected opportunity to learn more about David without revealing her lingering interest.

"*Goot meiya*, Maggie," Patricia greeted her warmly. "Looking for something special today?"

Maggie smiled at Patricia's greeting. "I need tender, sweet pie pumpkins for Thanksgiving."

Patricia selected a few of the finest specimens and handed them to Maggie. "These should be perfect." She hesitated briefly before adding, "I met your brother-in-law, David, at the

SEASONS OF THE HEART

Sugarcreek Harvest Dinner last year. He mentioned he might be traveling. Do you know if he's still away?"

Maggie paused, a thoughtful expression crossing her face. "He did spend some time in Tomah, Wisconsin, over the summer. But last I heard, he's back in Sugarcreek, working at Schrock Construction."

Patricia's pulse quickened at the mention of David's return. "It's good to know he's back home."

Maggie nodded with a curious glint in her eye. "*Jah*, he's been quite busy since his return."

Patricia offered a polite smile, her mind already racing with what that might be. As Maggie paid for the pumpkins and walked away, Patricia couldn't help but feel that this encounter was a nudge from above, a subtle sign guiding her toward the answers she sought.

As Patricia watched Maggie pull her buggy away from the stand, a spark of determination ignited within her. The thought of returning to Sugarcreek for the harvest dinner and possibly seeing David again consumed her mind. She turned to Rudy, who was arranging a display of gourds nearby.

"Rudy," she began, trying to sound casual, "when do you think we'll close the stand for the season?"

Rudy looked up, a playful glint in his eye. "Why? Are you that eager to be rid of me?"

Patricia couldn't help but laugh, a genuine giggle escaping her lips. "*Nee*, it's not that at all. I've actually enjoyed working here. But I was thinking of doing some visiting and need to make plans."

Rudy raised his chin, his curiosity piqued. "Visiting, huh? Anyone I know?"

Patricia felt a blush creep up her cheeks. "Just some friends in Sugarcreek. I thought the annual Harvest Dinner would be a good time to catch up."

Rudy nodded slowly, a knowing smile tugging at his lips. "I see. Well, if all goes as planned, we should wrap up here by the end of next week. That should give you plenty of time for your . . . visiting, *jah*?"

"*Jah*." Patricia's mind already raced with possibilities. Perhaps she could convince her parents to visit her *schwester's* family in Sugarcreek, or maybe she could take a bus on her own. The thought of seeing David again filled her with both excitement and apprehension.

Later that afternoon, Patricia and Rudy were arranging a pyramid of pumpkins at the stand's entrance. Engrossed in their conversation, they didn't notice the structure becoming unstable. Suddenly, the pumpkins began to wobble, and before they could react, the entire display collapsed, sending pumpkins rolling in all directions.

Patricia gasped, instinctively reaching out to stop the tumbling gourds. Rudy, quick on his feet, managed to catch a particularly large pumpkin before it hit the ground. They both stood amidst the scattered produce, eyes wide, before bursting into laughter.

"Well, that didn't go as planned." Patricia wiped her brow with the back of her hand.

Rudy chuckled, setting the rescued pumpkin aside. "I guess our pyramid-building skills need some work."

As they began gathering the runaway pumpkins, Rudy looked at Patricia, his usual teasing grin firmly in place. "You know," he said, his tone mock-serious, "I've always been there for you. Catching falling pumpkins, scaring off ill-mannered boys, making sure your buggy wheels don't fall off . . . you name it. I'm basically your knight in shining armor."

Patricia paused, a small pumpkin in her hands, and eyed him skeptically. "Knight? That's quite the title. Are you sure you're not just making this up to get out of fixing that pyramid?"

Rudy placed a hand over his heart, feigning offense. "Patricia Wengerd, you wound me. Here I am, a humble knight dedicating my life to your safety, and this is the thanks I get."

She rolled her eyes but couldn't help the smile tugging at her lips. "Alright, if you're my 'knight,' where were you when the pyramid started falling?"

Rudy shrugged, grabbing another pumpkin and tossing it in her direction. "Hey, I can't be everywhere at once. Even knights need a break now and then."

Patricia chuckled, shaking her head as they worked together to rebuild the display. Despite his joking manner, something in his words lingered.

As they finished, Rudy brushed off his hands and shot her a quick grin. "You know, you're pretty lucky to have me around. Without me, who knows how many pumpkins would've met their untimely end today?"

"Lucky," Patricia repeated, her words playful. "That's one way to put it."

She turned back to the stand, her attention drifting as the rhythm of their easy banter occupied the crisp autumn air. Rudy might always joke, but there was a comfort in his presence . . . a steadfastness she was only beginning to appreciate.

THE FIRST DROPS of rain splattered against the roof of the Farmstand as Rudy secured the last crate of produce. He peeked over at Patricia, who was pulling her sweater tighter against the sudden chill in the air.

"Looks like we closed just in time," Rudy pulled his buggy

closer to the stand. He turned to her with a casual grin. "Want a ride home? Can't have you getting drenched and ruining your *kapp*."

Patricia hesitated for a moment before nodding. "*Denki.* That would be helpful."

Rudy's heart did a little flip as she climbed into the buggy. Moments like this . . . just the two of them, no customers, no distractions . . . were rare, and he wasn't about to rush through it. He snapped the reins lightly, letting the horse set an unhurried pace down the rain-slicked road.

As they trotted along, Rudy couldn't help but bring up his favorite topic. "You know, I've been thinking more about the *haus* I want to build up on the ridge."

"Oh?" Patricia turned to face him, her expression soft in the dim light filtering through the rain.

"*Jah.*" Rudy straightened his shoulders. "I just got a call from the Sugarcreek auction house. They're interested in taking the rest of my fall produce if I can get it there by the end of next week. If it works out, it'll add a nice chunk to my savings. Might even help me break ground by early spring."

Patricia smiled. "That sounds promising. You've been talking about that ridge all summer."

Rudy chuckled. "Well, it's not just about building a *haus*. It's about building the right *one*. One that feels like home, you know? And since I don't exactly have anyone in mind to share it with yet . . ." He peeked at her out of the corner of his eye. " . . . I was hoping to get a woman's perspective on what makes a *haus* feel like home."

Patricia turned toward him. "What do you mean?"

"Well," Rudy kept his manner casual, "I figure there's more to it than walls and a roof. Things like the layout, the kitchen, and where the windows should go. That sort of thing."

Patricia seemed to consider this for a moment before nodding. "That's true. A home should feel warm and welcoming. The kitchen is important; it's where so much of life happens. And lots of windows would be nice, especially if you're building up on the ridge. You'll want to make the most of the view."

Rudy's grin widened. "Exactly what I was thinking. You've got a good eye for these things."

They fell into an easy rhythm of conversation as the buggy continued its slow journey. The rain softened to drizzle, and Rudy scanned the horizon, noting they still had a couple of hours of daylight left.

"You know," he said, almost hesitant, "we could take a ride up to the ridge. It's not far from here. I'd like to hear more of your ideas while you can see the spot for yourself."

Patricia looked at him, her eyes widening. "You want my opinion?"

"Of course." Rudy kept his words light but sincere. "Who better to ask?"

He held his breath as she seemed to mull it over, and relief flooded him when she nodded. "Alright. Let's go."

Rudy couldn't hide the satisfaction that crept onto his face as he guided the buggy toward the ridge. For once, he had the time and space to talk to her without interruptions. And as they made their way up the hill, he couldn't help but feel hopeful for his uncertain future.

THE BUGGY CREAKED to some extent as Rudy guided it along the winding path to the ridge. The rain had lightened to a gentle mist, and the cool autumn air carried the faint scent of wet leaves. Patricia pulled her sweater tighter around her shoulders and felt warmer as Rudy's voice, animated and excited, described his plans.

"And over there . . ." Rudy pointed as they neared the top

of the ridge. ". . . I'm thinking a big kitchen with enough space for a proper table. You know, one of those long, sturdy ones where a family could sit together, and you'd still have room for guests."

Patricia smiled at his enthusiasm. "Any woman would be excited about what you've got planned, it's . . . thoughtful."

Rudy glanced at her, his grin softening into something more earnest. "You think so? I've always figured it's the little things that matter, you know? Like where the windows go or making sure there's enough space for a rocking chair by the fireplace."

Patricia nodded; her heart warmed at his sincerity. She couldn't help but think how different this conversation was from the ones she'd had with Albert.

Her attention wandered back to her past relationship, and a pang of regret mingled with clarity. With Albert, there had been no talk of houses, children, or a shared future beyond his plans to take over his father's farm. Their practical conversations centered on cows and fields, not dreams or possibilities. Not once had Albert asked her opinion about anything concerning their future.

And yet there was Rudy, his eyes alight with enthusiasm, genuinely eager to hear her thoughts on the smallest details of a life not yet built. It wasn't just his plans that stood out; it was the way he included her, valued her input, even if it was imaginary.

Patricia turned her gaze to Rudy as he described how he wanted it to sit so the sunrise could be seen from the kitchen window. She couldn't help but notice how different he was from Albert. Rudy, with his joking, nonserious manner, managed to be attentive in ways Albert never had.

But as much as she appreciated Rudy's attentiveness, her mind couldn't help but drift to David. She thought of his broad shoulders and the confidence in his voice when he spoke.

Comparing Albert, Rudy, and David felt unfair, but the ideas came unbidden, each man highlighting something the others lacked.

"Patricia?" Rudy's voice pulled her from her ponderings.

She blinked, realizing she'd been quiet for too long. "I'm sorry, what did you say?"

"I was just asking what you thought about a wraparound porch." Rudy's question was light but tinged with curiosity.

Patricia smiled, her heart settling for a moment. "I think it's a wonderful idea. A porch like that would be perfect for watching the sunrise . . . or the rain."

Rudy's grin widened. "Exactly what I was thinking."

As they reached the ridge and looked out over the rolling hills, Patricia felt a whisper of what he had envisioned. The contrast between the men in her life and what she truly wanted grew clearer with every passing moment, even if the answers still eluded her. For now, she chose to enjoy the simplicity of Rudy's company and the inviting nature of his dreams while she worked on a plan to go meet the man who truly captured her heart.

As RUDY GUIDED the buggy down Willow Creek Road, the rhythmic clatter of hooves on the wooden planks of the covered bridge echoed around them. The rain had tapered to a gentle drizzle, adding a silvery sheen over the landscape. Below, a flock of geese descended gracefully onto the creek, their reflections rippling in the water.

Rudy pulled the reins, bringing the buggy to a halt. He nodded toward the geese, a smile tugging at his lips. "Look at that, even the geese know how to make a grand entrance."

Patricia watched the birds, their serene landing contrasting with the turmoil of her thoughts. She had been unusually quiet during the ride, her mind occupied with reflections on Rudy's plans and her own uncertain future.

Rudy turned to her, his eyes twinkling with gentle mischief. "Lost in thought, or just mesmerized by my riveting conversation?"

She managed a small smile. "You seem to find joy in the simplest things. I admire that."

He chuckled. "I've learned to appreciate the good things. Like a good meal, a sturdy roof, or a friend who listens, even when they're rambling about geese."

Patricia's smile grew, the weight on her heart lifting just a bit. "I suppose that's true."

Rudy's expression softened, his nature becoming more sincere. "Life's too short to dwell on what doesn't bring you happiness. Sometimes, you have to ask yourself what truly makes you happy and go after it, even if it means taking a leap of faith."

She looked at him, his words resonating deeply. The simplicity of his outlook was comforting, a stark contrast to the complexities she often found herself entangled in.

"*Denki,*" she said softly. "I needed to hear that."

He tipped his hat with a playful grin. "Anytime. Now, shall we get you home before the geese decide to take over the road?"

With a light flick of the reins, the buggy resumed its journey, the covered bridge fading into the mist behind them. As they traveled the familiar path, Patricia couldn't help but feel a sense of clarity emerging from the fog in her head, guided by the simple wisdom of a friend who found joy in the little things and encouraged her to take a leap of fate like none she had ever taken before . . . leading her straight to Sugarcreek.

CHAPTER 6

*P*atricia and Ellie sat cross-legged on the quilt-covered bed. Patricia's eyes sparkled with excitement as she shared her news.

"I've received permission to visit Rebecca in Sugarcreek," Patricia announced, her voice brimming with anticipation. "I'll be there just in time for the harvest dinner. I'm praying that *Gott* will answer my prayers and David Schrock will be there."

Ellie listened and after a moment, she asked, "What do you truly know about him?"

Patricia blinked, slightly taken aback. "Well . . . he was kind, handsome, and adventurous." Patricia swooned and brought her hands up to her chin before continuing. "We had a wonderful evening together just talking and sharing our lives."

Ellie nodded slowly. "I understand that, but can you truly know someone after just one evening?"

Patricia's enthusiasm waned as she considered Ellie's words. "I suppose I don't know much about him. But I . . . I hope if he shows up like we promised each other, then we can build on that one night."

Ellie reached out, placing a comforting hand on Patricia's.

"I don't want to dampen your spirits, but it's important to be realistic. *Gott's* plan may not align with your hopes. Have you prepared your heart for that possibility?"

Patricia sighed, her shoulders slumping. "I guess I haven't thought about it that way."

Ellie offered a reassuring smile. "It's natural to dream, but are you prepared to trust in *Gott's* wisdom? He knows what's best for you, even if it's not what you expect."

Patricia nodded, absorbing her friend's counsel. "*Jah.*"

Suddenly, Patricia leaped up and headed to her closet, her excitement rekindled. She pulled out two dresses, one blue and one light brown, holding each under her chin. "So, what do you think? Brown to bring out my eyes, or blue to complement my blonde hair?"

Ellie sighed inwardly, realizing that her earlier words hadn't fully settled in Patricia's mind. She feared her friend was setting herself up for disappointment, especially since it had been almost a year since Patricia had even spoken to David. How much stock could one really put in fate?

"Both are lovely," Ellie said tenderly. "I pray you're prepared for any outcome."

Patricia's smile faded, but she nodded. "*Jah,* I am."

Ellie returned the nod, hoping that her friend would find the balance between hope and realism as she embarked on her journey to Sugarcreek.

RUDY PROPPED against the wooden counter of the kitchen, absently running a hand through his hair as his thoughts swirled. He had spent the better part of the morning thinking about Patricia and her sudden excitement over the trip to Sugarcreek. It didn't take much to piece together that she had more than family on her mind. The way her face lit up when she mentioned the Harvest Dinner, the way her voice carried just a little more hope than usual . . . it gnawed at him.

The jealousy bug had bitten, and Rudy couldn't shake it. He didn't know for sure why she was so set on going, but something about it felt . . . off. And he wasn't about to let her go to Sugarcreek without him. Not when there might be someone waiting there to sweep her off her feet.

After calling nearly half a dozen of his regular drivers, Rudy finally found someone willing to take a load of winter squash to the auction house the week of Thanksgiving. It hadn't been easy. He even had to promise an extra day's pay to get the driver to stick around so Rudy could attend the annual Sugarcreek Harvest Dinner.

Once the arrangements were settled, Rudy felt a strange mix of satisfaction and nerves. He wasn't entirely sure what he was doing, but he knew one thing: he wasn't letting Patricia make that trip alone.

Later that afternoon, Rudy pulled his buggy into the Wengerds' drive. He spotted Patricia hanging laundry on the line, wisps of her golden hair that had escaped her *kapp* catching the afternoon sun. His chest tightened as he climbed down and made his way over.

"Afternoon, Patricia," he called, grinning as she turned to face him. "Do you have a minute?"

Patricia dried her hands on her apron and nodded. "Of course. What's on your mind?"

Rudy rested casually against the fence, trying to keep his tone light. "Are you still planning a trip to Sugarcreek?"

Patricia's eyes lit up. "*Jah*. I'm visiting my *schwester*."

"Well"—Rudy adjusted his hat—"as it happens, I'm heading that way myself. Got a load of winter squash to deliver to the auction house. Thought it might make sense for us to travel together."

Patricia gave a subtle look of surprise, a teasing smile

playing on her lips. "Is that so? Or are you just looking for free labor?"

Rudy chuckled. "Hey, you work at the Farmstand. It's only fair you help see the produce through to its final destination."

Patricia folded her arms, her smile widening. "And you're going to pay me for this work, right?"

Rudy faked a thoughtful expression. "Pay you? I'm offering you a free ride. Think of the bus fare you'll save."

Patricia laughed, shaking her head. "Alright, you've convinced me. But only if you promise not to make me load the squash."

Rudy tipped his hat with a grin. "Deal."

As they talked, Rudy felt a surge of relief. He might not know what Patricia hoped to find in Sugarcreek, but at least he'd be there to see for himself. And maybe, just maybe, he'd find a way to show her that what she was searching for might already be right in front of her.

JUST AT DAWN on Monday morning, Rudy and his *Englisch* driver arrived at the Wengerd farm to pick up Patricia. The horizon hinted at an approaching storm, adding a somber atmosphere over the early morning. The driver, a burly older gentleman, was eager to depart promptly to avoid the impending weather.

Patricia stood by the front door, her hands fidgeting with the strap of her travel bag. "I hope I haven't forgotten anything," she murmured, glancing back toward the *haus*.

Her parents stood on the porch, their faces a mix of concern as they looked up toward the sky. She exchanged hurried goodbyes, her mother's eyes lingering a moment longer than usual on the darkening clouds. With a final wave, Patricia approached the truck.

Climbing into the front seat beside Rudy, she found the space more confined than expected.

As the truck set off toward Sugarcreek, the rhythmic hum of the engine mingled with the darkening clouds, marking the beginning of their journey. The driver, Hank, navigated the winding roads with a heavy hand, and when he took a sharp turn too hard, Patricia slid closer to Rudy, their thighs pressing together.

In all the years she'd known Rudy, she had never been this close to him. The unexpected contact sent a jolt through her, and she realized she'd never noticed his clean, fresh scent before. It was comforting, a stark contrast to the overpowering aftershave of the driver.

Patricia felt Rudy subtly shift his leg closer as they touched. She tried to will herself to pull away, but there was a magnetic pull that held her in place. The moment startled her, and she found herself focusing intently on the road ahead, unable to muster the strength to break the contact.

She had never sat this close to another man. Even with Albert, their interactions had been reserved, rarely touching. This personal connection left her emotions scattered, a whirlwind of confusion at the unexpected event.

"Looks like we're in for some weather today," Rudy remarked, glancing at the darkening sky.

Hank nodded, his grip firm on the steering wheel. "Yeah, the forecast mentioned some heavy snow along I-80, especially near Youngstown and into Akron. Could make the drive a bit tricky."

Concerned, Rudy asked, "Any idea how bad it's supposed to get?"

Hank reached over and switched on the weather radio. A crisp voice filled the cab, detailing the latest storm warnings.

"... *Lake Effect Snow Warning remains in effect until 1 AM EST Wednesday. Additional snow accumulations between 6 and 12 inches in*

Mahoning County and 2 to 4 inches in Lawrence County. A warning is in effect until 1 AM EST Wednesday. The condition impacts all roads and especially bridges and overpasses will likely become slick and hazardous. Travel could be difficult . . ."

Patricia heard the words but found it hard to focus. The warmth of Rudy's leg against hers was a constant distraction, sending her emotions into a whirlwind.

Rudy, noticing her distraction, gave her a reassuring smile. "Don't worry. We'll take it slow and easy. Hank here is an experienced driver."

Hank chuckled. "Been through worse, that's for sure. I'll get you both to Sugarcreek safe and sound."

Despite their reassurances, Patricia couldn't shake the fluttering in her soul. It wasn't the storm that unsettled her, but the unexpected closeness to Rudy and the unfamiliar emotions it stirred within her.

APPROXIMATELY AN HOUR and a half into their journey, a sudden snow squall enveloped the truck, drastically reducing visibility. Hank immediately slowed to twenty miles per hour and activated the hazard lights. Recognizing the dangerous conditions, he decided to pull off at the nearest rest stop along I-80. A line of holiday travelers followed, forming a cautious procession down the service road leading to the welcome center near the Ohio-Pennsylvania border.

Inside the cab, Patricia's thoughts remained entangled with the unexpected closeness to Rudy, making it difficult for her to focus on the unfolding situation. Sensing her tension, Rudy maintained a lighthearted conversation with Hank about the weather, aiming to ease the atmosphere. "This snow came out of nowhere," Rudy remarked, glancing at the swirling flakes outside.

Hank nodded, his eyes fixed on the road. "Lake effect snow

can be unpredictable. One minute it's clear, the next you're in a whiteout."

Inside the cab, the atmosphere was tense, the howling wind outside seemed to mirror the blizzard within Patricia, each flake of snow adding to the accumulation of emotions she struggled to comprehend.

As they finally came to a stop at the rest area, Hank turned to his passengers. "We'll wait here until the worst passes. No sense in risking it."

Rudy nodded in agreement, then glanced at Patricia, his eyes searching hers for reassurance. "How are you holding up?"

Patricia managed a small smile, though her heart pounded in her chest. "I'm alright. I just . . . wasn't expecting this." As the storm raged outside, she found an unexpected small island of calm in Rudy's presence.

The rest stop bustled with stranded travelers, all seeking shelter from the relentless storm. Inside the welcome center, the air was crowded with murmurs of concern and the occasional cry of a restless child.

Patricia and Rudy found a quiet corner, settling onto a bench near a window obscured by frost. The cold seeped through the glass, but the warmth between them created a barrier against the chill.

Rudy scanned the crowded room, then back at Patricia. "Looks like we're here for a while."

Patricia nodded, her earlier anxiety slowly ebbing away. "I suppose so."

Rudy's eyes softened as he looked at her, a hint of something unspoken lingering in the air. "You know, sometimes unexpected detours lead to the best destinations."

Patricia met his gaze, her heart fluttering at the depth she saw there. "Perhaps they do."

As the storm continued to howl outside, the two sat in

companionable silence, the world around them fading into the background.

A crackling sound from the overhead speakers drew everyone's attention. The rest stop attendant's voice resonated through the room, carrying a sound of cautious optimism.

"Ladies and gentlemen, may I have your attention, please? Due to the severe weather conditions, both eastbound and westbound lanes of I-80 are closed until further notice. Authorities are working diligently to clear the roads, but for your safety, we advise remaining here until the storm passes. We understand this is an inconvenience, and we appreciate your patience. Please make yourselves comfortable; we have amenities available, and our staff is here to assist you."

A murmur spread among the travelers, a mix of frustration and resignation. Patricia studied Rudy, her earlier excitement about the trip now overshadowed by uncertainty.

Rudy offered a reassuring smile. "Looks like we'll be here for a bit. But hey, it's an adventure, right?"

Patricia managed a small laugh, appreciating his attempt to lighten the mood. "I suppose so. Not quite the journey we planned, though."

He leaned in, his voice gentle. "Sometimes the unplanned moments make the best memories."

As the snowstorm intensified, Patricia and Rudy found themselves among a growing number of travelers seeking refuge in the crowded rest stop. The atmosphere was tense, with families huddled together and individuals anxiously checking weather updates.

Amidst the murmur of concerned conversations, a young mother entered, cradling a crying infant and accompanied by a toddler clutching her coat. Her eyes scanned the room for a place to sit, but every seat was occupied. Noticing her predicament, Rudy immediately stood and approached her.

"Ma'am, please take my seat. You and your little ones need it more than I do."

The mother's face lit up with gratitude. "Thank you so much," she replied, settling into the seat with a sigh of relief. The toddler climbed onto her lap, and the baby began to calm in her arms.

Patricia observed the exchange; her heart warmed at Rudy's selflessness. His simple act of kindness spoke volumes about his character, revealing a depth of compassion she hadn't fully recognized before.

As the hours passed, the rest stop grew more crowded and tensions rose. A group of children, restless from the prolonged confinement, began to fidget and whine, their parents struggling to keep them entertained. Sensing an opportunity to help, Rudy approached the group with a playful grin.

"Who wants to hear a story?" His eyes twinkled with mischief.

The children's faces brightened, and they gathered around him eagerly. Rudy launched into an animated tale, complete with exaggerated voices and gestures, eliciting giggles and laughter from his young audience. The parents exchanged relieved glances, grateful for the brief respite.

Patricia watched Rudy with admiration, captivated by his ability to bring joy to others even in challenging circumstances. His playful nature and genuine care for those around him were qualities she found increasingly endearing.

Later, as the storm showed no signs of abating, an elderly couple seated nearby appeared distressed. The husband patted his pockets frantically, his face pale with worry. His wife leaned in, whispering something that deepened his frown.

Rudy noticed their unease and approached them kindly. "Is everything alright?" he inquired.

The elderly man looked up, his eyes bursting with concern.

"I've left my medication in the car," he explained. "I need it, but with this storm . . ."

Without hesitation, Rudy offered, "I can fetch it for you. Just point me to your vehicle."

The couple exchanged uncertain glances. "We couldn't ask you to do that," the woman began, but Rudy shook his head.

"It's no trouble at all," he assured them. "I'll be back shortly."

Braving the biting wind and swirling snow, Rudy ventured into the parking lot. Patricia watched anxiously as he navigated through the drifts, disappearing into the white haze. Minutes later, he returned, vaguely breathless but triumphant, holding a small bag.

"Here you go," he said, handing the medication to the grateful couple. "I hope this helps."

The elderly man clasped Rudy's hand, his eyes moist with gratitude. "Thank you, young man. You don't know what this means to us."

Patricia's heart swelled with pride and affection. Rudy's unwavering kindness revealed a side of him she hadn't fully appreciated before. His actions spoke of a man who put others before himself, embodying the very essence of compassion.

As the day wore on, the rest stop's resources began to dwindle. Noticing a family with young children who appeared hungry and had little to eat, Rudy approached Patricia with a thoughtful expression.

"We have some produce in the truck," he said quietly. "What do you say we share some with those in need?"

Patricia nodded, her admiration for Rudy growing with each passing moment. "That's a wonderful idea."

Together, they retrieved apples, carrots, and other items from the truck, distributing them among the stranded travelers. The simple act of sharing brought smiles and words of thanks, fostering a sense of community amid the storm.

Through these experiences, Patricia's perception of Rudy transformed. She saw not just a friend, but a man of integrity, generosity, and warmth. His actions during their unexpected detour illuminated the depth of his character, leaving an indelible impression on her heart.

As the storm continued to rage outside, Patricia found herself drawing closer to Rudy, and she realized that his quiet, selfless acts revealed the true nature of his heart.

THE FAINT GLOW of the morning seeped through the large-paned glass windows of the rest stop. Patricia stirred from her makeshift seat on the bench, the fabric of Rudy's jacket slipping from her shoulders as she sat up. Her heart softened as she realized he must have covered her during the night, his quiet thoughtfulness again evident.

She scanned the room, her observation settling on Rudy standing near the door with Hank. The two men seemed engrossed in a conversation, their faces framed by the pale light streaming in from the snow-covered parking lot. Moments later, Rudy stepped outside, shovel in hand, helping the rest stop attendant clear the snowy sidewalk.

Patricia grabbed his jacket and hurried toward the door, her shoes clicking against the tile floor. Stepping into the brisk morning air, she called out, "Rudy! Your jacket."

He turned, his breath visible in the frigid air, and his face lit up with a quick grin. "Why, thank you, Miss Wengerd," he teased, taking the jacket from her hands. His eyes twinkled as he added a wink.

She smiled despite herself, her cheeks flushing a little as he returned to shoveling with cheerful determination.

Back inside, Hank greeted her with a nod and a weathered smile. "Good news. They've reopened the interstate. If we leave now, we should hit Sugarcreek by mid-morning."

Patricia's heart skipped. The long night was over, and their impromptu adventure was coming to an end. A bittersweet feeling settled over her as she processed the news. Part of her longed to reach her destination and continue her plans, but another part regretted the end of this shared experience with Rudy.

When Rudy returned, he stomped his boots against the mat to shake off the clinging snow. His eyes swept the room until they landed on Patricia. The warmth in his eyes and the unrestrained joy in his smile sent a hint of something unfamiliar through her . . . an unexpected flutter.

"Well," Rudy said, his voice bright as he approached, "looks like we'll make it to Sugarcreek in plenty of time for the Harvest Dinner. Don't say I don't keep my promises."

Patricia laughed softly, appreciating his ability to lighten the moment. As they stepped back into the truck, the cold seat felt oddly welcoming after the night they'd shared. Rudy's voice filled the cab with a constant stream of jokes and observations, but Patricia's thoughts began to drift.

Her mind wandered to David, to the dinner that awaited her, and to the promise of the night she'd dreamed about for months. But now, the journey itself had already changed her.

She looked sideways at Rudy as the truck rumbled back onto the interstate, his profile framed by the fading snowstorm. The road to Sugarcreek stretched ahead, but Patricia couldn't shake the feeling that her heart was no longer entirely certain of its destination.

CHAPTER 7

*A*s Hank's truck came to a halt in front of her *schwester's* home, Patricia's heart fluttered with unease. The journey had been unexpectedly eventful, and now, standing on the cusp of her long-awaited reunion with David, she found her emotions in turmoil.

Rudy stepped out of the truck and turned to her, his eyes warm and earnest. "I've decided to visit my cousins here in Sugarcreek for a couple of days and stay through Thanksgiving. Since I'm in town, would you like me to pick you up later for the Harvest Dinner? I'm planning to attend myself."

His offer, though considerate, sent a ripple of anxiety through her. The prospect of Rudy's presence at the dinner, where she hoped to reconnect with David, complicated her already tangled feelings. She forced a smile, striving to keep her voice steady.

"Oh . . . that's thoughtful of you, but I can only imagine you're tired after sleeping on the floor last night." She paused for a moment, trying to find a tactful way of declining his offer. "I can find my own way."

Rudy's forehead creased, a hint of disappointment flickering in his eyes. "It's no trouble at all. I'm sure my uncle would have a buggy I could borrow. I'd be happy to accompany you."

Patricia's mind raced, her earlier resolve wavering under the weight of his sincerity. The memory of their shared moments during the storm lingered, blurring the lines between friendship and something deeper. She took a stable breath, her thoughts a whirlwind of confusion.

"I appreciate it, truly. But I think it's best if I go alone tonight."

He studied her momentarily, then nodded. "Alright, if that's what you want."

As she stepped past him and approached her *schwester's* porch, her heart ached with the burden of unspoken emotions. The prospect of seeing David, once a source of joy, now overshadowed by the unexpected bond she had formed with Rudy.

Inside the farmhouse, the familiar embrace of the family did little to quell her inner turmoil. As she prepared for the evening, her feelings remained a tangled web of anticipation and uncertainty, the faces of two men intertwining in her mind.

As RUDY WATCHED Patricia walk toward her *schwester's haus*, a sense of disappointment settled over him. He had hoped she would accept his offer, but her polite refusal left him questioning her reasons. Determined not to dwell on it, he reminded himself of his own plans.

"Hank, after we unload the produce, could you drop me off at my cousins' place? I've decided to stay in Sugarcreek through Thanksgiving."

Hank nodded. "Sure thing. Just give me the address."

As they drove toward the auction house, Rudy's focus drifted back to Patricia. Her hesitation and the subtle nervousness in her demeanor hinted at something more than just a casual visit. A realization struck him. He was sure she hoped to see someone special at the dinner.

The idea gnawed at him, stirring an unexpected pang of jealousy. He had always valued Patricia's friendship, but the prospect of her affection being directed toward another man unsettled him. Determined to confront his feelings, Rudy decided to attend anyway, not just out of curiosity but to understand his own heart.

After delivering the produce, Hank navigated the truck through the quaint streets of Sugarcreek, finally stopping in front of a charming farmhouse. Rudy's cousins welcomed him with open arms, their home brimming with the enticing aroma of home-cooked meals.

As the day wore on, Rudy found himself distracted, his mind continually returning to Patricia. As he prepared for the event, Rudy took a moment to steady himself. He knew that attending the dinner might reveal truths he wasn't entirely ready to face, but he also understood that avoiding them would only prolong his uncertainty.

As Patricia approached the lantern-lit barn, the warmth of the roaring bonfire outside evoked memories of the previous year's dinner. She recalled standing by the fire with David, their conversation light and etched with promise. A soft smile touched her lips at the recollection.

Stepping inside, she was enveloped by the comforting aromas of homemade dishes: freshly baked bread, savory meats, and sweet desserts filling the air. The barn was adorned with simple decorations: plastic tablecloths and modest arrangements of pumpkins and gourds on the tables, reminiscent of the displays at the Farmstand, where she had spent so much time with Rudy over the past few months.

Navigating through the mingling guests, her heart raced with anticipation. She bypassed the buffet table laden with traditional Amish fare, her appetite overshadowed by the fluttering nerves in her stomach. Spotting the hay bales where she and David had sat the year before, she made her way over and settled on one, her eyes scanning the entrance for any sign of him.

As she waited, the lively hum of conversations filled the barn, creating a festive atmosphere. Patricia's thoughts drifted to the adventures she envisioned sharing with David. His adventurous spirit had always intrigued her, and she imagined the two of them exploring new places, perhaps visiting markets in nearby towns or taking long buggy rides through the countryside. She pictured them working side by side, building a life jam-packed with shared experiences and unexpected adventures.

The prospect of such a future brought a hopeful smile to her face. She envisioned attending community events together, hosting gatherings in their own home, and raising a family grounded in the values they both cherished. The possibilities seemed endless, each one more exciting than the last, with the possibilities of their shared journeys.

Yet as the minutes ticked by and David remained absent, a seed of doubt began to sprout. She couldn't help but wonder if her dreams were just that . . . dreams. But she quickly pushed the thought aside, choosing instead to focus on the positive memories and the potential for a shared future. Taking a deep breath, she straightened her posture and smoothed her dress. She was determined to make the most of the evening, regardless of what it might bring.

As the lively hum of conversations filled the barn, Patricia's heart leaped when she saw David step through the doorway. His confident presence commanded the room as he paused just inside, his look scanning the crowd as though searching for someone. Her breath caught in her throat, and for a moment, the entire barn seemed to fade away.

Rising slowly from her seat on the hay bale, she smoothed her light brown dress, confident the color highlighted her eyes. She stood tall, silently willing his eyes to find hers. The faint smile that tugged at her lips masked the wild thrum of her heart. As he moved purposefully into the room, her anticipation soared, and she imagined his familiar warmth as he reached her side.

But his stare didn't land on her. Instead, it drifted past her, fixated on something or someone just beyond her.

Patricia's chest tightened, a wave of doubt crashing against the shore of her confidence. She stepped forward, her movement deliberate yet hesitant, positioning herself directly in his path. Surely, he would see her now.

"David," she said softly, her voice shuddering.

He stopped, his expression politely surprised. For a fleeting moment, his eyes met hers, and she held her breath, waiting for recognition to light his features. But instead, his brow furrowed, and a flicker of confusion passed across his face.

"Oh, uh . . ." David began, his voice trailing off as he searched for her name. Patricia's stomach plummeted as she realized he didn't remember her.

"Patricia," she offered quietly, her voice barely audible over the clamor of the barn.

"Right. Patricia," he said with a quick, apologetic smile, but his attention wavered, his eyes darting over her shoulder. Before she could respond, a young woman with radiant features approached, her presence commanding David's immediate attention. The air between them seemed to hum with unspoken connection, their eyes locking in a way that spoke volumes. "There you are," the woman said warmly, her voice effortlessly claiming his focus.

Patricia stepped back instinctively, the distance between them suddenly feeling insurmountable.

David turned to the woman with an ease that cut through Patricia's heart. "Oh, Sarah, this is . . . uh . . . this is Patricia," he said, stumbling over her name as though he'd just pieced it together.

Sarah's smile widened, her eyes glimmering with familiarity and comfort as she took a quick look at David and then her. It was clear in that instant that whatever connection Patricia had once shared with David had been eclipsed by something far more significant.

The barn seemed to tilt around her, the cheerful buzz of conversation a cruel contrast to the crushing weight at the center of her being. Heat rose to her cheeks, her hopes and dreams unraveling like threads pulled loose from a cherished quilt.

"Excuse me," Patricia murmured, her voice trembling as she turned away, desperate to escape the pitying glance Sarah offered her and the awkward smile David forced.

As she moved toward the door, the joyful energy of the dinner felt like a mocking reminder of her misplaced fantasies. The man she had built dreams around for nearly a year hadn't just forgotten her; he'd replaced her.

Her heart fractured, Patricia fled into the cool night air, the sting of rejection searing hotter than the cold wind against her cheeks.

RUDY STOOD near the back of the barn, scanning the room until his eyes settled on Patricia by the hay bales. Her posture was tense, and her fingers fidgeted with the hem of her dress . . . a telltale sign of her nervousness. Following her stare, he saw a man enter. Her eyes landed and stayed glued to the stranger.

Patricia stepped forward as the man moved through the crowd, her face lighting up with a hopeful smile. But when the man's attention shifted past her to another woman approaching, Patricia's shoulders slumped and her smile faltered. She took a step back, her hands clasped together tightly, knuckles white . . . a clear indication of her distress.

Rudy couldn't hear their conversation, but the scene unfolding spoke volumes. Patricia's downcast eyes and the way she hugged herself slightly were signs he recognized all too well. When she turned abruptly and made her way toward the exit, her movements were hurried, almost as if she were fleeing.

Concerned, Rudy waited only a moment before following her outside, determined to offer the support he knew she needed.

PATRICIA FLED THE BARN, the festive sounds fading behind her as she stumbled into the cold night. Snowflakes drifted lightly from the darkened sky, settling on her shoulders and mingling with the hot tears streaming down her cheeks. Her breath came in ragged gasps, each exhale visible in the frigid air.

Reaching the side of the barn, she rested heavily against the weathered wood, her stomach churning with a nauseating mix of embarrassment and heartbreak. The image of David's puzzled expression and Sarah's sympathetic smile replayed in her mind, each recollection twisting the knife deeper into her wounded pride.

An uncontrollable sob escaped her lips, and she pressed a trembling hand to her mouth as if to stifle the torrent of emotions threatening to overwhelm her. The cold seeped through her thin dress, but the chill was nothing compared to the icy realization that her dreams of rekindling a romance with David had been nothing more than a silly schoolgirl's imagination.

She had envisioned this evening so differently, imagining a joyous reunion, shared laughter, and perhaps the spark of renewed affection. Instead, she was confronted with the harsh truth: David had moved on, and she was left clinging to memories that no longer held meaning.

As the snow continued to fall, Patricia wrapped her arms around herself, seeking comfort in her own embrace. The festive atmosphere seemed a world away, replaced by the silent, snowy landscape that mirrored the desolation in her heart.

Patricia wiped her tears and took a moment to gather herself, the cold air filling her lungs and bringing a semblance of clarity. She moved toward the bonfire, its flames dancing and crackling against the darkness. Finding an empty log, she sat down, the heat from the fire seeping through her chilled skin.

As she stared into the flickering flames, her thoughts began to untangle. The initial sting of David's indifference gave way to reflection. She realized that her feelings for him had been more about yearning for adventure and change than genuine affection. David had represented a departure from her sure and steady routine with Albert to a symbol of excitement and new experiences.

Reflecting on their past interactions, Patricia recognized that she had idealized David, focusing on the possibilities he embodied rather than the reality of their connection. Her infatuation had been a projection of her own desires for something beyond the familiar confines of her daily life and the future laid out for her.

The glow of the fire comforted her as she acknowledged

this truth. Her heartache began to recede, replaced by a sense of understanding. She had been chasing an illusion, not a person. The adventure she sought wasn't tied to David; it was a journey she needed to embark on herself.

As fresh snow continued to fall quietly around her, Patricia felt a weight lift from her shoulders. Crossing her legs and resting her elbow on her knee, she massaged her temples with her hand as she closed her eyes. The gentle heat of the flames contrasted with the chill in her heart, and as she sought solace, a vivid dream resurfaced, a man standing across a room, his hand extended toward her. This time, the man's face came into sharp focus. Startled, she opened her eyes, and there he was, sitting across from her, his face etched with concern and something deeper, something that looked like love . . . it was Rudy.

"Patricia," Rudy's voice was gentle, cutting through the crackling of the fire. "Are you alright?"

She blinked, the remnants of her tears glistening in the firelight. The realization of Rudy's unwavering presence washed over her, bringing a warmth that the bonfire couldn't provide.

"I . . . I will be," she replied, her voice trembling but sincere.

Rudy moved to a log next to her.

In that moment, Patricia understood that the adventure she had longed for wasn't about distant dreams or unfulfilled fantasies. It was about the genuine connection and steadfast support that had been beside her all along.

Patricia felt a profound sense of peace in the shared silence with Rudy at that moment. His presence required no explanations; he yearned only to be close to her, offering unwavering support and understanding . . . just like he always had.

EPILOGUE

Willow Springs a Year Later

On Thanksgiving Day, Patricia stepped onto Rudy's family's front porch, clutching her famous Paper Bag Apple Pie. The aroma of roasted turkey and baked goods wafted through the crisp autumn air, mingling with the distant sounds of family chatter and children's laughter. She smoothed her dress nervously, her heart pounding with anticipation. They had kept their relationship a secret for nearly a year, and today was the day she and Rudy would share their news with his family.

Summoning her courage, she knocked on the sturdy wooden door. Moments later, it creaked open to reveal Rudy, his eyes widening in surprise and delight.

"Patricia," he exclaimed, a warm smile spreading across his face.

She returned his smile, holding up the pie. "I thought I'd contribute."

Rudy stepped aside, gesturing for her to enter. "Please, come in. Everyone will be thrilled to see you."

As she crossed the threshold, the cozy interior enveloped her. The dining table was laden with various dishes: mashed potatoes, stuffing, cranberry sauce, all prepared with love and care. Family members bustled about, setting places and sharing laughter.

Rudy led her to the kitchen, where his *mamm* was arranging a platter of rolls. "*Mamm*, look who's here," he announced.

His mother turned, her eyes lighting up. "Patricia! What a lovely surprise."

Patricia offered the pie. "I hope this can find a place on your table."

The older woman accepted it with a grateful nod. "*Denki.* It's wonderful to have you join us."

As the family gathered around the table, Rudy pulled out a chair beside him for Patricia. She took her seat, feeling a sense of belonging she hadn't anticipated. The meal commenced with a silent prayer, and soon, the room was filled with the clatter of utensils and the murmur of contented conversation.

Throughout the dinner, Rudy engaged her in lighthearted banter, his presence a comforting anchor amid the unfamiliar setting. He introduced her to his relatives, sharing anecdotes that elicited both laughter and blushes. With each passing moment, Patricia's initial nervousness melted away, replaced by a warm camaraderie.

After the meal, Rudy guided Patricia to a quiet corner as the family moved to the living room for coffee and desserts. "Are you ready?" he asked softly, his eyes reflecting sincerity.

She met his stare, her heart swelling with a newfound affection. "*Jah.*"

He reached out, squeezing her hand for only a second. "Not too much longer, and we may host Thanksgiving dinners of our own."

"I'd like that very much," she whispered.

He reached for her hand and gently pulled her toward the front room to share their news.

As the evening unfolded, filled with stories, laughter, and the warmth of family, Patricia felt a profound sense of belonging. The dreams she once harbored had transformed into a beautiful reality with Rudy by her side.

In a moment of quiet reflection, she closed her eyes and offered a silent prayer, thanking *Gott* for the unanswered prayers that had gently redirected her path. She acknowledged His wisdom in guiding her toward a destiny more fulfilling than she had envisioned. Grateful for His divine guidance, Patricia resolved to trust in His plan and follow His lead in all aspects of her life.

And so, amidst the Thanksgiving celebration, embraced by Rudy's family and the promise of new beginnings, Patricia and Rudy's story truly began.

PAPER BAG APPLE PIE

Filling

6 c. coarsely peeled and sliced apples
1/2 c. sugar
1/2 tsp. nutmeg
2 tbsps. flour
2 tbsps. lemon juice

In a large bowl, combine the apples, sugar, flour, nutmeg, and lemon juice. Mix well to coat the apples evenly. Transfer the apple mixture into an unbaked pie shell and pat down evenly.

Topping

1/2 c. butter
    1/2 c. flour
    1/2 c. brown sugar

Using a pastry blender, cut the butter into the flour and brown sugar until the mixture resembles pea-sized crumbs. Sprinkle

PAPER BAG APPLE PIE

the topping evenly over the apples and gently press it around the edges.

Baking

Slide the pie into a brown paper bag and fold the ends under the pie to seal. Place the bagged pie on a cookie sheet for easy handling. Bake at 425°F for 50 minutes.

Notes

• The paper bag helps prevent a scorched rim, ensures evenly baked apples, and avoids spills in the oven.
• Always monitor the pie carefully, as oven temperatures may vary.

ABOUT THE AUTHOR

Tracy Fredrychowski is a country girl at heart—an author, homesteader, and passionate advocate for simple living. Raised in Northwest Pennsylvania, she grew up immersed in the rhythms of Amish Country, where the clip-clop of horse-drawn buggies echoed outside her childhood window each morning.

Her deep connection to Amish life is both personal and profound. A tragic event involving an Amish murder left a lasting impact on her, shaping the themes of faith, forgiveness, and community that flow through her writing. Today, she channels that history into heartfelt Amish fiction rooted in authenticity and respect.

Whether tending her homestead or crafting stories, Tracy remains devoted to celebrating the beauty of a simpler, more intentional way of life.

You can read more about her and the stories she crafts at https://tracyfredrychowski.com

LETTERS OF GRATITUDE

RACHEL J. GOOD

CHAPTER 1

*E*arly morning light crept across the distant mountains and painted the weathered boards of the one-room schoolhouse in pale gold as Ruby Beiler, her breath visible in the November air, stepped onto the porch to greet the scholars. Inside, twenty-eight carefully sharpened pencils lay beside twenty-eight sheets of white paper—tools for the day's special assignment. At twenty-eight years old herself, Rebecca noticed the coincidence of numbers. Her recent birthday had once again reinforced her status as an *alt maedel*, reminding her that expectations, like autumn leaves, eventually fall away. Perhaps the time had come to give up on her dreams and accept that she'd always remain a teacher rather than a wife or mother.

She loved the children she taught. For now, that had to be enough. With a wistful smile, she smoothed her blue dress and apron, adjusted her *kapp*, and bowed her head.

Lord, you know the yearnings of my heart, but please help me to accept Your will for my life. I trust You to show me how to lead each scholar down the path You have chosen.

At the rattle of pony carts, zipping scooters, and chattering children, Ruby lifted her head.

The air filled with *gude mariye*s as the children streamed toward her, some eager to start their day, others dragging their feet. Ruby greeted each one, and they filed into the *schulhaus.* As usual, David Fisher, his face sullen, lagged far behind the others.

For his benefit, Ruby raised her voice. "Today we'll be starting with a special Thanksgiving assignment. Please do not touch the items on your desk."

None of the other scholars would do so, but David most likely would poke holes in his paper and snap off his pencil point before the day started.

Following morning prayer, Scripture reading, and hymn singing, Ruby motioned to the papers on every desk. "Who can tell me something they're grateful for?" Her voice carried to the back of the room, where David Fisher was trying to slip a fake grasshopper onto Sarah Zook's shoulder.

"David?" Ruby's sharp tone arrested David's hand in midair. "What are you thankful for?"

"I, um…" He dropped the rubber grasshopper, which bounced a few feet and landed beside Sarah.

Sarah shrieked and jumped from her seat.

David grinned, and most of the class giggled. Sarah, a nervous child, was easily startled, and David usually took full advantage of it.

Ruby gritted her teeth. She tried not to be charmed by David's innocent expression or his big brown eyes, so like his *onkel* Elijah's. David's eyes begged for love and understanding, unlike Elijah's, which remained shuttered and sorrow-filled since his wife's death.

Time after time, David melted Ruby's heart, and she struggled to scold him, even when he sorely needed it. He'd lost his parents in the same accident that had claimed Elijah's wife. Living with his sorrowing widowed *onkel* must be hard on such a lively child. But if Ruby let David get away with his pranks, the other scholars would follow his lead, and her classroom would dissolve into chaos.

Steeling herself against David's pleading eyes, Ruby kept her voice and expression stern. "Pick up the bug, and bring it to my desk. Then you will apologize to Sarah, and at recess today, you will write a list of twelve things you can do to help her and the other scholars."

She waited until David had obeyed and returned to his seat. "Now, back to my question. This November, we're going to focus on gratitude. Who can tell me something they're thankful for?"

Hands rose around the room, and she called on several scholars who always gave the right answers.

"My *mamm*." "My new baby *bruder*." "God's love." "Good food to eat."

"You, Teacher Ruby." Martha King, who longed to be teacher's pet, beamed at Ruby.

Ruby swallowed back a sigh. She hadn't started this project to gain praise for herself. To compensate, she called on one of the other troublemakers in class.

Sam Miller shot her a cheeky smile. "I'm thankful for David, who always makes me laugh."

Surprised and touched, David stared at Sam, making Ruby's heart ache. Most likely, the poor boy never heard anything good about himself. He spent more time getting into trouble in school, and his taciturn *onkel* wasn't likely to give David any encouragement.

Ruby didn't want David to become prideful, but she made a mental note to say more positive things to him. And she'd do the project she'd planned not only for people in the community but also for each of her scholars.

She wrote on the board, "*In every thing give thanks: for this is the will of God in Christ Jesus concerning you.* 1 Thessalonians 5:18." Then she clapped her hands to get everyone's attention.

"Every morning this month before we begin our lessons, we're going to write a letter of gratitude to someone we're thankful for. I want you all to practice your best letter-writing and handwriting skills."

Ruby handed envelopes to Sarah to pass out. Sarah ducked her head and gave Ruby a shy smile. The young girl seemed pleased to have the responsibility until she neared David's desk. Anna, a responsible ten-year-old with eight younger siblings, took her envelope, then held out a hand for David's.

"I can put it on his desk," Anna offered.

With grateful eyes, Sarah handed over the envelope, and Ruby sighed with relief. She'd made an excellent choice in seating Anna beside David.

"Hey, that's not fair," David burst out. "Anna got two envelopes, and I didn't get any."

"Here you go." Anna calmly set an envelope on David's desk.

David managed a grudging *danke*, but his pout revealed he'd been hoping to tease Sarah. Ruby thanked the good Lord those plans had been foiled.

After they all had their supplies, she gave her final instructions. "These letters will be anonymous. Who knows what that means?"

As usual, Martha King's hand shot into the air first. "It means nobody will know who wrote them."

Ruby tried not to grimace at Martha's *know-it-all* tone. "That's right. I don't want you to sign the letters with your names."

"So we're like spies?" David's face lit with delight.

Where had he learned about spies? Judging from the sinister edge to his words, it hadn't been from Bible stories.

Ruby continued, "When you're done, address the envelopes and put them in this basket. At the end of the day, each of you will take a few envelopes for people who live near you. Try to

248

sneak them into people's mailboxes without letting them see you."

David shivered with excitement. "Ooo, we really are like spies. This'll be fun."

In keeping with her plan, Ruby beamed at him. "I'm so glad you like this letter-writing idea."

A sullen expression settled on David's face. "I don't want to write letters." He crossed his arms. "I'll just do the sneaking part."

"Often to get to the fun part, we have to do things we don't really like." She kept her tone light. "I'm sure you'll do just as well at writing letters as you will at sneaking them into mailboxes."

He didn't look like he agreed, but he bent his head over his paper and chewed on his pencil.

Martha waved her hand frantically, her face filled with concern. "Do we have to do them for a different person every day?" When Ruby nodded, Martha groaned. "I can't think of thirty different people."

"It'll only be twenty-one because some November days are weekends," Sarah pointed out.

"Smarty-pants," David whispered, loud enough for the whole room to hear.

And Martha glared, not liking to be shown up by a younger girl.

Ruby frowned at both of them. "Let's get to work."

"What if I can't think of anyone?" a timid voice asked.

"Start with your family members and relatives, your friends, people at church, people in the community. . ."

David's head popped up. "*Englischers?*"

"Of course. We can thank everyone. You might want to think about shopkeepers, neighbors, or others who have helped you. Many times, we don't think about the people who do things behind the scenes like—"

"Firefighters." David's face lit with excitement. "That's who I'll write to."

"Good idea." Ruby smiled, and an idea struck her. "Other people help us in ways we don't even realize. Like Elijah Fisher, our next-door neighbor, who owns the land this school is on."

"My *onkel*?" David sat up a little straighter.

"*Jah*, and your *dawdi* Simon. He and many other grandparents built this school forty years ago."

"He did?" David gazed around him in wonder. "My family gave the land for this school?" At Ruby's nod, he glared around at his classmates. "Then you all better thank me for that."

One of the older boys snickered. "You mean blame you for it?"

"That's enough." Ruby rubbed her temples, wondering how her gratitude project had gone so far off track. "Spend the next twenty minutes writing. If you finish before that, do your silent work." She gestured to the blackboard where she'd listed that day's assignments for each group.

Then she settled at her desk to write her own letter of gratitude.

CHAPTER 2

A worried frown creasing his brow, Elijah Fisher hurried to the mailbox. One of his *Englisch* neighbors had stopped by to complain that David had egged their house last night. His nephew must have slipped out after he'd been sent to bed early for disrespect.

Elijah had no idea how to handle a rebellious ten-year-old, a problem that would only grow worse as David became a teen. Elijah dreaded thinking of all the trouble his nephew would get into during *Rumschpringa*.

Opening the mailbox, Elijah stared at the handwritten letters among the bills. Four of them bore childish writing. Lovely feminine script adorned the other envelope. The beauty of it took his breath away as longing flooded through him. He and his wife had written letters to each other while they were courting. How his spirits had lifted when he used to open the mailbox to find a precious missive. Now his heart clenched as pain and sorrow washed over him. Why had God taken her away from him? Along with his beloved sister and brother-in-law? And his unborn child?

Before the accident, he'd been happy in his faith, but the

past three years had been nothing but heartache. Every morning when he woke, the first question on his lips was *Why, God, why?*

He doubted he'd ever be free of his fury at the unfairness of it. And, as hard as he tried, he could barely struggle out of the quicksand of grief holding him prisoner to care for David properly, who seemed more of a trial every single day. David, who needed his parents' care and love. A love Elijah had no capacity to give. All of that had died the day he buried his beloved wife and precious unborn child.

Elijah couldn't bear to look at the loopy letters of his name, sent by a woman. He had no desire to have anything to do with women. Never again would he give his heart, only to lose the one he loved.

He tossed the mail onto the kitchen counter, being sure to turn the worst one upside down. Part of him wanted to toss them all in the trash, but if someone had gone to the trouble of writing them, he should at least be courteous enough to open them and respond, if necessary.

A terrible thought struck him. What if they were other complaints about David? Reports of more vandalism? Of him bullying other children? Why else would children and women write him letters?

He should open them now, but the day was too bleak, and he had too many woodworking projects to complete before Christmas. He'd do it later.

But the whole time he worked, his mind strayed to those envelopes. He should open them before David came home from school because Elijah might need to add more infractions to his planned lecture about egging the neighbor's house. The messages might be five more potential problems to handle.

Since his wife died, Elijah kept to himself and avoided interactions with neighbors and the community. He took orders for his woodworking business and attended church, but he stayed away from all social gatherings. David's misbehavior, though, had forced him into frequent confrontations with others. Not arguments really, because Elijah stayed silent while others ranted on about his nephew. After listening, Elijah gave his usual apology and promised to speak to David about it. For all the good it did. Scolding and punishing David didn't work. If Elijah set a new rule, David found loopholes and weaseled his way around the restriction. Or outright defied it.

The wall clock ticked its way to school dismissal time. Elijah hurried to organize his woodworking shop. When he finished, he put away his tools, locked the metal cabinet, and pocketed the key. He'd made the mistake of leaving his tools out once, and David had rampaged through the workshop, gouging chunks out of all the projects.

It had taken Elijah months to repair or replace everything. Though he'd earned a reputation of not doing timely work, he'd never told anyone why their orders were late. That disaster left him scrambling for customers and struggling to pay bills and put food on the table. After steadily meeting all the deadlines for more than a year, he'd begun erasing the community's negative opinion, and he now earned enough to cover the bills.

Like his mother had done when he was young, Elijah set out cookies and milk for David every day after school. Only these cookies came from a package rather than the oven. As much as Elijah regretted it, he'd barely learned to cook a few simple meals. Baking was not something he did often, except for helping his wife make pies to sell at the Green Valley Farmer's Market. How he missed baking them together.

His gaze strayed to the overgrown pumpkin patch outside the window, untended for the past three years. Knee-high weeds had taken over the area in many places. Bits of orange peeked through in spots. Elijah turned away. Much like his faith, the abandoned patch was weed-choked and neglected.

David burst through the door like a whirlwind and tossed his lunch container onto the kitchen counter where it clanged against an unwashed pot, giving Elijah an idea. Make David wash dishes for egging. Then his nephew should write an apology letter, and Elijah would march him across the street to clean off the lady's house.

HIS NEPHEW PLOPPED into a chair at the kitchen table and reached for some cookies.

"Mrs. Keller stopped by the woodshop this morning." Elijah plunked each word down like a stone in a *you'd-better-pay-attention* tone.

David's hand stopped in midair. A second later, he feigned innocence, grabbed three cookies, and stuffed one into his mouth. "What'd she want?" he mumbled around it. Cookie crumbs sprayed everywhere.

"I think you know." When his nephew started to protest, Elijah held up a hand. "Best not add lying to your offenses." He tossed a dishrag to David, who caught it and pretended to be interested in wiping up the crumbs.

"Mrs. Keller is—"

"Stop right there before you get yourself in more trouble than you already are."

With a mutinous expression, David crossed his arms, but he kept silent.

Elijah motioned to the sink. "I had to rush out to drop off customer orders this morning, so I didn't wash the breakfast dishes." He hadn't even soaked them, leaving the skillet with burned-on scrambled eggs, the pan with congealed bacon grease, and the plates crusted. Everything needed major scrubbing.

Unconcerned, David reached for another cookie, but Elijah

closed the bag and put it away. Then he stood in front of David to get his full attention.

"For egging Mrs. Keller's house—"

"Who said I did that?"

"Mrs. Keller saw you."

"She did not."

Elijah bent over and splayed his fingers on the table so he and David were eye to eye. "Are you calling her a liar?"

David avoided Elijah's gaze.

"As I was saying . . . for egging her house, you will clean our own egg-encrusted dishes."

David expelled a slow breath as if he'd gotten off easy.

"After that, you will write an apology letter—"

A loud groan interrupted Elijah. "Teacher Ruby already made me write a letter today."

"Don't tell me you had to apologize for something else."

"*Neh*, it was only a dumb school lesson."

"*Gut*, then you know how to write one. After that, you'll give it to Mrs. Keller and tell her you're sorry."

"If I say I'm sorry, why do I hafta write a letter?"

"To show you're sincere."

David's mouth puckered. "I won't mean it neither time."

"Well, perhaps scrubbing all the egg off her siding will make you sorry you did it."

"What?" David screeched.

"It's not fair for Mrs. Keller to have to clean up a mess you made. Now get started on the dishes. You'll need to scrape the bacon grease into here first." Elijah pulled out a container and lifted off the lid. "And do the skillets last."

While David gulped down his milk, Elijah filled the sink with sudsy water and slipped the blue stoneware under the froth. Each time he stood there, the clouded kitchen window framing the ragged pumpkin patch accused him of sloth. If Sarah had been here, the windows would be sparkling and the

RACHEL J. GOOD

pumpkin patch perfect. Never would the breakfast dishes sit until suppertime, and a mouthwatering meal would be simmering on the stove. How Elijah missed his beloved wife. And the loss of her daily presence and the homey touches she'd brought to his life pierced him each and every day.

He clenched and unclenched his fists as slow-burning anger smoldered in his gut. Why had she and their unborn baby been taken from him? Elijah struggled to tamp down the feelings roiling within. Instead, he focused his attention on David.

"Finish these dishes." Elijah kept his voice low and firm. "Then you'll write that apology to Mrs. Keller. And once the ink's dry, we'll hurry over there. You'll scrub every bit of egg off her siding before bedtime."

David's dark curls bobbed in defiance. "I don't want to."

"You did the damage." Elijah turned away so the boy couldn't see his warring emotions. "This is your chance to make it right."

Grumbling, David lifted a plate from the water. The first splash drenched his sleeves. Water dribbled onto the floor.

"If you aren't more careful, you'll need to mop the floor as well." Elijah wished he didn't nag over every little thing, but David seemed to irritate him purposely.

His nephew huffed, but stopped sloshing. After he finished the plates and reached for the skillets, he spotted the envelopes, still scattered on the counter nearby. He reached for the top one, just as Elijah's hand closed around it.

"Those aren't for you."

"But you haven't opened them."

"I will when I have more time to read them." And deal with their contents.

Once the dishes had been dried and put away, Elijah settled into a chair across from David, whose moans sounded as if a horse were trampling on his foot. Elijah could barely concentrate on the *Die Botschaft* article he was reading. It

256

wondered him if Teacher Ruby had to put up with such behavior every time David did his school assignments. Finally, David's pencil clattered to the tabletop, and the groans stopped.

As David folded the paper in half, Elijah held out a hand. "Let me see what you've written."

David snatched up the letter and pressed it to his chest.

"The letter," Elijah insisted.

"Have to fix something first." David unfolded it and scribbled hard. With a defiant look, he passed it across the table.

Elijah studied it. *I'm sorry your*— Two blackened patches almost covered the words *stupid old*. They were followed by *house got egged*.

He frowned. These were the words his nephew had agonized over? "You haven't taken responsibility. Pencil please."

Underneath David's scrawled sentence, Elijah printed, *I'm so sorry I egged your house yesterday. I promise not to do it again.* He pushed it over to his nephew. "Get a clean sheet of paper and write something like what I have there. Without complaint this time."

David glared, but he obeyed.

When at last the word had been written and checked, they set off across the street with a bucket of soapy water and an assortment of brushes and rags. As they approached, Mrs. Keller stepped outside onto the porch, arms folded, expression unreadable behind her rimless spectacles. David stole a glance and quickly looked away, his cheeks reddening.

Elijah cleared his throat. "David has something he'd like to say."

David stared at the siding, one hand gripping the brushes so tightly his knuckles turned white. His other fingers crinkled the envelope. He thrust it out.

"I'm sorry." His words sounded insincere, and he didn't meet Mrs. Keller's eyes.

Elijah wasn't quite sure, but he thought David added under his breath, *Sorry I have to clean it up.*

Mrs. Keller held the letter in two fingers and frowned as if trying to make out the mumbled words.

To distract her, Elijah gestured toward the brushes and bucket. "David will clean it all up for you."

She didn't respond right away. The breeze tickled the hem of her apron as she studied him. Then, slowly, her lips curved into the faintest smile. "I appreciate your apology, David. And your elbow grease."

David blinked. "My what?"

"It means hard work," Elijah explained. "You're doing the right thing."

"Just be sure you don't damage the siding."

David curled up his nose at the dried streaks of egg trailing down the wall in brittle ribbons, crusted and sour-smelling.

Elijah handed David the bucket of warm soapy water and pointed to the soft-bristled brush. "Start with that. Don't scrub too hard."

David muttered something, but he dropped to his knees and dipped the brush in the suds. Elijah watched for a while to be sure his nephew was doing it correctly, then he picked up a soft rag and went over the spots David had cleaned to remove the last bits. The two of them formed a silent rhythm—scrub, rinse, wipe, repeat. David shot Elijah a grateful glance, then quickly looked away.

When the last streak was gone, Mrs. Keller stepped outside. "I must say, you're a hard worker." She inspected the siding more closely. "And a thorough one too." Then she handed David a ginger cookie wrapped in wax paper. "If you ever want to make a little money, I have some jobs you could do around here."

David held the cookie in stunned silence. "You'd trust me?"

She studied him with shrewd eyes. "Taking responsibility for a mistake and fixing it shows you're trustworthy."

David hung his head. "My *onkel* made me do it."

"But you did the work."

"I did, didn't I?" He broke into a crooked grin. "*Danke.*" He nodded toward the cookie, but Elijah realized the thanks was for more than the small treat.

They walked home together, the scent of ginger accompanying them—and Elijah prayed Mrs. Keller had planted the first seeds of change in David's heart.

CHAPTER 3

*T*ired and weary, Ruby dragged home at the end of the school day. Normally, she enjoyed teaching, but today David had tested her patience all day long. He'd irritated the good scholars and riled up the mischievous ones. She had to find a way to channel all that energy into productivity.

As she neared her house, Ruby's steps slowed. A fancy *Englisch* car stood in their driveway. *Mrs. Vandenberg?* Everyone in the surrounding Lancaster County communities knew that Bentley belonged to the wealthy elderly woman who owned the Green Valley Farmers Market and ran many charitable projects in town.

Ruby's spirits rose. Mrs. Vandenberg always brought good news and happiness wherever she went.

The minute Ruby opened the door, the ninety-three-year-old woman hobbled across the room, her cane tapping on the polished hardwood floor. "Just the person I wanted to speak to. I have a favor to ask you."

"Of course. It's *gut* to see you, Mrs. Vandenberg."

"And it's always delightful to see your cheery face, Ruby."

The tiny, birdlike woman clasped a notebook. She opened it to a page marked *Ruby*.

Ruby strained to read the list of bullet points under her name, but Mrs. Vandenberg clasped it to her chest.

"Why don't we sit, dear?" Mrs. Vandenberg grasped a nearby chair arm and lowered herself to the seat on shaky legs.

After Ruby sat on a nearby rocker, Mrs. Vandenberg spread the notebook in her lap. "I'm planning a Thanksgiving dinner at my STAR center, so I'm asking for donations. Can I put you down for two dozen pumpkin pies?"

Ruby gasped. "I, um. . ."

"Don't worry, dear. All the ingredients will be provided. Except for the pumpkins, that is."

"It's not that. I'm happy to bake cakes or cookies. I can make lemon bars and sticky buns. But pies? Ask my family. They'll tell you I've never made a decent one in my life."

Mrs. Vandenberg tapped her pen against her notebook and shook her head. "I've already had commitments for all the other desserts. All I need is pumpkin pie."

Ruby's fingers pleated wrinkles in her apron. How could she refuse this request? The STAR center fed hungry inner-city children and their families, got gang members off the streets, and helped the homeless. No way could she say *neh*.

When she glanced up, she met Mrs. Vandenberg's keen gaze. "Perhaps one of my sisters can make them?"

"Or maybe you should trust God for help," Mrs. Vandenberg offered, her voice gentle. "I've given each of your sisters a task already."

Ask *Gott* for help? Wouldn't it make more sense to find someone who already baked good pumpkin pies?

"You don't believe God helps with small things as well as large ones?"

"Of course He does."

"Wonderful. I'm glad that's settled." Mrs. Vandenberg made a checkmark on her list. "Thank you."

Dazed, Ruby wasn't sure how her agreement about God's power had committed her to baking pumpkin pies. Next time, she'd be prepared with better excuses. She wished she could see the rest of the items.

"All in good time," Mrs. Vandenberg assured her.

Squirming, Ruby wondered if Mrs. Vandenberg had read her mind.

"Now, about the pumpkins." The pages of her notebook flipped rapidly. "There's an overgrown pumpkin patch beyond the oaks that shade the *schulhaus* playground."

Ruby closed her eyes to visualize the property. The thick stand of trees blocked the view, but beyond them, the land sloped steeply. That area had once held a garden, now overgrown. Some distance beyond it, David lived with his *onkel*.

"That land is owned by Elijah Fisher," Ruby said. "It's not part of the *schulhaus* grounds."

"I'm sure Elijah wouldn't mind if you harvested the pumpkins. In fact, he might be grateful if someone cleared the weeds."

"I-I wouldn't feel right doing that. It's his land. And weeds have probably choked off the pumpkins' growth."

"You might be surprised. With so many pumpkins rotting there over the past few years, it's possible the patch is more productive than you imagine."

"I'll check into it." Just looking at the overgrown garden didn't mean she had to get the pumpkins there. Surely, *Daed* would let her use part of her salary to buy pumpkins for a charity donation. And several Amish neighbors who grew pumpkins would sell them cheaply or even donate them once they heard Mrs. Vandenberg's plan.

Pumpkins would be no trouble. She'd get those. But learning to make a decent pumpkin pie in the three weeks leading up to Thanksgiving? Now, that would be a major problem.

"Nothing is a problem. Unless you don't turn it over to the Lord." Mrs. Vandenberg pushed herself to her feet.

Once again, the elderly woman had answered Ruby's internal questions. And introduced more. The word *problem* reminded her of David. Now that was a huge one. Making bad pies was a small worry when compared with his constant misbehavior. She'd stewed about it and agonized over it and tried different techniques. But had she actually prayed about it?

Ruby couldn't remember bringing it to the Lord. She sent up a silent plea: *Lord, please show me a way to reach David.*

Mrs. Vandenberg smiled as she reached the door. "Now you're heading in the right direction."

Bobbing her head in agreement, Ruby opened the door and accompanied Mrs. Vandenberg to the car. The driver came around to assist her.

Before the door shut, Mrs. Vandenberg caught Ruby's eye. "You may find prayers—and pumpkins—are the answer to all your problems." She grinned at Ruby's puzzled expression.

Ruby stared after the departing car, her mind in a whirl. Prayers, definitely. But pumpkins? What did they have to do with any of this?

THE CHILLY FALL air penetrated Ruby's coat as she walked to school extra early the next morning. Mrs. Vandenberg's comment stayed with her. Pumpkins. She failed to see how that might help with David's behavior, which was her greatest problem at the moment. Second only to learning to bake pies.

Instead of heading up the gravel road to the school, she walked past it and the dense grove of oaks that blocked her view of the Fisher property. From time to time between the thick trunks, she glimpsed the roofs of a barn or a house, but after the grove ended, towering pine trees lined the edge of the main road and blocked her view of the property. Unless she stood in the driveway beside the hand-carved *Fisher Woodworking* sign—the only opening between the trees—and craned her neck, she could barely see the house or the woodworking shop because a row of smaller evergreens lined the curving dirt road into the property.

Ruby returned to the school driveway and climbed the hill. She crossed the playground and wound through tree trunks and underbrush, not sure why she was going to so much trouble for an overgrown pumpkin patch that belonged to someone else. When she emerged, she followed the ridge of the slope. Below her, bits of orange showed through overgrown patches of weeds that stretched for hundreds of yards. Pumpkins!

Her first instinct was to race down the hill and yank the weeds that stunted the pumpkins' growth. Were any of those pumpkins worth saving?

Several yards away, a rough path wound down the hill. Vines and brambles twined over it. Ruby hesitated. School would be starting soon. And she had no idea how far school property stretched, but it definitely didn't include the pumpkin patch. Still, it wouldn't hurt to just look.

She picked up a fallen branch and cautiously picked her way down the rough path, pulling vines out of her way and avoiding brambles. The closer she got, the more her fingers itched to yank up weeds and free the pumpkins. It would take a massive amount of work, but this could be returned to a productive garden.

She reached level ground and bunched up her dress and apron to keep them from getting stained or snagged. Then she squatted in the field and tugged at the nearest weeds. She uprooted some, but others needed a hoe. After much pulling and tossing weeds into a pile, she uncovered the first pumpkin.

When Ruby's family had moved here from Gratz two years ago, she'd heard about Sarah Fisher's legendary pumpkins. This must be one of them. Round and plump and huge, it had survived the weeds. Maybe it wasn't as large as it would have been if it hadn't competed with all these weeds to grow, but it would make magnificent pumpkin pies—if only she knew how to make them.

Ruby twisted it free of the other surrounding weeds. She wished she had a knife, so she could cut it off the vine. Wait, what was she thinking? This wasn't her garden, and she hadn't asked permission to harvest these pumpkins. Reluctantly, she set it down.

Ruby couldn't resist freeing a smaller pumpkin nearby. But when she did, the lower half had turned to mush. Pumpkin innards oozed onto the ground. What a shame it had gone to waste. Still, it would seed a new crop. Brushing off her hands, Ruby stood and surveyed the vast field. It would take a lot of work to unearth all these pumpkins.

She smiled to herself as an idea formed in her mind. If Elijah Fisher would let her, she'd turn this pumpkin patch into a gorgeous garden again. Right after school today, she'd ask him. He had to say *jah*. He had precious treasure in this field, and she'd enjoy unearthing it.

CHAPTER 4

*E*lijah turned from the stove, where scrambled eggs bubbled in a skillet. Once again, he'd forgotten to get out the spatula before starting. Ever since he'd lost Sarah, he struggled to remember basic steps. Even in his woodworking, which he'd been doing since age five beside his father, he sometimes needed enormous concentration to recall what to do next. Some days, he'd stand there, tool in hand, uncertain of how to begin.

As he dug through the utensil drawer, a quick flash outside the window startled him. He stopped, hand in drawer, to study the pumpkin patch.

Nothing shifted nearby. Perhaps it had been a swooping bird or a deer pawing at a pumpkin buried under the weeds. But no animals stirred. Then the movement came again. Far across the field, a woman bent and weeded. His heart leaped. *Sarah!*

He sucked in a breath. Many mornings, he gazed out the window, wishing fervently to see her as he had in the past, tending her garden after breakfast. He closed his eyes and shook his head. But when he opened them again, the woman was still there. Grief did strange things to the brain, but this was the first time his imagination had actually come to life.

David bounded into the kitchen. "Whatcha looking at?" He elbowed his way into place beside Elijah. "Hey, who's that in our garden?"

The woman stood, brushed off her hands, and turned. From this distance and with his eyes blurred with tears, Elijah couldn't make out her features, but her petite, slim frame reminded him of Sarah.

"That's Teacher Ruby. What's she doing out there?"

The acrid odor of burning stung Elijah's nose, and the kitchen filled with smoke. He wrestled the skillet from the stove.

"Open the back door," he commanded.

For once, David obeyed without arguing. He flung it open and propped open the storm door, waving to remove the choking clouds surrounding them. Frigid air blew into the house, chilling them both.

Elijah set the smoking pan in the sink, dug in the open utensil drawer, pulled out a spatula, and spooned the scorched, but not blackened, top layer onto his breakfast plate. Then he ran water into the skillet, sending hissing puffs of hot, smelly mist into the air.

David's face settled into grumpy lines. "Burned eggs again?"

"They're only lightly browned." Elijah spooned the less singed bits onto his nephew's plate. "You'd better close the door before we turn into icicles."

"If I do, we'll choke." David clutched at his throat and hacked dramatically.

"The door," Elijah repeated.

Guilt overtook him as he set the plates on the table. He'd forgotten to start the bacon and the toast. At least he didn't have to worry about burning those. But David needed more than eggs. Sighing, Elijah took out the loaf of bread and buttered two pieces for each of them.

By the time, he'd fixed both plates, he only had a second to glance out the window. The woman was gone. Had it been his imagination? Or had David been right? If so, why had his teacher been weeding in the pumpkin patch?

Elijah sank heavily into his chair. Between the charred food and the sight of a woman in the garden, he was emotionally drained. He didn't have energy to deal with his nephew's antics.

David curled up his nose at the breakfast on his plate and glared when Elijah indicated he needed to bow his head for silent prayer.

"What if I'm not grateful for this?"

"Be glad you have something to eat in the morning. Some children don't."

"They can have this."

"Enough." Elijah's voice thundered around the kitchen, and David jumped.

His nephew closed his eyes and bowed his head.

For a moment, Elijah wondered if he should explode in a temper more often to get David to listen. But Elijah regretted that his anger had gotten David to cooperate in prayer. Somehow, it didn't seem right.

Elijah added a plea for forgiveness to his own prayer.

When he lifted his head, he debated about apologizing, but David was shoveling in his breakfast without complaint. Elijah didn't want to risk upsetting the positive result.

David even packed his own lunch and raced out the door to school without being nagged and scolded. Elijah relaxed back in his chair for a moment, savoring the peace in the still cloudy room before he stood to do the dishes.

As he scoured the skillet, his gaze kept drifting to the pumpkin patch. The woman had stirred a longing deep within his soul. The yearning grew to an unbearable ache. *Why, God? Why did You leave me alone?*

Elijah scrubbed the charred eggs so hard his hands ached. If only that woman hadn't disturbed his peace of mind. Now, he couldn't get her or Sarah out of his thoughts.

USUALLY, if Elijah lost himself in carving or sanding wood, the pain of missing of Sarah lessened. Today, though, not only couldn't he concentrate on his work, but memories flooded past his eyes. He kept looking up, expecting Sarah to walk through the door to share lunch with him. Her voice echoed on the air. Several times, he had to stop himself from reaching out for her.

Frustrated, he ended his work early and headed for the kitchen. He had to find a way to stop the images flooding through his brain, but as he reached for the cookies that would be David's afternoon snack, the stack of mail caught his eye. He should read those letters and respond. And deal with David's misbehavior if that's what these notes were about.

He picked up the stack and settled at the kitchen table as the late afternoon sun slanting across the wood in faded ribbons. The envelopes lay before him, their edges slightly curled. He exhaled slowly and forced himself to reach for the first. Clumsy printing misspelled his name as *Elyja*.

He cracked a smile, but quickly sobered. No doubt one of their younger neighbors—a young one, most likely—had written about David's bullying. Elijah unfolded the slightly crumpled paper that smelled faintly of grape jelly.

I'm glad for the land. I like to play ball there. I hit far and run fast.

The handwriting wobbled, and the writer had pressed down hard with effort. *Odd.* The letter was unsigned. *Land?*

What land? Had the letter been misdirected? *Neh*, it had his name on the envelope.

He reached for the second one.

Thank you for the Schule and the land. *I like learning new things.*

Slowly, light dawned. *The schulhaus* sat on his *dawdi*'s land. The teacher must have insisted they write letters to him. He hoped twenty more letters didn't fill his mailbox.

Elijah didn't deserve gratitude for something his family had done a generation ago. But he couldn't help being touched by the children taking time to express their appreciation.

The third letter, written in a competent cursive hand, nearly burst with earnestness.

Dear Elijah Fisher,

Thank you so much for the land, the playground, and the schulhaus. *It was very kind of your* daed *to build it. His gift is special to everyone who goes to school here. May God give you a blessed day.*

Elijah blinked hard. The young writer had wished him a blessed day. The kindness of it touched him. Even if it had been an assignment, the child had written that line just for him.

He turned the final envelope over in his hands. Crisp white paper. Handwriting that slowed his breath—delicate, graceful. The curve of each letter reminded him of the way Sarah used to dot her "i"s with a careful touch, before folding her notes and sealing them with prayer.

His chest tightened as he unfolded it slowly, then scanned every stroke.

To the one whose generosity made the schulhaus *possible,*

Thank you for the land and building and for letting our scholars grow roots where your family once planted them. The trees your daed *left standing at the edge of the property have stood for hundreds of years, reminding us of God's wonderful creative hand. Like those trees, the scholars grow tall and strong in knowledge and faith on the property your family donated.*

With much gratitude,

A friend of the schulhaus

Though, it was unsigned, gentleness had been woven through every line. He swallowed hard as the beauty and meaning of the words washed over him. People cared. They appreciated him and had taken the time to let him know.

Despite the kindness of the sentiments, the letters opened a gaping wound inside, reminding him of the seasons before his heartbreak—when the letters he and Sarah exchanged offered comfort, hope, and an anchor during their courtship.

Elijah sat back, the paper trembling slightly in his hands, and his heart, long locked tight with grief, pulsed quietly with longing.

Each thank-you note felt like an unearned gift. His heart expanded with gratitude until it pressed against his ribs. And something inside him shifted—like a door closed so long, it could only creak open an inch.

He laid the letter atop the others. Thought better of it. For some reason, he didn't want David to mock the letters or taint them with his scorn. He gathered them up and hastened to the workshop, where he slid them into his desk drawer.

He started to leave, but changed his mind. He pinned the children's notes to his bulletin board. Just knowing someone cared enough to write to him eased some of his loneliness. He left the longer letter in the drawer. That one, he couldn't bear to read again.

He made it back to the kitchen a few minutes before David rocketed into the house, clanging his lunch pail and making a beeline for the cookies.

Elijah's hand, as unsteady as his heart, shook a bit as poured milk into a glass for his nephew. A sharp rap on the front door startled him, and milk dribbled down the outside of the cup.

"Please clean up the spill while I get the door."

"But you did it."

"It's good to help others." Elijah strode across the kitchen and to the door.

He hesitated a moment. No delivery truck had rumbled in. No customer's horse had clip-clopped down the driveway. People rarely walked down his long, curving driveway. All his senses warned him of danger. Perhaps he should ignore the knock.

Someone rapped again. A bit softer this time.

Elijah twisted the knob and opened the door a crack. He'd been right. He should have left the door closed.

CHAPTER 5

A woman stood on Elijah's porch with a sunny smile. "Hello, I'm Teacher Ruby."

It was all he could do to offer a semi-polite nod. His whole body sent off alarm signals, urging him to flee. The warnings choked his throat, making a response impossible.

That didn't deter her. "I wondered," she said, her voice light and sweet, "if I could weed your pumpkin patch. The weeds are choking out the pumpkin vines."

Elijah froze. Up close, Ruby looked nothing like Sarah. The setting sun touched Ruby's hair with golden highlights. Sarah had light brown hair. Ruby's white teeth shone in her generous smile and distracted him.

Suddenly, he realized he'd been staring. He dropped his gaze and fumbled to remember her question. She wanted to weed the pumpkin patch.

He couldn't bear to see her—or anyone—in the field. Looking out there this morning had been enough of a shock. A shock that had stayed with him all morning and messed up his whole day. He needed to be able to concentrate on his large workload this time of year. He already had a backlog of

RACHEL J. GOOD

Christmas orders, and more flowed in every day. He couldn't possibly agree to her plan.

"*Neh.*" The word exploded from his lips before he could soften it.

She blinked. "I just thought it might—"

"The field's worthless." His voice came out flat and firm. "Doesn't need tending. Waste of time." He tightened his grip on the door knob to steady himself. "Leave it be."

Ruby opened her mouth, but before she could utter anything more, he pushed the door harder than he'd intended to. It shut with a sharp thud.

David padded into the living room, trailing cookie crumbs. "Who was at the door?"

Eliah would rather not answer, but David never let questions drop. He'd pester until Elijah told him. "Your teacher." He tried to pass it off in a low, casual tone and not show Ruby's presence had shaken him.

"Teacher Ruby?" David asked warily.

"Are you in trouble at school?"

David's head whizzed back and forth in an emphatic *neh*. Then, he appeared thoughtful. His *neh* came out hesitant. "Did she say I was?"

"She didn't mention you."

"What'd she want then?"

"Never mind. It's not important."

"But I want to know."

Frowning, Elijah pointed to the crumbs. "Finish that cookie in the kitchen. And clean up the mess you made."

Elijah wished he could clean up the mess he'd just made as easily.

STUNNED, Ruby remained on the front porch, staring at the wooden barrier Elijah Fisher had banged shut between them. When he'd slammed the door, dried leaves had skittered across the porch. Ruby had crunched through those leaves as she'd mounted the steps earlier. Evidence they rarely used their front door and had no wife or mother to sweep the porch each day.

In her pocket, she carried a utility knife she'd taken from the *schulhaus* toolbox. Ruby planned to ask to cut off the pumpkin she'd unearthed that morning. She wondered how Elijah Fisher would respond to unexpected company.

He always kept to himself. Never had he attended a school program in the two years she'd been teaching. And he scurried in and out of church, avoiding socializing. Even during the after-church meals, he barely said a word. He kept his head down, shoveled in his food, and left a short while later.

Ruby always felt sorry for David. He never had time to have fun with his friends like the other children did after they ate the church meal. His face sullen, he followed Elijah out to the buggy, glancing over his shoulder at the others playing ball or games of tag.

Maybe that's why he had trouble making friends at school. That and the constant pranks he played on people. Those revealed how desperate David was for attention, even if it was negative. Ruby remembered how his face had lit up when Sam praised his jokes. She made a mental note to find ways to encourage the positive things David did.

But right now, she had to figure out what to do about Elijah's answer. She'd expected some awkwardness when he came to the door, like him shifting his feet and struggling to speak. Or a hesitancy to respond to her question. But never that short, sharp *neh*.

She'd jumped when his front door had creaked halfway open. He'd filled the space like an old oak—rooted, weathered, reluctant. His stare unnerved her. And his obvious reluctance to be around her had been off-putting.

But that explosive *neh*? And *worthless*?

That pumpkin she'd uncovered this morning had been far from worthless. It might not have been one of his wife's gigantic prize-winners at the county fair, but even with its growth stunted by weeds, it had been large enough to fill two or three pie crusts.

Ruby still couldn't believe his rude and abrupt response. Her lips pressed tight, she stared at the closed door. Then, with determination, she stepped off the porch and spun toward the field. Her skirt caught a breeze as she strode across the yard, brisk and defiant. Those pumpkins deserved care and tending.

Near the row of tumbled vines, half-buried in dirt, sat the pumpkin she'd uncovered that morning. It was plump, orange, and perfectly shaped. She pulled out the utility knife. The blade clicked up smoothly.

She should Elijah's permission before cutting off the pumpkin, but she had to prove he was wrong. This field was not worthless. She sawed at the vine until the pumpkin came free.

Although she brushed the pumpkin skin several times, dirt still clung to the underside. Ignoring the marks it made on her dress and apron, Ruby cradled it in both arms and turned back toward the house, her back straight and resolve in every step.

This time her knock bounced off the wood with firmness. Again, she waited a long time for an answer.

Elijah opened the door more slowly now, warier. Ruby held up the pumpkin as proof.

"You said the field was worthless." She lifted it, her gaze steady. "I found this under the weeds."

His jaw worked silently. The skin around his eyes creased. He looked down at the heavy orange pumpkin she held, his eyes brimming with sorrow.

"I don't want help," he muttered, but quieter now.

"Maybe not," she replied. "But have you ever thought that not tending God's bounty is unkind to others?"

Surprise flickered in his eyes, and she pressed her advantage.

"Your pumpkins could help the hungry. If you don't want or need them, they could be given away as food or sold to feed the hungry."

This time, he blinked, and silence stretched between them, full of unspoken words and heavy with regret. Minutes ticked past, before his voice, low and rusty, revealed his remorse. "I had not thought of that."

Ruby kept her words gentle. "I want to help restore the patch and hope to receive a few pumpkins in return."

Elijah startled her by reaching out—not for the pumpkin, but to push the door wider. Not an invitation. Not yet.

But a sliver of softening.

He grimaced at the pumpkin in her arms. "Leave it there," he said gruffly, nodding to the steps.

Ruby set it down gently, hiding her smile. When she turned, Elijah pain-filled eyes studied it—round, healthy, and undeniable proof that even the forgotten things could thrive. She'd made her point. Now to gain his cooperation.

ELIJAH COULDN'T BELIEVE he was considering her suggestion, but her words had filled him with guilt. What would Sarah think of the way he'd treated her treasured garden? Even worse, despite lecturing David this morning about hungry children, Elijah had been letting God's bounty rot.

He sank into the wooden rocker he'd made as Teacher Ruby settled onto the couch across from him. She sat primly, hands in her lap, but the tension in her face and shoulders showed he made her nervous. He didn't blame her. He'd barked at her and shut the door in her face much more forcefully than he'd intended.

"I'm sorry for—" Still choked with emotion at the image of that pumpkin in Ruby's arms, Elijah gestured helplessly toward the front door, relieved it blocked his view of the fruit of his wife's labors.

"And I apologize for going onto your land without asking permission."

Ruby's melodic voice touched a part of Elijah that he'd pushed deep down. He forced himself not to compare her to Sarah, but it wasn't easy. Absorbed in the struggle not to look at Ruby, he missed what she said until the words *Mrs. Vandenberg* jolted him to pay attention.

"What did you say about Mrs. Vandenberg?" he asked.

Ruby appeared taken aback. "She suggested I get pumpkins for the STAR pies from your garden."

"What are star pies?"

"Perhaps you haven't heard about her STAR Center in the inner city?"

Elijah stared at her blankly. *Star center? Star pies?* It seemed she was speaking a foreign language. He made the mistake of meeting her sparkling eyes. They drew him in. Made him forget his resolve.

"A few years ago, Mrs. Vandenberg started a program in the city to keep children out of gangs. The STAR Center has classes, lessons, and fun activities for all ages. It also provides food for hungry families, shelter for the homeless, and job training for former gang members. It's a wonderful set of programs."

"Sounds like it."

While she described the center, Ruby's pretty hands flashed in and out, distracting Elijah. She must be excellent at keeping the scholar's attention during the school day. He had a hard time keeping his eyes off her.

"Anyway, Mrs. Vandenberg asked me to make pumpkin pies for the STAR Center Thanksgiving dinner. I have no idea why. I make terrible pies. Anyway, she insisted I should get the pumpkins from here."

"Why?"

"Because it's close to the school? And your field has so many unpicked pumpkins?" Ruby sounded uncertain.

"Or knowing Mrs. Vandenberg, maybe because I needed to be woken out of my selfishness?" he said drily.

Her cheeks flushed crimson. "I didn't mean—"

"I know you didn't. But it can't be denied." Now that it had been pointed out, shame filled him at how his grief had made him shut everyone out. Though he wanted to crawl back inside his cocoon of anger and self-pity, the thought of rotting pumpkins made him regret how self-centered he'd been.

Sarah would have hated what had become of her carefully tended fields. She'd be the first to donate every single pumpkin she had to help others. All Ruby wanted were a few pumpkins for pies. It was the least he could do after slamming the door in her face.

Seeing someone else in the pumpkin field would be unbearable, but he could avoid the window for a few days. Taking a deep breath, he made himself say, "Take as many as you need."

"I'll need enough for two dozen pies and perhaps some experimental pies to improve my recipe. But that wasn't the only reason I came. I'd like to restore the whole patch."

"What?" Surely, he hadn't heard her right.

"I appreciate the pumpkins for the pies, but it seems a shame to let the rest of the pumpkins go to seed when they could help others."

"You have no idea how much work a field that size takes." His wife had spent her days weeding, baking pies, and selling them at the Green Valley Farmers Market. And she'd kept the ground clear by weeding six days a week. With the present overgrowth, it would be impossible for a teacher who spent most of the day in school to clear even a small section for her pies.

Ruby broke into his thoughts. "I didn't plan to do it alone. It would be a good project for the scholars. They could devote an hour a day to the work. That would add up to 29 hours of labor every day. It makes 145 hours in a week."

Elijah chuckled. "I see you like math."

"I do. How many hours do you estimate it will take to clear the whole field?"

"I don't know, but I suspect you've measured the field and figured out how fast each child will work."

Ruby's bell-toned laugh twisted his insides. How long had it been since he'd heard such a joyful sound?

"I haven't gone that far," she insisted. "But I think we could harvest most of the pumpkins—those that haven't decayed, that is—over the next two weeks."

Two weeks, and then she'd be gone. For some reason, the cold winds of loss swept over Elijah. He hid his emotions and focused on facts. "What do you plan to do with the rest of the pumpkins?"

"You're letting us keep them? I thought they'd be yours."

"I don't need them." Or want them. The fewer reminders he had of his losses, the better.

"If you're sure?"

"Positive."

"Then I'll ask Mrs. Vandenberg to sell them at the market and—" When he cringed, she stopped, then asked, "Are you all right?"

As a newcomer, Ruby may not be aware that his wife used

to have a market stand. *Neh,* she must have heard gossip because her eyes overflowed with sympathy.

"I'm so sorry. I didn't mean to bring up—"

Elijah waved a hand to dismiss it. He didn't want pity. "What will you do with the proceeds?"

"I thought we could donate the money to feed hungry children who come to the STAR center during the school vacations. Often school lunch is the only meal they get all day. When school is out . . ."

She didn't need to finish. His wince wasn't for himself but for the children.

"That's a good cause. I'm pleased to help."

Ruby's brilliant smile almost knocked him over.

"*Danke.* I'm so glad you've agreed to let us do this. I like to teach the scholars life lessons in addition to reading and arithmetic. This will be a wonderful opportunity."

She acted as if he'd done her a favor instead of the other way around. Seeing the pumpkin patch tended and harvested would lessen his guilt and sadness when he glanced out the window. As long as he didn't watch her when she was out there.

She sprang to her feet. "I'd better go, or I'll be late helping *Mamm* with dinner."

As he showed her to the door, he asked a question that he'd wondered about earlier. "Did you ask your scholars to write me *danke* letters?"

"David didn't tell you about it?"

She looked so surprised, Elijah couldn't admit his nephew told him nothing. Perhaps because Elijah didn't ask. Was this another example of his selfishness? He suspected, though, if he asked about school, David would refuse to answer.

Ruby's gaze remained fixed on Elijah, waiting for a response.

He shrugged. "David doesn't talk much about school."

Inside, Elijah squirmed a little. How much of that was his own fault?

"I see." Ruby seemed to understand much more than he wanted her to. "I've asked the scholars to write a letter of gratitude to someone in the community every day until Thanksgiving."

"So you didn't encourage them to write to me?"

"I did mention your *daed* gave the land and built the *schulhaus*, so I imagine some of them may have written to you."

He nodded. "They did." He wanted to ask if the other anonymous letter had come from her, but he was pretty sure it had.

CHAPTER 6

*T*he next morning, Ruby couldn't wait to share her exciting surprise with the scholars. She left for school before sunrise, pushing a wheelbarrow full of hoes, spades, trowels, and clippers, many borrowed from neighbors whose gardening duties were done for the year. As she reached the ridge above the pumpkin patch, the sun peeked over the horizon, painting the sky in streaks of crimson, tangerine, and plum.

Ruby set to work clearing the path down to the field. Her breath fogged the air, but she grew overheated inside her heavy wool coat and scarf. Once she'd removed any roots, vines, and brambles that might trip her scholars, she smoothed out the dirt and pushed the wheelbarrow down to the garden.

Never had she been so excited to begin weeding. First, though, she drove upright sticks into the hard ground to mark where each scholar would start. Then she dug in. Over the next hour, she cleared a good-sized section, uncovering three usable pumpkins—one large and two tiny—and several smushy, oozing messes. What a shame they'd been left to decay.

With reluctance, Ruby gathered up her tools, shook off the

dirt, and rose. As much as she'd like to keep going, she needed to get to school to prepare for the scholars' arrival.

Wiping her sweaty brow with the back of her glove, she surveyed her work. The part she'd labored over appeared to be a tiny speck in a vast field that stretched endlessly. Chances were they'd only have a week or so until frost set in and harvest-time ended. How would they ever weed such a huge expanse? The numbers she'd thrown at Elijah seemed insignificant. Had she taken on more than she could handle?

Even if she had, all she could do now was forge ahead and accomplish whatever she could before the first frost. Ruby took off her gardening gloves, brushed off her skirt and apron, placed her gardening tools in the wheelbarrow, and climbed the hill to the *schoohaus*.

THOUGH ELIJAH PROMISED himself he wouldn't look out the window at breakfast time, his gaze was drawn to the ridge, where Ruby stood silhouetted by the rising sun. Through the dusty pane, the sky blazed with vivid colors behind her as she hacked a path down to the field. He regretted not doing that before she arrived.

Once again, it reminded him of his self-centeredness. The time had come to think about others instead of his own grief.

Ruby knelt in the dirt, her black bonnet bobbing as she tugged stubborn vines from the soil. Sarah used to kneel just like that—hands dirt-speckled, humming hymns as she weeded between rows. Her presence had once filled this home like morning light, and Ruby working in Sarah's special place sliced through him. The rhythm of Ruby's movements echoed Sarah's. Each twist of a spade, each toss of a weed onto a pile stirred deep memories.

Ruby lifted a small pumpkin, held it up, and examined it.

Elijah sucked in a breath. If he blurred his vision a little, he could believe Sarah was working out in the garden. He longed to call to her the way he often did. She'd raise her head and smile across the distance between them.

Stop, he ordered himself. *You must let her go. Don't dwell on the past.*

But how could he? The idea of moving on brought images of emptiness and loss. How could he accept he'd never see or touch her again? Not on this earth. Pain engulfed him, shaking him to his core.

Yet alongside the ache, something else bloomed. Ruby's lilting voice, her brilliant smile had strummed long-silent chords within his soul. For the brief time she'd visited, she brought peace. While he sat with her, she'd erased his loneliness.

Last night, his dreams had brought not Sarah, but Ruby to him. She'd helped and comforted him. While he slept, Ruby had tiptoed into his life and set everything right. Her sunshine brought lightness to the darkness engulfing him. Her sweetness had softened wild and wary David. This morning, he'd fought against awakening because he didn't want to leave that place where he'd been safe and comforted.

Elijah's chest tightened—not only with loss, but with longing. Was it possible to hope in a space still lined with grief?

He hadn't realized he'd been standing at the window for so long until someone nudged his arm. David appeared beside him, holding a half-eaten apple. Elijah shifted his stance and blinked, trying to bring himself back to reality.

David squinted through the smudged glass. "*Ach*, it's Teacher Ruby. She's pulling weeds again. Why's she doing that? You told her the pumpkins weren't any good."

Elijah didn't answer right away. His eyes lingered on her bent form, her hands strong and firm as she tugged a stubborn vine. "She sees things others overlook."

David frowned. "Like buried pumpkins?"

A smile tugged at Elijah's mouth. "Exactly like that."

David studied Ruby for a long beat. "She's always helping people, even when she doesn't have to. She does that at school at lot too."

Elijah didn't need David to tell him that. Even from his short conversation with Ruby, he could tell she cared about others. "*Jah*, she does."

Brows drawn, David turned to Elijah. "Then why'd you run away yesterday after she came to the porch?"

Elijah turned the question around on David. "You mean you?"

"No, I mean you." David licked apple juice from his fingers. "First, you didn't open the door. Then when you did, you yelled at her and slammed the door. After that, you stomped out to your workshop so fast and didn't come back for a while. When she knocked again, you almost didn't answer."

Elijah picked up a dishcloth and rubbed at the grimy window. "She caught me off guard, that's all."

What had he been thinking? Using a dishcloth? And worse yet, clearing the glass for a better view?

He turned away and concentrated on the filthy dishcloth. He'd have to turn it into a cleaning rag.

David tilted his head. "Is it 'cause she's pretty?"

Elijah nearly dropped the cloth. What had put a thought like that in David's mind? Words bubbled up that Elijah's *mamm* had repeated often when he'd first mooned over Sarah. His nephew might need to hear them. "*Don't look at outward appearance, but pay attention to the heart*," he told David.

With a quick flick of the hand, David dismissed the advice. "Do you like her?"

"I hardly know her." That didn't quite answer the question.

David placed his hands on his hips and stared Elijah down.

Time to change the subject. "Why did *you* hurry off when

she came inside?" Elijah examined his nephew's nervous gestures.

Then David shrugged. "I thought she was mad about my prank. Or maybe she came to tell you I should write more thank-you letters."

Elijah should ask about the prank, but bone-deep weariness overtook him. He was not up to cooking after yesterday's disastrous charred eggs along with today's churning feelings about Ruby, so he plunked a bulk bag of puffed wheat on the table. "Better eat your breakfast so you're not late for school."

"I don't like—" David clamped his mouth shut.

Had the lecture about hungry children made an impact? Elijah hoped so. Ruby had hammered that point home for him yesterday. Perhaps David had overheard his teacher's comments about children here in Lancaster who had only one meal a day.

"Did you listen in when I talked to Teacher Ruby yesterday?"

David ignored the question. He took a bowl from the cupboard, filled it, and drowned his puffed wheat in milk and sugar. He pretended disinterest as he spooned cereal into his mouth.

Elijah didn't press for an answer, the figure outside the window distracted him as he rinsed out the dishrag. He dried his hands and turned away, but the image of Ruby stayed with him, kneeling in soil he'd abandoned—bringing life where he'd only seen ruin.

To Ruby's surprise, the first scholar to arrive was David. He raced onto the playground and straight up to her. Normally, he dragged up the hill at the last minute and mumbled the expected *gude mariye* without looking at her.

Today, he demanded, "What were you doing in our garden?"

Ruby considered correcting his rudeness, but thought the better of it. This was the first time he'd addressed her in a voice that held no sullenness or anger. She could discuss manners later.

"Your *onkel* gave me permission to weed the pumpkin patch."

"How come he's letting you do that? I'm not allowed to step a foot in there."

"I stopped by yesterday to—"

Fear flickered in David's eyes.

"Not to talk about you."

He hung his head and mumbled, "I know."

Evidently, David had eavesdropped. "So you also know what we'll be doing this morning."

Before he could respond, Martha skipped up to them. "*Gude mariye*, Teacher Ruby," she gushed.

While Ruby responded, David slinked away. She wished she'd had more time to talk to him. They'd been on the verge of a conversation. She'd have no time to connect with him now because the lot filled with scooters and pony carts.

She did note David strutting up to various groups to brag, "I know what we're going to do today, and you don't."

Ruby clapped her hands for them to gather. She didn't want him to make enemies of everyone this morning when they'd all need to work together. But his need for attention gave her an idea. He pushed his way to the front of the line, his shoulders thrown back proudly.

Ruby leaned over to whisper, "I have an important job for you. Will you help me?"

David eyed her warily, but he nodded. He probably expected to be asked to do one of the disliked school chores.

After they'd finished their morning routine, Ruby

announced, "Today we're going to do something very different."

David wriggled in his seat and interrupted, "I know what it is."

Ruby ignored his outburst. "David's excited because we'll be going to his *onkel's* pumpkin patch this morning. We will be uncovering hidden pumpkins to sell at market."

Excited murmurs buzzed through the room. She'd hoped to stir their interest, and it seemed she'd succeeded. Hunting for pumpkins sounded more appealing than weeding. Ruby held up her hand for silence.

"The money we make will buy food for hungry children."

Martha waggled her hand in the air. "I love to help people."

"That's wonderful." Ruby managed to keep the sarcastic edge from her voice. "I hope you all remember helping people also can include being kind and not criticizing others." She didn't look directly at Martha, though Ruby's words were directed toward the prideful, judgmental girl.

Martha didn't take the hint. She only beamed proudly.

Ruby sighed inwardly. A few lessons in *hochmut* might be needed. "I've set up sections for each of you, but David will be in charge of telling you which one is yours."

David's eyes rounded. "I will?" he breathed. But he recovered quickly and acted as if he'd known all along. "*Jah*, I will."

"Put on your outer garments, and we'll head to the pumpkin patch. Please dress extra warmly the next two weeks." As the scholars scurried to get ready, Ruby called over the din, "On the days we search for pumpkins, we'll write our gratitude letters at the end of the day."

Several scholars groaned, but David's was the loudest.

After she herded the children down the path, she gathered them at the edge of the field. "As most of you know, this patch belongs to David's *onkel*, Elijah, so wait for David to tell you which row to search.

Martha waved her hand in the air. "You said *search*, but this field is full of weeds. How can we find anything in it?"

Ruby wanted to grit her teeth. Leave it to Martha to point out the negatives. "You may have to pull weeds up or aside to find the pumpkins. All of you know how to get rid of weeds. And I have a wheelbarrow of tools if you need them."

By that time, David had recovered. He sorted his classmates into their rows. Most were delighted with his choices. He'd placed best friends in adjoining rows and separated those who annoyed each other. He put himself and Sam beside each other, so they could joke. And for the first time in a long time, Sarah, who'd been tucked alone on the opposite end of the field, relaxed enough to smile.

"Good job, David." Ruby's compliment came from the heart.

He beamed and set to work with vigor. Ruby determined to tap into his leadership abilities and give him positive attention. Maybe she'd found a secret for getting him to behave.

CHAPTER 7

$\mathcal{C}$hildish laughter drew Elijah's attention as he headed out to his workshop. He drew back into the shadows, where he could observe without being seen. Pangs struck him each time Ruby bent over to listen to a child, assist with a stubborn root, or call out encouragement. As hard as it was to see Sarah's fields being weeded without her, gratitude filled Elijah that Ruby, David, and other small children were caring for the neglected field.

He sneaked into the woodshop to avoid being seen. He didn't want Ruby to think he'd spied on her. Even if he had.

Although he kept busy sanding the Martins' table, his ears stayed tuned to the distant calls of joy as children discovered pumpkins. Loud *ewws* or groans echoed when they found rotted pumpkins. Through it all, Ruby's sweet voice floated on the air, touching his heart and soul.

After Ruby and the children returned to the *schulhaus*, he missed the lively voices. The silence of his shop weighed on him. How had he gone so long without friendship and the company of others? As the bishop reminded Elijah often, *It is not good for man to be alone.*

His grieving mind finally agreed. He'd always ignored the bishop's advice because he couldn't imagine moving on and allowing anyone else into his life. Was he ready to take some small steps in that direction?

At lunchtime, Elijah pulled Ruby's letter from the drawer and reread it several times. Now that he'd spent time with her, he had no doubt she'd sent it. Debating with himself, he pulled a sheet of paper from his desk drawer and penned the feelings overflowing inside. The words came slower than carving wood, but they were as deep and long-lasting.

Dear Ruby,

You'll never read this, and perhaps that's best. But I needed to say the things that have stirred in me since I saw you in the pumpkin patch this morning.

It's strange how watching you pull weeds brought back memories I'd buried—memories of Sarah laughing, bending beside me in the sun. For a moment, I felt her there again. And yet . . . it wasn't only memory. It was you.

Your kindness has crept into corners I thought I'd sealed shut. You remind me of what faith looks like in motion—not in words, but in care freely given. I saw it every time you encouraged a child, every time David smiled because you noticed him.

Today I realized I've been hoarding pumpkins—not just the fruit, but the good they were meant for. I've kept God's bounty tucked behind weeds and grief. But you . . . you saw something worth saving.

Thank you. Not just for tending neglected soil, but for showing me that even when we don't feel worthy, others may still be grateful for the tiny things we share. You took my reluctant gift, as weed-choked as it is, and turned it into a blessing for others. And for me. You've brought small rays of sunshine into my life that give me hope I can move on from my grief.

Your lilting voice, your smile—it stays with me.

Yours in quiet thanks,

Elijah

He folded the letter with care, slid it into an envelope, and wrote her name on the front. Then he tucked it into the drawer with hers. He'd never be bold enough to send this to her, but his heart lightened at expressing the thankfulness stirring inside.

DAVID ARRIVED home late that afternoon, breathless and beaming.

"Where have you been?" Elijah demanded. "You're supposed to come straight home."

"I can't tell you. It's a secret." But David didn't say it in his usual defiant manner. "Teacher Ruby asked me to do something." He glowed with pride.

Elijah glanced at his nephew askance. Somehow, he couldn't imagine Ruby asking David to help or David agreeing so enthusiastically, but Elijah wasn't about to probe and spoil the mood. He only hoped David hadn't gotten in trouble again.

"After you finish your snack, can you get the mail? I need to get back out to the workshop." Watching Ruby and the children weeding along with writing his gratitude letter had put Elijah behind on his orders.

When he exited his shop two hours later, he stopped in shock at the small figure weeding the pumpkin patch. He rubbed his eyes. David?

Spying Elijah, David jumped up and raced toward the house. "I found five more pumpkins."

"Great. That will help Teacher Ruby make her pies."

"She's making them into pies? Are we doing it with her?"

"I'm sure she doesn't need our help." Then he remembered Ruby's confession that she didn't make good pies. Maybe she did need help.

As they entered the kitchen, Elijah sucked in an annoyed

breath. Envelopes had been torn open, and the contents scattered across the table. He opened his mouth to scold David, but he caught sight of the name scrawled on one envelope.

"Look!" David scooped up the letters. "I got six *dankes*. Some people from my class liked that I put them next to their friends. And some thanked me for letting them hunt for pumpkins. I think they like me."

Elijah berated himself. How long had David been feeling left out at school? He'd been so caught up in his own grief, he hadn't paid attention to his nephew's struggles.

"I just weeded for the ones who didn't get very far today. Now everyone will be at the same place tomorrow. That way they can stay close enough to talk to their friends."

"That was thoughtful of you."

David jumped up and carried several letters to Elijah, who took them eagerly. His spirits fell when none of the envelopes held the lovely handwriting he'd reread earlier. But he couldn't expect her to send him more letters. He set aside the bills and opened three childish letters thanking him for letting them pick pumpkins. For the first time in a long time, his heart brimmed with gratitude.

LONG AFTER ELIJAH had gone to bed, David's question about pumpkin pies kept jabbing Elijah awake. He tossed and turned all night. When he rolled out of bed exhausted in the morning, he did something he hadn't done for three years. He bowed his head. Until now, his only communication with God had been shaking his fist toward heaven and demanding, *Why, God, why?*

Today, he humbled himself before the Lord and asked for forgiveness for not accepting His will. Then he bared his heart.

Father, I want to help Ruby, but I'm torn about sharing Sarah's and my special secret. If this is what You want me to do, please give me the strength to offer it.

Elijah lifted his head. A deep sense of calm settled over him, and he knew what he needed to do. He set the cereal bag on the table again, promising himself he'd cook breakfast tomorrow, and headed out to the pumpkin patch.

RUBY HUMMED a tune as she headed into Elijah's field. They'd unearthed a surprising number of pumpkins already. Half of them had been decaying, but they'd found quite a few usable ones too.

When she drew near, she halted. Elijah, hoe in hand, uprooted a waist-high mullein along with its taproot.

"What are you doing?" Ruby blurted out.

He jumped, then turned to face her. "These might be hard for the children to pull out. They've been growing wild for several years now."

"How thoughtful of you."

He seemed pleased by the compliment. "I thought I could come out every morning to remove some of the large stubborn weeds."

Ruby's heart sang. "It would be nice to have company."

He rewarded her with a crooked smile. "Don't know how much help I'll be in that. I'm rusty at conversation."

She grinned back. "Never too late to learn."

"Spoken like a true teacher." He sobered. "I don't know what you did with David, but he's changed so much. In a *gut* way."

"I'm so glad. I discovered he's a natural leader, so I put him in charge of handing out garden rows. He did an amazing job. And he loves doing spy work."

"Spy work?"

Ruby laughed at Elijah's concerned expression. "That's what I call it when scholars sneak the gratitude letters into mailboxes without being seen. I gave David a big stack yesterday because he seemed so eager."

"Ah, so that's why he was so late getting home. He told me he was doing secret work. I'm glad to know he's not getting into trouble." Elijah paused and cleared his throat. "The gratitude letters have been helpful. For David. And for me."

"I'm so glad." She fidgeted. As much as she enjoyed talking to Elijah, she should get to work.

Elijah noticed her *rutsching*. "I'm sorry. I've been keeping you." When she waved her hand to dismiss it, he pressed his lips together. After drawing in a deep breath, he pushed out words as if each one hurt him. "I, um, wanted to . . ."

Ruby ached for him. Whatever he was about to say seemed to be torn from the depth of his being. She wished she could set him at ease.

"I could, um, help you bake pumpkin pies."

"I don't think—" A nervous giggle escaped her lips. "It's just that I'm so bad at it, I'd rather not do it in front of anyone."

"*Neh, neh.* I meant I could teach you."

"Teach me?"

"*Jah.* You didn't live here then, but my"—he closed his eyes and swallowed hard—"my wife was a champion pumpkin pie baker. I used to help her make them. From her *mammi*'s recipe."

Elijah's generous offer left Ruby speechless. He'd share this with her even though it obviously hurt him deeply?

She blinked back the moisture in her eyes. "*D-danke.*" What more could she say? If she tried, she'd start babbling. Or sniffling.

"Would you want to come here after school?" He sounded so tentative, so unsure.

"I can do that. *Danke* again."

Elijah turned and, his voice rough with emotion, said, "I should be thanking you." Keeping his back to her, he continued yanking up the tall weeds.

Ruby tried to steady her pattering pulse. The idea of learning to make award-winning pumpkin pies left her giddy. But she wasn't sure how much of it stemmed from mastering a skill that had eluded her for years or from spending more time with Elijah.

CHAPTER 8

*H*eart hammering, Ruby stood on Elijah's doorstep that afternoon, hesitant to knock. An image of him blasting her with a *neh* through the partially opened door last time held her frozen. Suppose he'd reverted to his unwelcoming self. That wasn't the only thing stopping her. The possibility of his charming, welcoming smile made her even more nervous.

As much as she denied it to herself, Elijah had intrigued her ever since her family had moved to town. His broody silences and avoiding people made her long to reach out, but she'd never had the courage. Something inside her had always longed to comfort him.

But yesterday, when she'd seen his honesty and raw emotion, it had given her a glimpse of his depth. And confronted with his selfishness, he'd made no excuses. He'd faced it and gone out of his way to fix it. And now he'd made this generous offer.

Ruby couldn't let time slip away when she needed these lessons so badly. She steeled herself and knocked. The door opened so rapidly, Elijah must have been waiting for her.

"You came." He sounded as if he'd doubted she'd show up.

"This way." He led her into a spotless, well-appointed the kitchen.

She gasped at the size of the workspace. They could easily make dozens of pies on the massive island.

Ingredients stood on the counter, organized into groups. "I already baked the pumpkin so it wouldn't take too long." He pulled out a battered recipe card. "We can start with the crusts. Then while they're baking, we can make the filling."

Elijah surprised her by pulling a bowl out of the kerosene-powered refrigerator. It contained cut-up bits of butter and shortening. "The colder everything is, the flakier the crust gets. We"—he gulped—"used to do that. And we also added vinegar to tenderize the crust and make it easier to roll out."

After he helped her mix everything, he had her divide the dough and hand him half. Their fingers brushed. Sparks zinged through her. Elijah jerked back as if burned. They both took a moment to compose themselves. Then, side by side, they rolled out the crusts and prebaked them.

Elijah laid two recipe cards in front of her. "You have two choices. One is for regular baked pumpkin filling. The other is for a fluffy unbaked version. We called it Pumpkin Dream Cloud."

Ruby leaned in to read the small, neat printing. Elijah stood so near, the light scent of sawdust and a hint of pine tantalized her. In the intimacy of the kitchen and with their closeness, Elijah's uneven breathing matched hers. Ruby tilted her head to meet his eyes.

David slammed into the house and galloped into the room, clutching a handful of mail. Elijah and Ruby jumped apart, sending the recipe cards fluttering to the floor. They both swooped down to pick them up and bumped heads. Their gazes connected again and held.

David screeched to a halt. "What are you doing?"

~

ELIJAH SHOT to his feet and sent his nephew a warning look. "Manners."

"Willkumm, Teacher Ruby. Why are you here?"

Elijah's breath hissed out from between his teeth. What would Ruby think of this rudeness?

Ruby took it all in stride. "Your *onkel* is teaching me to make pumpkin pies."

"Can I help?" David pleaded with puppy dog eyes.

"That's up to your *onkel*."

"Can I? Can I? *Mamm* and I used to help *Aenti* Sarah every summer."

David's casual comment cut into Elijah like a barb. He squeezed his eyes shut a moment to lessen the hurt. A gentle touch on his arm startled him.

"Are you all right?" Ruby's soft voice soothed him.

He opened his eyes to the compassion on her face. Before he could stop himself, he confessed, "This is harder than I expected." And he realized he didn't only mean dealing with all the old memories. Having her here in the kitchen was confusing him. She'd removed her hand, but his forearm still tingled from the warmth of her fingers.

"I'm so sorry." Her glance confirmed she meant every word. Then she took in David bouncing impatiently. "I'm fine with David's help if that's all right with you."

Steeling himself, Elijah broke her gaze and turned to his nephew. "If you wash your hands."

When his beaming nephew rushed to obey, Elijah's gratitude overflowed. "He's cooperating. That's all your doing."

"*Neh*, it's yours too. He's happy to be a part of the baking."

For the first time in a long time, David followed instructions and eagerly participated. Elijah found himself enjoying the experience of baking again, especially with Ruby for company. From time to time, thoughts of Sarah drifted through his mind, but he believed she'd be pleased to see the lively kitchen conversation. And his heart lifted.

AFTER THEY ALL tasted a sliver of each pie, Elijah insisted Ruby take them home to her family. She left slices for David and Elijah, then hurried home with the two partially eaten pies and the recipe cards. Ruby still couldn't believe Elijah had entrusted them to her, but he'd insisted he wanted her to have them. She intended to recopy and return them, but for now, she held them as tightly as she clung to her precious memories of the fun she'd had with Elijah and David.

And Elijah had suggested practicing again next week. Ruby's pulse pitter-pattered at the chance to get to know him better.

The next afternoon as the children wrote their gratitude letters, Ruby penned several of her own. She started with quick notes to three scholars to thank them for kindnesses or hard work in class. But then she had a very special person to thank, and this one wouldn't be anonymous.

Elijah,

Thank you so much for sharing your recipes and teaching me how to make pumpkin pies. They're the most delicious I've ever eaten. The crust is so much flakier than mine ever was. And Pumpkin Dream Cloud is well named. If I become an expert pumpkin pie baker, I'll have you to thank.

Spending time with you and David was so much fun, and it made for a special end to a busy day. You both have brought much joy into my life.

Ruby paused. She'd like to say more about what he meant to her, but it might be too soon. She added one last line.

Looking forward to working with you again next week,

Ruby

She put it into an envelope, addressed it, and slid it under other letters in the basket on her desk. Then she wished she'd thanked him for meeting her in the garden and clearing the weeds each morning, but she could always send another letter.

Ruby really appreciated his help clearing the largest weeds. And it gave them time alone together to talk and get to know each other. She hoped he'd continue to join her in the early mornings.

She drifted off into daydreams until Martha's voice startled her back to the classroom.

"Teacher Ruby, it's dismissal time."

Reluctantly, Ruby pushed away her fantasies. "*Danke.*" She sorted letters into piles and called different children to her desk to assign them notes for their neighbors. David received an extra thick stack to keep him occupied after school while someone else delivered the envelopes addressed to him and Elijah.

After the children left, all eager to give out the letters, Ruby could once again indulge in her memories of the times she and Elijah had shared.

In dreamy bliss, she drifted into her driveway but jolted when she spied Mrs. Vandenberg's Bentley in the driveway. Ruby hurried into the house, eager to spill all her news.

When she entered the room, Mrs. Vandenberg was forking the last bite of pumpkin pie into her mouth. "I must say, both of these were delicious."

Ruby grinned. "Elijah taught me how to make them."

Mrs. Vandenberg's eyes twinkled. "Either you're a fast learner, or he's an excellent teacher." She studied Ruby's pinkening cheeks. "Or both."

"He's a good teacher and he let us harvest the pumpkins in the field and he even helped pull mullein and the scholars are excited to hunt for pumpkins in the morning and—"

Mrs. Vandenberg held up a hand. "Take a breath, dear. It

sounds like many good things are happening. God is wonderful, isn't He?"

Ruby responded with a hearty *jah*.

"Wonderful. Now I have another small favor to ask."

Whatever it might be, Ruby couldn't wait to do it. She owed Mrs. Vandenberg so much for the joy the pumpkin patch had brought into her life.

"I've decided to have a Harvest Fest at the market. All proceeds will go toward feeding the hungry. I'd like a booth with pumpkins. I assume Elijah would be willing to provide some."

"*Jah*, he would. He said I could donate the ones I don't need for the Thanksgiving pies."

"I figured as much. And would you be willing to staff it next weekend?"

"Of course."

Mrs. Vandenberg opened her notebook and checked off several items. "Perfect." As she stood to leave, she pinned Ruby with a searching look. "And I assume you solved your problems with David."

That brought Ruby up short. She'd worried about David's behavior to herself, but she'd never mentioned it to Mrs. Vandenberg. Or had she? How else would Mrs. Vandenberg know?

"God gives me nudges from time to time." Mrs. Vandenberg answered Ruby's unspoken question.

Those must be powerful nudges. Still startled, Ruby explained how putting David in charge at the pumpkin patch had turned him around. Then it dawned on her. "You said I'd find prayers and pumpkins were the answer to all my problems."

The elderly woman gave her a knowing smile. "And have you found that to be true?"

"Definitely." And as Mrs. Vandenberg headed out to her

car, Ruby realized pumpkins had provided another answer to prayer. Pumpkins had filled one of her deepest longings—the companionship of a man. And it might even be the start of something more.

Ruby hugged herself. Many people said Mrs. Vandenberg was a matchmaker. Could Elijah be the one for her? Was that why Mrs. Vandenberg had suggested his pumpkin patch and requested pumpkin pies? Ruby almost squealed out loud, but she didn't want to attract her family's attention. She wasn't ready to share this yet. Her joy bubbled over as she held the secret close.

CHAPTER 9

O ver the next week, Elijah showed up every morning to help her weed. Those early morning hours together were precious. They shared their life stories and deepest secrets —except the big one Ruby hid deep inside—her growing attraction for him.

They joked and teased each other, and Ruby marveled at how Elijah's responses had changed. He had begun with constricted chuckles, but now he'd relaxed into full, open belly laughs. Her happiness skyrocketed each time she made him laugh.

Gone was the man who barely uttered a word. Conversation flowed freely. And the dark shadows in his eyes disappeared. His face lit up when he talked to her. He seemed as thrilled to see her as she was to see him. And Ruby had their Thursday pie-making to look forward to. He'd asked her to come. Did that count as a date? To her, it did.

On Thursday, she hurried to his house after school. She'd given David an extra large stack of mail to deliver, hoping to have a little time alone with Elijah before his nephew arrived home. This time, she didn't hesitate to knock. But before she could lift her hand, the door swung open. Elijah had watching for her. Her spirits soared even higher.

Their hands brushed as they worked together, and this time Elijah didn't pull back. It almost seemed as if he purposely moved close enough to touch often. Several times their eyes met and held. The messages in his gaze seemed to mirror hers. Ruby could barely believe it. Was her dream about to come true? Would Elijah ask to court her?

David's arrival brought them back to earth. Ruby told them both about Mrs. Vandenberg's plans for the Harvest Fest. "And she'd like to have a pumpkin booth."

David stopped pressing pie dough into a pan. "Can I help with that?"

Ruby turned to Elijah for the answer.

He looked thoughtful for a moment. "I don't see why not. You can come along when I drop off the pumpkins."

David whooped and jumped up and down. Ruby wanted to do the same thing. She couldn't believe she'd get to spend a whole day with Elijah, working together and enjoying his company. Her life just kept getting better and better.

This time they made six pies. Elijah made two, with Ruby following his steps on two of her own. And they both helped David bake two. All of them looked and smelled delicious.

Ruby looked at their creations. "These are so beautiful, I wish we could sell them at the Harvest Fest."

"You can. The pie business was in my name, and I've renewed the license every year in Sarah's honor."

"How *wunderbar*."

"If you want, we could make more tomorrow."

Was this another date? Ruby planned to count it as one. "I'd love that."

He beamed at her, his eyes brimming with happiness, and Ruby thanked the Lord for His many gifts. This Thanksgiving season had turned into a harvest of many blessings.

WHEN RUBY ARRIVED at Elijah's the next day after school, pumpkin pies lined the counter. He must have baked all day. Some were already boxed and stowed in shelved wooden carriers.

When she exclaimed over the pie carriers, Elijah shuffled and stared off into the distance. "I made them years ago from scrap lumber. They'll make it easier to transport the pies tomorrow."

Next, he showed her how to assemble white cardboard pie boxes. As they tucked in the flaps, he said, "These were stored in the shed along with cartons of foil pie plates." His eyes clouded briefly with sadness. "May as well use them for charity."

Ruby touched his arm to comfort him. He turned forlorn eyes to her, then gave her a wobbly smile, placed his hand over hers, and gave it a tiny squeeze. Her pulse galloped long after he removed his hand.

Once they'd boxed up the pies he'd made, they set up an assembly line to create another large batch of pies. When David returned, he joined them in baking and mixing pie fillings. They worked well as a team, assembling pie after pie. Ruby disliked leaving before they finished the third batch, but *Mamm* needed her help with dinner.

Elijah appeared as regretful as Ruby that she had to go. "I'll bring the pies along when I drop off the pumpkins tomorrow. What time will you get to the market?"

"I'll come two hours before it opens. That should give us enough time to set up."

"I'll get everything there by then. See you tomorrow."

"Me too," David chimed in.

Ruby beamed at both of them. "I can't wait."

She wasn't sure, but she thought Elijah said, "I can't wait either." But the words were so low, she couldn't be sure.

~

After Ruby left, David and Elijah completed the final batch and boxed them up. The kitchen smelled of spice and home, but the spark had gone out of the air. Elijah missed the companionship, the fun, the laughter.

David plopped down for supper without any of his usual fuss or attitude. He sighed wistfully. "I wish Teacher Ruby could come again. She's so nice."

Elijah agreed. He would have liked to have her here at the table tonight—and every night. Where did that thought come from? Was he falling for her? The idea scared him.

He wasn't positive, but she seemed to be giving off signals that showed her interest. Twice now she'd touched his arm, awakening feelings that worried him. Loving someone meant losing them. Once this pumpkin harvest ended, he had to put her out of his mind, stop the relationship before it got started. Although the possibility of not spending time with Ruby left him bereft, he couldn't bear to face another heartbreak. He could never go through that agony again. Better to cut it off now before he got more involved.

After washing the dishes, Elijah headed out to the barn. He had to load up tomorrow's deliveries. As he hefted pie crates and pumpkins onto the wagon bed, his eye caught the small wooden box he'd made to sell at a consignment shop in town. He'd been thinking of Ruby as he designed it and carved pumpkin leaves onto the top. He wouldn't sell that box. Since he couldn't have her in his life, he wanted it as a keepsake to remember their times together.

Once he'd loaded everything into the wagon, he carried the box into the office and set it on his desk. It was the right size to hold envelopes. He opened the drawer and slipped his letter and hers inside the pumpkin box, his heart heavy at having to end things with Ruby.

In some ways, he wished he'd never answered the door when she'd knocked the second time. *Neh*, he wouldn't have wanted to miss all the good times they'd had—laughing and talking in the pumpkin patch, working together in the kitchen like a couple, a family.

His thoughts snagged on those last words. *Couple? Family?* And at the supper table earlier, he'd longed to have her seated beside him. As a *wife? Neh, neh, neh* to all these words. No matter how painful, he had to end things now.

But he couldn't just stop seeing her without offering any explanation. Maybe he could write her a letter. That would be easier than telling her face to face. He sat down and picked up a pen. His first words flowed easily:

Dear Ruby,

David and I had so much fun with you tonight. Your kindness and laughter made our time together enjoyable.

You're a special woman who has a gift for spreading joy wherever you go. God's love shines through you, and I pray He will give you all the happiness you deserve for sharing His light with others, including David and me.

It seemed a bit stiff and formal, but hopefully, she'd get the message behind the words. How did you tell someone you didn't want to see them again, especially when you did? And was he presuming they had enough of a relationship that she'd notice if he disappeared from her life? He clicked the pen open and closed unsure how to write the words he had to say. He didn't want to hurt her.

"Elijah?" David's voice, small and scared, came through the open doorway. "You're late coming inside."

Folding the letter with one hand to conceal the words, Elijah reached for the carved box but not fast enough.

"What's that?" David pounced on the box and examined it. Elijah hoped David wouldn't peek inside.

"Pumpkin leaves." David traced a finger over the design. "Did you make this for Ruby?"

Elijah snatched at the box, but David opened it and examined the letter on top. "It is for her. You wrote her a letter."

"Give it back," Elijah commanded. "It's rude to look other people's mail."

David handed over the box. "I can give it to her."

"*Neh.*" Elijah slid the unfinished letter into the box and closed the lid. "It's past your bedtime. Head into the house. I'll be right in."

If he left the box on the desk, David might sneak out here to read the letters. Elijah waited until the door closed behind his nephew before hiding the box on a top shelf and draping a soft rag over it. He'd complete the letter to Ruby tomorrow.

THE NEXT MORNING, Elijah woke David at five. He'd deliver the pumpkins before Ruby got there. Then he'd leave David to keep guard over them until she arrived. He wouldn't have time to finish the letter this morning, so he would do his best to avoid her until he could put the words down on paper.

When they arrived at the farmers market parking lot, a huge heated tent had been erected on one side. A painted banner announced, *Harvest Fest.* In smaller print, it said, *All Proceeds Donated to Charity.* Elijah drove the wagon as close to the entrance as he could. Several other vendors were hanging quilts, setting out buckets of asters and chrysanthemums, or filling tables with fall crafts. A man with a clipboard circulated, checking off names.

Elijah approached him. "I'm here with pumpkins and pies for Ruby Beiler."

"Right over there." He indicated a large empty space near the heavy plastic door flap. "They haven't assembled those tables yet. Ruby won't be here for an hour yet, but pile everything as close to the opening as you can without blocking the entrance."

David and Elijah unloaded their cargo swiftly. Elijah had to get out of here before Ruby arrived.

"I'll be back to pick you up later, David." Elijah smiled at him and hurried off.

He'd almost made it to the wagon when Ruby pulled in. She stopped her buggy near him. It would be rude to leave without at least greeting her. The chill in the air matched the one in his heart as he headed by her buggy window.

Her smile poured over him like sunshine. He braced himself not to react in kind.

"You've already unloaded the pumpkins?" The happiness radiating from her made Elijah feel lower than a worm. "Are you pulling your wagon around to the shelter? I'll follow you."

His *neh* came out gruff. "I, um, have work to do in my shop."

Ruby looked crushed. "*Ach*, I thought we'd spend the day together."

Elijah couldn't bear to look at her. He hadn't meant to hurt her. His insides were being ripped in two. Part of him wanted to stay with her, but his need to escape overpowered that longing. "I'm sorry" was all he could manage.

He climbed into the wagon. "I'm sorry," he mumbled again as he drove away and left her standing there, staring after him with sorrowful eyes.

As soon as he left, he regretted turning her down, but it was all too much, too fast. Falling for her had been an emotional shock already, but leading her on would only make it worse. The whole way home, he kicked himself for being so cruel.

At home, he hurried into the workshop and threw himself into his work, hoping it would erase the picture of Ruby's disappointment. But her sad eyes haunted him. She'd done so much for him. Why couldn't he do this for her?

Even if he didn't plan to continue a relationship with her, he still could have helped. What had he been thinking? He should have lifted those heavy wooden pie carriers. And he should have put the pumpkins on the table and assisted with customers. Once again, he'd only considered his own feelings, not hers.

Would he ever get over his selfish behavior?

If he hurried back, he could help her set up the stand and . . .

He couldn't do this under his own strength.

Lord, give me the courage to assist Ruby today. And please help me to think first of others rather than myself.

CHAPTER 10

*A*s fast as possible, Elijah hitched his horse to the wagon, which he'd need to bring home the pie carriers after the fest ended. Then he urged the horse into a trot. In the market parking lot, he wove around cars and other buggies to reach the horse shelter. Ruby's horse stood nearby, and Elijah gave it a pat before rushing through the vendors pushing carts piled high with goods.

One of the sellers lifted the thick plastic that covered the opening and waved others in. Elijah, who had nothing in his hands, took over to hold up the flap. To his left, Ruby, her back to him, maneuvered tables into place. At the opposite end, Merv Allgyer flashed her a *more-than-friendly* grin. Elijah's heart sank.

His hands dropped to his sides. Someone took over from him to push the plastic higher, bumping Elijah out of the way, trapping him behind oncoming throngs. With the waves of people scurrying by, he was practically invisible. He stood mesmerized by the glimpses of Ruby he caught between passing paintings, armloads of boxes, extravagant fall wreaths,

313

and clothing racks holding quilted dresses and vests in autumn colors.

She and Merv talked and laughed as he helped her smooth patterned cloths over the tables and arrange the wooden pie carriers. She waved a hand to direct him to place them at different angles. The looks Merv shot her spoke of his interest. He couldn't see Ruby's face, but from her patter, she enjoyed Merv's company. The two seemed well suited as they worked together to arrange the pumpkins—pumpkins from Elijah's patch, pumpkins he'd helped her weed—in a pleasing display. David handled the smaller pumpkins and joined in the fun as Merv made silly faces.

No point in sticking around. Elijah couldn't bear watching. Ruby had already found someone to replace him. Someone closer to her age. Someone who'd make her happier than Elijah ever could.

Then Ruby's bell-like laughter rang out, its sweet sound a sharp blow to his newly discovered feelings for her. Despite his determination to end things between them, a pang of desire to be with her sliced through him. Somehow, he'd expected letting her go would ease his pain, but his sadness only increased.

Elijah turned and blindly wove through the crowd, hoping Ruby wouldn't spot him. He jogged to his wagon and rushed home faster than he'd come. With each mile he put between Ruby and him, his heartache increased. He'd never run away from this.

It would be torture watching her court and marry another man. But he had no choice. This house and land had been in his family for generations. He couldn't leave it. He'd have to get used to seeing her with someone else.

314

AFTER ELIJAH HAD TURNED and hurried off earlier that morning, Ruby had stared after him, stunned and hurt. Maybe he really did have to work today, but the way he'd cut their conversation short and avoided her gaze made her think he didn't want to be with her. She'd built up a whole fantasy of them courting, getting engaged, being married. It had only been wishful thinking.

What puzzled her most was the change in him from last night to this morning. He'd been so open and caring and happy. Today, he'd turned closed, sharp, and moody. The way he'd been the first time she came to his door. Perhaps he had a changeable personality—upbeat sometimes, grouchy at other times. That would be hard to live with.

"Teacher Ruby?" David stood nearby, staring at her with a worried expression. "Are you all right?"

Ruby straightened and pasted on a smile, but she couldn't lie. "I'm a little sad this morning."

"Because Elijah didn't stay?"

"*Jah*, I was looking forward to his company. But I'm glad you're here to help. I'll go tie up my horse, so we can get the stand set up."

After she'd settled her horse, she rubbed his neck. But all she wanted to do was bury her head against him and cry. *Maybe getting married isn't God's will for me.*

She gathered her bags and forced herself to hurry back to the tent, determined to make the day a happy one for David and for herself. Selling these pies and pumpkins would help hungry children. But when she walked into the tent and found the pumpkins piled in a heap, her stomach plummeted. He'd come early to avoid her and hadn't even waited for the tables to be set up. If she'd come at the time she'd told him, he would have been long gone.

"Ruby Beiler?" A man with a clipboard approached.

"Sorry we haven't put out your tables yet. We weren't expecting you for another half hour."

"That's all right. I'm early, and I guess my delivery person arrived even earlier."

The man checked off her name on the sheet and motioned to a young man who'd just set up a nearby table. He held up two fingers, and the young man nodded.

"He'll bring out your tables as soon as he can." The man headed off to talk to another newcomer.

When the tables finally arrived, Ruby smiled at David. "I guess we'd better get everything put out. It would be better if these tables were closer together and maybe moved to—" Her head tilted, she stepped back to assess their positions and bumped into someone.

Strong hands steadied her elbow. "Sorry. I didn't see you."

"It was my fault." Ruby turned. "Merv? What are you doing here?"

"Bringing in *Mamm*'s canned pickles and chow chow for sale. Several of her friends have a table together." He gestured toward the haphazard pile of pumpkins. "Those yours?"

"*Jah.* I was trying to decide on how to arrange the tables when I bumped into you."

"Need any help?"

David puffed out his chest. "I can do it."

Merv smiled at him. "I'm sure you can, but an extra pair of hands is always useful."

"I can't keep you from your mother," Ruby protested.

"I've already finished. Happy to help you and David."

Merv went to their church, and he and Ruby had taken baptismal classes together. She'd always been comfortable around him.

"OK, David, why don't you and I move the tables while Ruby tells us where they should go?"

A huge smile stretched David's face at being treated like a man. Ruby appreciated Merv's thoughtfulness to David and his willingness to assist. Within a few minutes, they had the tables positioned, and Merv helped her drape Thanksgiving cloths over both tables. Then Merv lifted the heavy pie carriers, and Ruby directed their placement.

While they'd been working, David had sorted the pumpkins by size. "My *aenti* charged more for the big pumpkins," he informed her.

"Great idea." Ruby scooped up a few medium-sized ones and centered them on the table. Merv handled the huge ones. David piled small ones at the far end, and scattered a few around the pie crates.

Ruby thanked Merv, who had to leave for work, and then she admired David's table decorations. "You're really good at that."

He ducked his head shyly. "I helped Sarah whenever we visited. She also put out sample pies, so people can see what they look like."

"Another great idea." One they implemented. The pies attracted several people from neighboring stands, who stopped by and purchased a few.

While they'd been working, Ruby had pushed the hurt from her mind, but now as they stood behind the tables waiting for the Harvest Fest to open, it washed over her.

David studied her. "You're still sad."

She needed to change the subject. "Did you want to go around and check the other stands before it gets busy?"

David darted off, leaving Ruby to wonder what had changed between her and Elijah. She went over last night's conversation in detail, but found no clues. He'd seemed eager to spend time with her today.

Once the Harvest Fest opened, customers poured in, so she

had no chance to mull things over. She and David stayed busy, and after the pies ran out, she took orders. People paid in advance to make sure their donations went to charity, and Ruby promised to make and deliver the pies. She'd make those along with the ones for Mrs. Vandenberg. She couldn't help wishing she could do it in Elijah's kitchen, laughing and talking and having fun.

When the Harvest Fest ended, Elijah pulled up outside, sending Ruby's pulse racing. But he'd only come to collect David and the pie carriers. To avoid awkwardness between them, she hurried across the tent to talk to Merv's *mamm* and other church ladies she knew.

While they were talking, Merv joined them. "Anything to pack up, *Mamm?*"

"Just my empty baskets." She handed them over.

"How did you do, Ruby?"

Ruby made her answer as animated as she could. "We sold out of pies and had to take orders. I think we have three tiny pumpkins left."

Merv pulled out his wallet. "How 'bout I buy them for charity?"

She wished she could stay here. But she lifted her chin, straightened her back, and strode to the table, where Elijah was removing the last pie carrier. Surprise—and was that hurt?—flashed in his eyes as he nodded a greeting to her and Merv.

"Goodbye, Teacher Ruby," David called from the doorway. "I had a fun time today."

"I did too." The words came out automatically. Although they weren't completely true, she did have some fun. She added more honest ones that came from the heart. "You did a wonderful *gut* job."

She left David smiling and turned her back to remove the tablecloths only to find Merv had already done it. "*Danke.* I appreciated your help." She took the folded cloths and turned to avoid Merv's assessing eyes.

Had he been able to tell how she felt about Elijah? She hoped not. Ruby wanted to keep those feelings to herself.

CHAPTER 11

*E*lijah berated himself on the way home. He had no right to be upset if Ruby liked someone else. He didn't want to date her. No, that wasn't correct. He longed to date her, but he couldn't face the chance of losing her.

Beside him on the bench seat, David piped up, "Teacher Ruby was sad today."

"She was?"

"*Jah.* She was sad 'cause you weren't there."

Startled, Elijah glanced at his nephew. "She told you that?"

"Not eggs-act-ly. But I could tell."

"But she had Merv for company."

David nodded. "And he's nice."

Elijah gritted his teeth. Jealousy reared its head again. He should be glad Ruby had found someone nice. But he couldn't get his mind off her. He'd gotten very little work done today because his thoughts kept straying to Ruby. He'd have to work late after supper.

He heated up vegetable soup for supper and made ham sandwiches. Then he sat at the table in brooding silence.

David picked up on his mood and chewed thoughtfully. "Did you have a fight with Teacher Ruby?"

"Of course not."

"But you're both sad. And you don't look at each other. That's what people do when they're mad."

"I. AM. NOT. MAD. AT. RUBY."

"You sound like you are."

Elijah blew out a sigh. Since when had David paid so much attention to people's feelings? Elijah *rutsched* under his nephew's scrutiny.

"Maybe if you give her the pumpkin box and say you're sorry, you'll both be happy."

Neh, that's the last thing he needed to do. He was glad he'd hidden it last night.

Yet, once he entered his workshop that evening, the only thing on his mind was Ruby. Merv must have spent the whole day with her, while Elijah sat in the workshop pining for her. Getting over her would be harder than he'd expected.

Before he left the shop for the night, he checked that the cloth still covered the box. Actually, if she was dating Merv, he could probably take the box down and throw those letters away. He didn't need to let her know his feelings or "break up" with her. She'd moved on from him. Too tired to do something that emotionally draining tonight, he'd wait until Monday morning after David left for school.

Thank heavens, tomorrow was an off-Sunday. He wouldn't need to see Ruby or Merv.

OUT OF HABIT, Ruby woke extra early on Monday morning. She'd gotten used to hurrying to the pumpkin patch. But today Elijah wouldn't be there, so she had no need to rush. She did need more pumpkins for the pie orders and for the STAR

Center. With frost predicted for later in the week, she needed to pick as many as she could in the next few days.

When Ruby reached the ridge, her eyes stung. No Elijah. She'd be doing this alone. Disheartened, she knelt and bent to work. After she'd collected several pumpkins, the back door creaked opened. Ruby lifted her head, filled with hope, but her excitement died at David's small figure darting down the path to the workshop.

Half an hour later, he emerged, holding a lumpy object. He glanced toward the house, then raced toward her. He held out a rag-covered box.

"Elijah made this for you."

When she lifted off the cloth to reveal the carved box, her breath caught in her throat. She removed her gardening gloves before running her fingers over the raised pumpkin leaves and vines on the lid.

"It's gorgeous," she breathed. *And so meaningful.* Surely if he'd made her a gift this precious . . .

"I gotta go." David took off running.

Ruby rose, cradling the box close. She picked up her tools and deposited them in the wheelbarrow, eager to get back to her classroom and examine the box more closely.

Ten minutes later, she sat at her desk, all four letters spread out in front of her. He'd kept both her letters, so he must care. She read and reread both of his until she almost knew them by heart. Perhaps he'd been overwhelmed with emotion when he showed up at the Harvest Fest tent. He'd wanted to finish this second letter and give it to her. His letters revealed his struggle with grief, his uncertainty over approaching her, and most of all, although he never came right out and said it, the depth of his love.

He'd also let her into his life by sharing the special pumpkin pie recipes and teaching her how to make them. He'd surprised her by baking pies all day Thursday and donating all the supplies. And what about his gift of the pumpkins, allowing the children to pick them, and removing the mullein to make it easier? He'd done all that for her.

Even if he couldn't express his love in words, Ruby could read it in his actions.

But if he struggled to express himself, that left everything up to her.

After David left for school, Elijah went out to his workshop determined to finish the orders he had lined up. No more distractions. He put up a mental wall to hold back unwanted memories and emotions. He'd do his work precisely, mechanically, and rapidly. Nothing and nobody would interfere.

His resolve lasted ten minutes. He unlocked the toolbox and selected the ones he needed for the first job. Once he'd laid out everything and chosen the wood, he began measuring, but as he measured, the empty spot on the top shelf arrested his movements.

Dropping everything, he turned his attention to the shop. He tore through every cupboard, cabinet, shelf, and toolbox. He opened every desk drawer and searched the closet. The box had to be here somewhere. Perhaps in the barn or house.

He spent the morning combing through every nook and cranny of every building, even the abandoned chicken coop. Where had his nephew hidden it? Elijah dashed out to the field and dug through the wheelbarrow. No box.

All afternoon he paced, waiting for David to come home from school. Several times, he'd been tempted to march into the *schulhaus* and confront his nephew. Only the thought of facing Ruby stopped him.

Finally, feet pattered on the front doorstep. David had

taken to coming in that way after delivering his secret gratitude messages so he could check their mailbox. He burst through the door, leaving it wide open. Full of energy and happiness, he almost barreled into Elijah's chest.

David skidded on the hardwood floor, and Elijah grasped his nephew's shoulders, both to prevent a fall and to keep him in place.

"Where did you hide the pumpkin box?"

"I didn't hide it."

"Then where is it?" Elijah tried not to bellow.

"Right here." The soft voice came from the open doorway. Ruby stood in the entryway, the wooden box cupped reverently in her hands. "It's so beautiful, Elijah. And so meaningful."

Elijah closed his eyes, his face hot with shame. Had she read the letters inside? If so . . .

As if she'd heard his silent question, her answer floated out —sweet and gentle and caring. "*Jah*, I read every word many times. And I've replied."

His eyes opened as she held out the box to him. He hesitated, but she stepped closer. When his hands closed around the box, she turned to David.

"Maybe you could weed the garden. We need a lot of pumpkins for those pie orders. And it would give your *onkel* and me some privacy."

David grinned. Then he spun around and scampered off.

Heart thumping against his ribs, Elijah lifted the lid and drew out the envelope with his name written in her lovely feminine script.

Dearest Elijah,

I thank the Lord He's brought you into my life. When I read your letters, my heart bonded with yours in a way that transcends words.

Your grief reveals the depth of love and commitment you bring to a relationship. I will never ask you to forget the past. I only ask that you let me walk beside you into the future.

I know it's hard for you to speak your feelings aloud. But your actions have shown me more than words ever could about how much you care.

And my answer is jah, *I'd love to be your wife.*

Together, we can build a life rooted in faith, love, and gratitude.

Ruby's words poured over Elijah's shadowed heart like a healing balm. How had she known his true feelings hidden under the pain?

He set down the letter and the box to take her hands in his. "You know me better than I know myself. You saw past my fears to my deepest longings. And I'd like more than anything to be your husband."

A rustling in the doorway drew their attention. David stood there, his face filled with hope, as he stared at their clasped hands. "Does this mean we're going to be a family?"

"*Jah,*" Ruby and Elijah answered in unison.

With a whoop, David sprinted toward them, and they enveloped him in a group hug. Elijah's eyes met Ruby's over David's head. "You've made both of us very happy."

Then he whispered the words he'd tried to suppress for so long, "I love you, Ruby, with all my heart."

She breathed out a sigh. "You've just made me the happiest woman in the world."

"And I'm the happiest man."

"And I'm the happiest kid." David hugged them both.

Elijah overflowed with gratitude that Ruby had understood his nephew's needs; the changes in David had been remarkable. Even more, Elijah thanked the Lord she had seen past his fears to the truth, and he prayed he'd be able to do the same for her.

When they all stepped back, Elijah picked up the pumpkin box and held it out to Ruby. "You were on my mind as I carved every leaf and vine. I hope we can add more letters to this box over our years together."

Tears sparkled on Ruby's lashes. "I have so much I want to say."

Elijah did too, but no words could express all the love and joy spilling over in his heart for her, but he sent a message with his gaze. And Ruby's eyes sparkled with a lovelight that made it clear she understood and returned his feelings. Together, they'd reap a harvest of blessings.

~

Looking for more Amish warmth this holiday season?

AFTER THE BLESSINGS OF THANKSGIVING, come gather around *An Amish Christmas Table*—a heartwarming collection of four Amish Christmas romances from beloved authors Mindy Steele, Rachel J. Good, Jennifer Beckstrand, and Tracy Fredrychowski.

STEP INTO SNOW-DUSTED VILLAGES, cozy kitchens, and candlelit barns, where love blooms, forgiveness is found, and unexpected blessings arrive just in time for Christmas. Whether it's a quiet act of generosity, a long-held secret, or a pair of mischievous twins with a knack for trouble, each story reminds us of the true meaning of the season.

MAMMI'S PUMPKIN PIE

Mammi's Pie Crust

3 c. pastry flour
½ tsp. salt
½ c. shortening + ½ c. butter (cold)
½ c. ice water (cold water with ice cubes)
1 tbsp. distilled vinegar
2 pie pans
1 beaten egg white

In a cold bowl, sift flour and salt into a large cold bowl. Use a pastry cutter to cut butter and shortening into the flour mix to make coarse crumbs. Mix water & vinegar. Add to flour and mix until it's in small clumps. Don't overmix. Varying sized chunks make for a flakier crust. Gather dough into a soft ball, and divide in half. Roll out each ball into a circle 1" larger than the pie pan. Lightly press one circle into each pie pan, and crimp the edges. Place the crusts in the freezer for 15 mins. or refrigerate for 30 mins.

Preheat oven to 375°F. Line the crusts with parchment

paper or foil. Spread pie weights, dried beans, or uncooked rig evenly across the paper. Bake for 20 minutes. Remove the weights and parchment paper. Poke holes in the pie crust bottoms and bake for 10 more mins. Cool completely before adding filling. When ready to fill (only for a baked filling), brush the crusts with a beaten egg white to prevent a soggy crust. Do not use egg white for the unbaked pumpkin cloud filling.

Pumpkin Pie Filling

1 ½ c. (12 oz. can) evaporated milk
3 eggs
1 ½ c. pumpkin puree
¾ c. light brown sugar, packed
¾ tsp. cinnamon
¾ tsp. dried ginger
½ tsp. salt
⅛ tsp. freshly grated nutmeg

Preheat the oven to 325°F. Mix evaporated milk, eggs, pumpkin puree, sugar, and spices. Pour filling into blind-baked crusts. Bake for 50–60 minutes until the pumpkin filling is set, slightly puffy, but still a little jiggly in the center.

Pumpkin Cloud Filling

1 tbsp. unflavored gelatin
¼ c. cold water
3 eggs, separated into yolks and whites
1 c. granulated sugar
2 c. pumpkin puree
½ tsp. kosher salt
1 tbsp. pumpkin pie spice
½ c. milk

Sprinkle gelatin into cold water and let sit for at least 5 mins. Beat 3 egg yolks and stir in sugar, pumpkin puree, salt, pumpkin pie spice, and milk. Cook mixture in a double boiler for 30 mins. or until mixture is thick, stirring often. Add softened gelatin and stir until gelatin mix melts. Remove from heat and let mixture cool completely. Beat egg whites to stiff peaks and gently fold into cooled pumpkin mixture. Spoon filling into prebaked crusts or graham cracker crusts. Chill for at least 3 hours to set.

ABOUT THE AUTHOR

USA Today bestselling author **Rachel J. Good** writes life-changing, heart-tugging novels of faith, hope, and forgiveness. She grew up near Lancaster County, Pennsylvania, the setting for her Amish novels. Striving to be as authentic as possible, she spends time with her Amish friends, doing chores on their farms and attending family events.

Rachel is the author of several award-winning Amish series in print or forthcoming, including the bestselling *Love & Promises*, *Amish Sisters & Friends*, *Unexpected Amish Blessings*, *Surprised by Love*, *Amish Detective Benuel Miller*, *Amish Hometown Heroes*, and two books in the *Hearts of Amish Country*. In addition, she has written more than two dozen anthology stories and novellas along with the *Amish Quilts Coloring Books*. She enjoys meeting readers and speaking at events across the country about Amish life and traditions. http://www.racheljgood.com

For more stories about Mrs. Vandenberg's match-making and the Green Valley Farmers Market, visit her book page.